TURN MY WORLD AROUND

KAIT NOLAN

Turn My World Around

Written and published by Kait Nolan

Cover design by Lori Jackson

Copyright 2016 Kait Nolan

To everyone who's ever felt trapped by the mistakes of their past,

This love story is for you.

With love,

Kait

A LETTER TO READERS

Dear Reader,

This book is set in the Deep South. As such, it contains a great deal of colorful, colloquial, and occasionally grammatically incorrect language. This is a deliberate choice on my part as an author to most accurately represent the region where I have lived my entire life. This book also contains swearing and pre-marital sex between the lead couple, as those things are part of the realistic lives of characters of this generation, and of many of my readers.

If any of these things are not your cup of tea, please consider that you may not be the right audience for this book. There are scores of other books out there that are written with you in mind. In fact, I've got a list of some of my favorite authors who write on the sweeter side on my website at https://kaitnolan.com/on-the-sweeter-side/

If you choose to stick with me, I hope you enjoy!

Happy reading!

Kait

CHAPTER 1

IS THERE ANYTHING MORE pitiful than a man drinking alone on a Friday night?

Tucker McGee pondered that from his seat at the bar of The Mudcat Tavern. In the wake of wrapping up an ugly divorce trial and a property dispute this week, he'd wanted to unwind with his friends. But those days of regular socializing seemed to be over. Brody had been back from Portland for almost a month and they'd hung out twice—once for his welcome home party and one hurried lunch. Tucker didn't blame his buddy for making up for lost time with his fiancée, Tyler. God knew they deserved all the happiness in the world.

But his other friends had been just as scarce. Cam was busy being half of Wishful's power couple, saving the town alongside *his* fiancée, Norah Burke, the new city planner. And poor Piper was busy puking her guts up, though her first trimester was past. She and her new husband, Myles Stewart, were sticking close to home until she was more human again. Hell, even his law partner, Vivian, had tied the knot earlier this summer with her long-term beau, Darius Greeley. That left Tucker high and dry, feeling like the last single guy in Wishful, and wishing the beer in his hand was a plate of pie.

Be honest. It's not about pie—it's about the owner of the hand that delivers the pie. Corinne with the wounded eyes.

Tucker took another pull on his beer. When, exactly, was the right time to make a move on a woman who was busy trying to rebuild her world from the ground up? He'd been trying to figure that out for the better part of a year, which had resulted in a lot of pie and an extra six miles a week on the treadmill at the gym. No date, though. He hadn't asked. Not because he was some kind of pansy afraid of rejection, but because he didn't want to be the rebound guy. But biding his time hadn't gotten him anywhere.

Irritated with himself, Tucker finished off the beer. He didn't even like his own company tonight.

"Tucker, my darlin', you are just the man I was looking for."

He swiveled on his stool to find Norah cutting a swath through the Friday night crowd. Cam was nowhere to be seen. Tucker slid off the stool and gave her a hug. "And where is your other half this evening?"

"Taking advantage of the long summer hours to finish up a job for Mamie Landon. She got it into her head to turn her backyard into a Zen garden, complete with Asian-inspired pergola."

"Better Cam than me. The heat index was over a hundred today."

"Welcome to August in Mississippi."

"Buy you a drink?" Tucker asked.

"I'm buying because I have a favor to ask."

Tucker recognized the gleam in her dark eyes. She had another grandiose scheme in the works. Norah Burke never did anything small, which meant whatever she had in mind would probably be a good distraction from his lack of a love life.

"I'm intrigued. What's the favor?"

"Drinks first." She lifted a hand to wave at the owner of The Mudcat, who was working taps behind the bar. "Hey Adele! Can I get whatever hard cider you've got on tap and another of what Tucker's having?"

"Coming right up."

Drinks in hand, they retreated to one of the high top tables along the far wall.

"Okay, spill it. What have you got up your sleeve?"

"You do volunteer work at the women's shelter, right?"

Not the segue he'd been expecting. "Yeah. I offer up free legal services. Divorces. Restraining orders. That kind of thing. Why?"

"Well, you know they're really in need of a bigger place, right? They want to be able to take in more women with children, and right now the house simply isn't big enough."

That was true enough. The shelter was, unfortunately, bursting at the seams—a sad testament to the need for its services.

"You want to do a fundraiser," Tucker said.

"I want to do a fundraiser," she confirmed.

"What did you have in mind?" *Please don't say a bachelor auction.* As much as he wanted some companionship right now, the kind of women who'd be bidding on him at a fundraiser like that were not a road he wanted to travel down again.

"Well, you know how *Dancing With the Stars* is in its bajillionth season, right? Way more popular than the showrunners ever expected it to be."

"Yeah..."

"I want to do a local version. Dancing With Wishful."

Tucker frowned. "How would that work?"

"Same kind of format as the show, with some minor modifications. The Babylon is hosting the competition in its ballroom. There will be—well, I don't know how many performances since I haven't nailed down all the dancers yet—but maybe four or five shows. One a week. We'll sell tickets to those. The whole thing will be streamed live online, and people will be able to vote for their favorites each week, just like on the actual show. There will be some built-in revenue on the site, via ad space and the like. And there will be a panel of three judges, like on the show, too."

"People tune in to watch *Dancing With the Stars* because there are pro dancers and famous people."

"People will tune in to watch this because we'll be pairing beloved town figures with the town's best dancers. That's where you come in. I want you to be one of our pro dancers."

"Oh really?"

"Tyler and Brody already agreed. Piper begged off because growing a human is hard. But she offered up the names of a couple of other people I should ask. You've been in court all week, so I haven't made it to you until now. Think about it, Tucker. You nobly gave up your role as Phil in *White Christmas* to get Brody and Tyler back together. Now's your chance to show off those happy feet of yours for all to see."

A spark of inspiration flared in his brain. "And who would my partner be?"

"To be determined. I wanted to have all my pros lined up before I started asking local businesses to sponsor someone, so I know how many I need. Cam volunteered to sponsor himself on behalf of the nursery, so he's dancing with Tyler."

"And you have the double whammy of him being an elected official." Tucker nodded. "People will tune in to see City Councilman Pretty Boy. What about you, Miss City Planner?"

Norah laughed. "Please. I know my limitations. I nearly broke your feet when you tried to dance with me last year. Surely you've learned your lesson."

As it was an undeniable truth that Norah possessed not a shred of natural rhythm, Tucker was privately relieved. And that potentially left the door open to a crazy plan. He did love a crazy plan. "What about Mama Pearl?"

Norah clapped her hands in glee. "Dinner Belles is the center of *everything* in this town. If you can talk her into dancing, the public would love it!"

"Oh, so I'm on recruiter duty now, am I?"

"You're the one who brought it up. Besides, you're a smooth talker, Tucker. If anyone can do it, you can."

He was, and Norah was falling right into his hands. "You could do it, too. I'm reasonably sure no one has actually said no to you about anything since you moved to town."

"True, but I'll be busy sweet talking everyone else. Can I count on you? To dance and to work on Mama Pearl?"

Tucker loved to dance, loved to perform, and it would give him yet another legitimate excuse to drop into the diner. And if he could get Mama Pearl on board, it just might give him the opportunity to break this stalemate he'd been in with her sad-eyed waitress. He lifted a hand in salute. "I'm your man, General Burke."

"ONLY TWENTY MORE MINUTES AND we are *done!* Girl, give me a high five."

Corinne Dawson slapped Malika Hobbs's uplifted hand before returning to her patient charts. The next twenty minutes were all that stood between them and the completion of the clinical hours required for their nursing program. With finals finished, this was the last requirement for graduation. Thank God. The last two semesters of juggling online classes, clinical hours, and her job as a waitress at Dinner Belles had meant little sleep and even less time with her son. But the end was in sight.

"We should totally go out for drinks to celebrate. Or ice cream. A big ass banana split," Malika continued. "And then a three hour nap."

The idea of that nap almost made Corinne whimper. "I wish. I've still got a shift at the diner when I leave here." Another eight hours on her feet after eight here at the hospital. She'd forgotten what it was like not to operate past the threshold of permanent exhaustion.

The younger woman stuck out her lip in a pout. "With clinicals done, when am I going to see you?"

It gave Corinne warm fuzzies that her classmate still *wanted* to see her. She hadn't exactly been welcomed back to Wishful with open arms when she'd come slinking home, a divorced single mom, eighteen months before. Friends had been hard to come by.

"You could both apply for jobs here at the hospital." Rosemary Newsome reached past them both to pluck a chart out of the rack.

Corinne looked at the charge nurse. "I didn't think they were hiring."

"They weren't. But they will be. It's a good gig. Hard work, but part of the job perks is that the hospital will pay for you to continue your education. You come in as LPNs, you can work your way up. Two years working here for every year of schooling."

A means of furthering her education without going deeper into debt? With that kind of option, she could afford to finally move out of her mom's house, get her own place and start paying off all the debts she'd accrued trying to get back on her feet since the divorce. "Where do I pick up an application?" Corinne asked.

"The posting will go up in a few weeks. You can swing by HR then, put in an application. They'll have it online, but better to have your face seen. We're old school around here. Then the board will interview candidates," Rosemary said.

"The hospital board?" Corinne asked.

"That'd be the one."

Damn it. Of the nine board members, Corinne knew at least three of them would turn her application down on the spot. She'd been back long enough to know nobody had forgotten high school and no one cared about giving her a chance to make up for her less than sterling behavior. But maybe it didn't have to be a unanimous decision. She'd just have to make sure she was the best candidate for the job.

"I'm going to go check on Mr. Lennox in 104," Malika announced.

As her friend hustled down the hall, Corinne turned to Rosemary. "I know clinical hours are over, but is there any chance I can continue volunteering?"

The older woman blinked. "You need to be studying for your NCLEX exam."

"And I am. But I'm serious about going for that job." She needed it to make a better life for her son. "It seems like going above and beyond would help set me apart from the crowd."

"Your work should speak for itself. You've done a good job here, Corinne."

She'd worked her tail off. But Corinne had her doubts about whether it would be enough. In all likelihood, she'd end up having to leave Wishful to start a new life for her and Kurt. As difficult as coming home had been, going somewhere entirely new was a mountain she wasn't sure she had it in her to climb.

One step at a time, she reminded herself. It had been the mantra echoing through her head for a long time now. It had gotten her away from Lance, found her a job, gotten her back in school. It would get her a little bit further.

At the end of their shift, she and Malika walked out to the parking lot together.

"Oh! Oh! Final grades are posted!" Malika furiously punched at her smartphone. "Thank you, baby Jesus, I passed."

"Could I borrow your phone to check?" Corinne held up her dumb phone. She hadn't been able to afford anything with a data plan.

Malika handed over the iPhone. Nerves danced in Corinne's belly as she logged into her own account on the student portal and scrolled to check her grades. Her breath wooshed out.

"All A's." She'd been terrified with all the extra hours she was pulling at the diner that she'd tank her classes.

"Damn, girl! You kickin' my ass. Making my A's and B's look shabby."

Corinne handed the phone back. "The important thing is we're both officially graduating!"

The pair of them executed a little happy dance, ending with a hip bump and a tight hug.

"Come by the diner to see me, now, you hear?" Corinne ordered. "I'll be there until I finish my test and find something else. We can get in some more study sessions for the NCLEX."

"I will. See you on the flip side."

With a wave, Malika slid into her little Nissan and headed out. Corinne took a long look at Wilton Memorial Hospital before climbing into her ancient Toyota and pointing toward downtown Wishful.

The town green was edging more toward brown in the late summer heat. Rather than parking behind the diner as usual, she took a space across from City Hall. She felt foolish as she made her way up the path to the huge fountain that was the town's pride and joy. Over a hundred and fifty years old, the fountain was central to Wishful's identity. People came from far and wide to toss a coin into the basin and make a wish. Fed by nearby Hope Springs, local legend had it that most of them came true—though not always the way the wisher expected.

Corinne had never been one for wishes. But under the circumstances, she didn't think it could possibly hurt. Standing at the edge, she dug in her purse for a coin. The biggest one in the handful she pulled out was a nickel.

Well, nobody ever said denomination counted.

Holding the coin tight, she pressed her fist over her heart. *I wish for the chance to be seen as who I am now, not who I used to be. Please don't let my past mistakes negatively impact my son.*

She tossed the nickel. It flipped end-over-end, flying through the air to ping off the central stone pedestal, before dropping into the water with a splash.

Well, that was that. She'd finished her LPN classes with a 4.0. She'd finished her clinical hours. And she'd made a wish of the Universe. The only thing left to do was study her butt off for her certification exam. With one last look at the fountain, she turned toward the diner with a bit more of a spring in her step.

CHAPTER 2

*T*UCKER TIMED HIS VISIT to Dinner Belles when he knew Corinne wouldn't be on shift. He chose to believe the fact that he knew this was simply due to his superior powers of observation and frequent patronage of the diner, rather than a slight edge toward stalker behavior. The Saturday lunch crowd was thinning. He scanned the restaurant, nodding at a few clients and former classmates. None of his friends were here, and thank God for it. He didn't want any opining from the peanut gallery regarding what he was about to do.

Squaring his shoulders, he headed for the counter.

"Tucker McGee!"

His feet did an automatic redirect at the hail before he'd registered who the speaker was.

Aw hell. The Casserole Patrol. The trio of elderly women, who provided home-cooked sustenance to everyone in town in the name of joy, illness, or sorrow, were clustered in a corner booth. Empty plates with crumbs of pie crust were shoved to the center of the table, testament to the sugar fueling their current knitting session. Skeins of yarn spilled over their laps, needles clack clacking away, except for Betty Monroe, who'd paused to crook her finger in his direction.

"Afternoon Miss Betty. Miss Delia. Miss Maudie Bell." Tucker nodded to each of the women in turn.

"Hear you're dancing in this newfangled fundraiser Norah's cooked up," Miss Betty said.

Word traveled fast. He suspected Norah had done everything she could to make it travel faster. For a transplant, she'd certainly learned how to make the most of the local grapevine.

"Yes ma'am. You heard right."

"Who's your partner?" Miss Delia wanted to know. The Casserole Patrol's favorite pastime was poking into everybody's love life. He'd heard a rumor earlier this summer that they were trying to talk Norah's old intern into teaching them how to blog so they could put in for a weekly column in the local paper. So far Myles was maintaining a firm "No" in his editorial capacity at *The Observer*, but Tucker only gave him another few months before they wore him down.

"Don't know yet. I'm here to sweet talk Mama Pearl into joining the competition. Norah wants to showcase some of the major business owners in town." *The truth. It's always safest to stick to the truth.*

Miss Maudie Bell pouted. "When's she gonna do a good bachelor auction? Got all these handsome, single men floating around town that need to find a good woman."

"You just want to win the bid so you can have one of them work shirtless in your yard for your ogling pleasure," Delia cackled.

"Well, why not get some fun out of things until they manage to find that good woman?" Miss Maudie Bell sniffed.

Tucker wasn't sure whether to laugh or run. Schooling his face in neutral lines, he said, "That sounds like an interesting idea. Maybe you should take that to Norah directly." And by the time they convinced her, maybe he'd be off the market.

"I do believe I'll do that," Miss Maudie Bell said.

Spying his quarry behind the counter, Tucker grinned. "Ladies, y'all have a good afternoon. I need to go have a chat with Mama Pearl."

When he escaped the encounter without having his ass pinched, he decided he'd received his quota of miracles for the day.

Mama Pearl turned from where she'd slid a fresh pie into the rack. "What can I get for you, Tucker?"

He eyed the rack. "Is that coconut cream?"

"It is."

His afternoon was free. He could squeeze in an extra workout. "A few minutes of your time. In private. Then a slice of that and a cup of coffee."

If she thought the request odd, she didn't show it. "All right then. Come on back to the office."

Tucker skirted the counter and followed her through the swinging door into the kitchen. The scents of grease and sugar hit him like a fist, making his mouth water. Oh yeah, the workout would be worth it. At the grill, Mama Pearl's youngest son flipped burgers with precision.

"Hey Omar."

"Tuck. Usual?" he asked.

"Just your mama's pie today. How's it going with the lovely Simone?"

Ahead of him, Mama Pearl made a grunting noise. She clearly hadn't made up her mind about Omar's girlfriend, the new reporter for *The Observer*.

"Lay off, Mama," Omar warned.

"What's the matter, Mama Pearl? Marrying Vivian off this summer didn't satisfy?" Tucker teased.

"Still got three more to go," she said.

"Then focus your attention on Violet. She and Reuben are a lot closer to the altar than I am," Omar suggested. "Simone and I are fine, just as we are."

With a fulminating glance, Mama Pearl shuffled into the office. Tucker followed her inside and shut the door.

"I'm not going to insult you by asking if you've heard about Norah's latest fundraising scheme," he began. Mama Pearl was the undisputed queen of gossip in Wishful. If the Casserole Patrol knew, she definitely did.

"You wanna pull me in. How?"

He explained what Norah wanted to do.

"You want me to dance," she repeated dubiously.

"People in Wishful would love to see that. Everybody loves you."

"Doesn't seem like the best exposure for my sponsorship. You may be good, but you can't make these old bones move like young ones again. Don't expect we'd last past the first week."

"You *would* get more long-term exposure from a longer run in the competition. There's no rule saying it has to be you. The diner is free to sponsor anyone it likes if you have someone else in mind." Look at him being all blasé about this.

"Mmmhmm." Those two syllables belied her bland expression. Mama Pearl was not a stupid woman. No judge Tucker had ever faced made him sweat like that single, raised eyebrow.

Before he could say anything to further his cause, the office door burst open. And there she was. Corinne Dawson, former Homecoming Queen, student body president, and head cheerleader. The girl who was wrong for him on every possible level. One fist shot into the air in a posture he'd seen a thousand times at pep rallies and football games when they'd been teenagers.

"I did it!" Her blue eyes sparkled until she realized Mama Pearl wasn't alone. She dropped her arm and pulled back a bit.

He was sorry to see any of her happiness dimmed. Happy had never been Corinne's default state and he wished boatloads of it for her.

"Did what?" Mama Pearl prompted.

"Oh, hey Tucker. Sorry to interrupt."

"Not interrupting at all. Good news should always be shared. What's up?" He thanked God for all his hours in a courtroom and on the stage. It kept his voice from reverting to the awkward tremble he hadn't been able to shake around her back in high school.

"I'm done. I officially passed all my nursing classes and finished my clinical hours. I am graduated!" Tucker hadn't seen her smile like that since he handed over her bouquet of roses for the homecoming parade. The sight of it sucker punched him right in the gut.

"That's awesome," he said, and meant it.

He'd watched her clawing her way back to something since she'd come back to Wishful. She'd fought tooth and nail against less than friendly odds. It was good to see her finding some success.

Mama Pearl rose to hug her. "That's wonderful, child. And there's pie to celebrate."

There was no such thing as a celebration in Wishful that didn't include Mama Pearl's pie.

Corinne squeezed her back, gratitude written clear on her face. "Thank you. But pie can wait. I've got tables."

With a quick wave at Tucker, she was gone again.

He stared at the empty doorway as the last flash of her long, dark hair disappeared.

"Mmmhmm," Mama Pearl said again.

Tucker pokered up, but not before she shot him a Look that made it clear she'd noticed him noticing Corinne. "So how about it? Will the diner be a part of the competition?"

After a long, assessing study that had him wanting to squirm in his chair, at last Mama Pearl nodded. "I'll do it."

~

EXHAUSTION DOGGED Corinne's steps as she slipped quietly into her mother's house after ten that night. Automatically, she avoided the third and eighth steps as she went up for bed, knowing the old wood would creak beneath her weight. That skill had been mastered well before she'd finished high school, back when she'd ruled the school, before the Universe had proved she'd been a big fish in a microscopic pond. One easily chewed up and spat back out.

Quiet as she could, she opened Kurt's door and looked in on him. In the glow of the firetruck night light, she could see the crescent of his dark lashes closed in sleep. His limbs stuck out at all angles in a forest of stuffed animals, with the stuffed Chewbacca doll tucked tight in one arm. For long minutes, she stood in the doorway watching him, her heart aching. She hadn't seen him at all today—gone before he woke, back after he'd gone to bed. There'd been far too many of those days in the past several months.

It's not forever, baby boy. I swear it.

A door opened down the hall. Corinne held in a wince. No luck sneaking in tonight. Shutting Kurt's door, she turned toward her mother. Marianne Dawson stood in a silky, floral robe, arms folded, annoyance etched on her face. It was her default expression these days.

"Hey Mama."

"You're home late."

Corinne didn't bring up the fact that she'd already reminded her mom that she'd be working a full shift at the diner after winding up at the hospital. "I know. I'm sorry. Did I wake you?"

"I was watching *The Tonight Show*. Julia Roberts was on talking about that new movie of hers."

Corinne made a noncommittal noise. She couldn't remember the last time she'd actually been to a movie. That kind of frivolity called for money and time she didn't have. Though she had been planning to take Kurt to the next big animated flick now that he'd settled down enough to sit all the way through one.

"How was Kurt today?"

Her mother grunted and moved past her, toward the stairs. "Come sit with me while I have some tea, and I'll tell you."

All Corinne wanted was a horizontal surface for longer than a span of six hours, but she dutifully followed to the kitchen. She was more starved for news of her son than she was for sleep.

Because it gave her something to do with her hands, and therefore kept her vertical and conscious, Corinne took the kettle from her mom's hand. "Why don't you let me do that?"

As she filled it, set it on the burner, Marianne sat at the kitchen table. "We did our school shopping today."

Corinne's hand froze with a mug halfway to the counter. "What?"

"Went ahead and got all the supplies and some new school clothes."

Corinne choked back the bitter words wanting to spill out. Her baby was starting kindergarten in a few weeks. She'd been looking forward to taking him shopping. To letting him pick out his backpack and lunch box. He wanted *Star Wars* everything. Did her mother know that?

"I was going to take him next week."

"Didn't figure you'd have time. You've hardly seen him the last few months."

The guilt stabbed deeper, made her want to lash out. But she bit back the impulse. "I know. And I don't know what I would've done without you, while I juggled school and work and my hours at the hospital. I really appreciate all your help, Mama." Corinne did her best to inject as much legitimate gratitude into the statement as she could. Because for all her faults, her mother had been there for her when Corinne had come crawling home.

"Wouldn't be having to do all this if you'd finished school the first time instead of going off and marrying that man."

That man. Lance Lindau. Bane of her existence and the worst mistake she'd ever made. Except he'd given her Kurt, and she could never, ever regret that. He was the best part of her world, and she'd become a better person because of him.

Corinne could have reminded Marianne that she'd been in favor of the marriage at the time. That she'd seen Lance's money and position and thought her daughter had made a smart match. She hadn't changed her tune until Corinne had ended it. And then only after considerable effort was made to place the blame for the disaster of a marriage squarely on her daughter's shoulders.

"You're right," Corinne said, because agreeing with her mother was the quickest way to end this conversation. Ending it was the only viable option. There was no winning an argument with Marianne Dawson. "But I can't change the past. I'm working really hard to give Kurt a better future. I'm done with clinicals and school. I'll have more time now that I'm down to the diner. Once I pass my licensure exam, I'll start applying for nursing jobs."

Marianne shook her head sadly. "You could've been so much more, Corinne. All that promise, all that momentum you built in high school, just thrown away."

And this, this was the price she paid for her mother's help. A perpetual recitation of her failings—which were many. Corinne said nothing, wishing desperately for a cigarette and the quick hit of nicotine to dull the edge of anxiety. After almost a year without them, these conversations with her mother always brought the craving roaring back.

She'd learned long ago that there was no meeting her mother's expectations. Her father had finally conceded that a few years before and divorced Marianne. He'd since remarried and moved to Florida. When her own marriage had fallen apart, he'd made it clear she and her son wouldn't be welcome additions to his new life for longer than a brief visit. So she'd taken the only option she'd had, returning to the house she'd married young to escape.

Hand trembling, Corinne poured boiling water over the

teabag. "I'm sorry I disappointed you." Setting the mug on the table, she straightened. "Thank you for all your help with Kurt. I need to get to bed."

As she climbed the stairs again, hitting both the third and eighth steps this time, Corinne wrapped an arm around her middle and wondered that words could hurt just as badly as fists.

CHAPTER 3

ON WEDNESDAY MORNING, TUCKER slipped in to Dinner Belles to tell Mama Pearl about the orientation meeting for the competition. Norah had pulled off her usual organizational miracle. Not that he was surprised. As he wasn't due in court until eleven, he had ample time for a hot breakfast. And he wasn't above admitting—to himself, at least—he hoped to run into Corinne.

Having Mama Pearl agree to be his partner wasn't exactly what he'd had in mind when he'd approached her. But maybe she thought Corinne wasn't ready. Or that he wasn't right for her. Or, hell, maybe that Corinne just flat wasn't interested—in him or the competition. Tucker wasn't about to fault the older woman for watching out for her employee. Corinne had few enough allies in her corner. But he'd hoped for the chance to be one of them.

Luck was with him. Moments after he slid into a booth, Corinne was at his elbow filling his coffee cup.

"God bless you," he murmured with feeling, already reaching for the sugar. "There's extra in it for you if you can apply your new nursing knowledge to giving me coffee in an IV drip."

Her lips quirked until the dimple he used to fantasize about in homeroom fluttered in her cheek. "I keep telling Mama Pearl there's a market, but she says we'd have a traffic jam of all the IV poles."

"Oh, I don't know. You could mount them to the sides of the booth right here. Like a coat rack."

Corinne laid a finger over her lips in a considering gesture. "You may be on to something."

"It makes sense," he drawled. "Got a nurse on staff and everything."

"Not a nurse quite yet."

"Pretty damn close. Congrats on finishing school, by the way."

"Thanks."

"What's next? The NCLEX?"

Her eyes widened in surprise.

"I remember from when Piper went through," he explained.

"Oh right. Yeah, I'll be taking it in a few weeks. I'm waiting on the school to send my transcripts to the testing center so I can register. Studying like a maniac in the meantime. After that, who knows?" She shrugged. Beneath the feigned nonchalance, he could see the worry it would all be for naught.

"You'll do great. Anybody who can juggle everything you have the last year can pass that test with flying colors."

Her cheeks flushed a pleased pink at the compliment. "From your mouth to God's ear. Or the testing board, anyway. What'll it be this morning?"

Tucker didn't need to check the menu. "Biscuits and gravy."

"Anything else? Grits?"

"Pass. I'd be in a food coma in front of Judge Carpenter, and I need to be on my toes."

"Biscuits and gravy it is. I'll just get this in for you."

"Thanks. Oh, and can you let Mama Pearl know I need to talk to her?"

"Sure thing."

The bell over the front door rang and a female voice called out, "Corinne, girl, it's up!"

Corinne's head whipped toward the newcomer. "Already? But it's at least two weeks early!"

"Rosemary said we should be at the head of the line to apply. They'll be taking applications for a couple of weeks, but she said they'll start looking at the applicants right away. You need to find time to sneak away this morning." The slightly out of breath woman glanced his way and flashed a smile. "Hi."

"Hey there. What do you need to apply for?" Tucker asked.

"A job at the hospital," Corinne said.

"Yeah? That's great," he said.

"Would be if I could get there to apply for it. I don't know if I can get away until tomorrow. Mom flaked on me, and I've got Kurt in the kitchen." She bit her lip. "Maybe Mama Pearl can watch him for half an hour after the breakfast rush is over."

"I'll wait on you. Get some breakfast since I'm here," said the other woman.

"There's room at the counter. Grab a stool, and I'll get your order in a minute. Tucker, are you good on your coffee?"

"Just fine."

She spun away, clearly in go mode. She stopped by another table on the way to the kitchen.

"About time."

Tucker recognized the voice as the opposing counsel he'd be facing later that morning. Jefferson Barksdale was a boatload of asshole. Had been since junior high. His disposition hadn't improved any since he'd finished law school and joined his father's firm. If anything, he'd become an even bigger douchebag.

"Maybe you don't realize the rest of the world doesn't operate on the Homecoming Queen's time table, but some of us have places to be. This isn't high school anymore and the world doesn't revolve around you and your social schedule. I need my check."

The Corinne he'd known in high school would've eviscerated

him on the spot, customer be damned. Instead, the faint glow of accomplishment that'd lit her face faded and she seemed to shrink in on herself, as if diminished by the contact. "I apologize for the wait. Would you like a to-go cup for the rest of your coffee?"

"Just the check."

"Right away, Mr. Barksdale." Shoulders slumped, she headed straight for the register.

Mr. Barksdale. As if he hadn't been one of the many guys fawning over her back in the day. As if he was better than she was.

Fists clenched, Tucker seethed. No one had a right to be an asshole to servers. He was still trying to decide whether to say anything when Corinne brought Jeff's bill back to the table.

The smug bastard had the nerve to look down his nose and check her out as he took the check. A long, slow perusal of her body that made Tucker want to jam a knee into Jeff's balls.

Corinne didn't flinch. "I'm happy to run your card now." The *better to get your ass out of my diner* was implied.

"No need. I'm paying in cash."

"You have a nice day then," she said in the precise, sugared tone of *fuck you* that only a true Southern belle could manage.

As soon as she'd disappeared into the kitchen, Tucker was out of his seat, blocking Jeff from getting out of his. "That was uncalled for, Barksdale."

"Excuse me?" Jeff's eyes narrowed.

"I realize you're justifiably scared shitless of me decimating you in court this morning, and therefore, want more time to prepare, but that's no excuse for being a dick."

"I'm not at all worried about facing you in court, McGee. As to the rest, it's nothing less than she deserves after how she treated everyone in high school."

"So you're going to be an asswipe to a hard-working single mom just because she turned you down back then? Classy." Absolutely nobody deserved be punished forever for the mistakes they'd made in high school. Especially not when she was making every effort to be a better person.

"What do you even care? Your crowd didn't like her either." His gaze turned speculative as he pushed back from the table and stood. "Or maybe she's working hard some other way to make ends meet."

Tucker was a nanosecond away from planting his fist in the other man's face when a massive crash sounded from the kitchen. In the instant his attention was dragged away, Jeff shoved past him and the moment for an easy sucker punch was past. Probably just as well. Brawling in the diner wouldn't accomplish anything. He'd take his pound of flesh in the courtroom.

"Mama, don't move."

The sound of Omar's distressed voice had Tucker skirting the counter, shoving through the swinging door.

Mama Pearl lay prostrate, half in, half out of the storeroom. Broken crockery littered the floor around her. She was fighting both her son and Corinne to get up. "I'm fine, damn it. I slipped, is all."

"Be still," Corinne snapped. "You're not moving until I look you over. And let us get this glass up before you cut yourself. Kurt stay back, baby."

A dark-haired half-pint stood off to the side, worrying his lip exactly the way his mother did.

Tucker automatically moved forward, grabbing a nearby trash can and kneeling to pick up the biggest shards of what had evidently been a stack of plates.

"You know you can't reach the top shelf. Why didn't you ask me to get these down?" Omar demanded as he knelt to do the same.

"I been running this diner since well before you were born, Omar Buckley. I don't need to pull you off the grill every time I need something off the damned shelf." Arms folded in irritation,

Mama Pearl glowered at the lot of them as they cleaned up the broken plates.

"Does anything hurt?" Corinne asked. "Did you put your hand out when you fell? Catch yourself with your wrist?"

"I caught myself with my behind, thank you very much. The only thing bruised is my pride."

"Let us help you up there, Mama Pearl." By tacit agreement, Tucker and Omar each took an arm and raised her to her feet.

She immediately sagged onto Tucker as her ankle gave out.

"Whoa there." Tucker readjusted his grip to take more of her weight, and they shuffled her over to a chair in the office.

"Mama Pearl, are you okay?" asked a tiny voice.

"I'm fine, Kurt. Everybody's fussin' for nothin'."

As soon as she was seated, Corinne nudged them both out of the way and reached for Mama Pearl's foot. "Tell me if this hurts." With great care, she probed the ankle.

Mama Pearl hissed. "It's a mite sore," she admitted through gritted teeth.

Corinne carefully rotated the joint, stopping as soon as her boss winced again. "Omar, go make your mother an ice pack. Tucker grab me that chair, please."

Once Mama Pearl's foot was elevated and draped in an ice pack, Corinne crossed her own arms and scowled. "What else hurts?"

"Nothing."

"You said you landed on your backside. You could've damaged your tailbone. Does it hurt to sit?"

"Not as much as your fussing does."

"Deal with it," Corinne retorted. "I want you to go see a doctor."

"It's just a sprain. It'll be fine tomorrow."

"Which one of us is one step away from a nursing license? You can't dance in this competition on that ankle."

"Um, I'm guessing this is a bad time to mention the orientation meeting is tomorrow night," Tucker added.

Mama Pearl's face turned mutinous.

"Don't even think about arguing with me. No publicity stunt is worth hurting yourself. You need to see a doctor," Corinne repeated.

"Fine," Mama Pearl gritted out. "I'll go to the doctor, and *you* go dance."

The expression of absolute control slipped from Corinne's face. "Excuse me?"

"I've already paid the sponsorship fees. Somebody's gotta do it. If you're benching me, that leaves you."

"What about Darlene? Or Cindy?"

"Darlene has the rhythm of a fence post, and Cindy doesn't have the flexibility. You do."

"But—"

"That's the deal, sugar. You want me to take the time to go have this total waste of time appointment at the doctor, you dance."

Tucker very deliberately didn't look at Corinne.

After a long pause, she huffed out a breath. "Fine. We'll have to discuss my schedule."

"Fine," said Mama Pearl with an ornery *hrmph*. "Now both of you get back to work. There are still customers."

Corinne glowered.

"What about the job application at the hospital?" Tucker asked.

She shot him a glare. "It'll have to wait."

"I can watch Kurt."

One dark brow winged up. "You're dressed for court."

"I don't have to be in until eleven. Seriously, he can hang out with me for the morning. Y'all can get things sorted here with Mama Pearl, and you can go get your application filled out before everybody else. Win-win for everybody."

She stared at him. "How is that a win for you?"

"I like kids." Which was absolutely true. "Let me help, Corinne."

"Don't look a gift babysitter in the mouth," Mama Pearl ordered. "Soon as breakfast rush is through, you get on to put in that application."

Corinne closed her eyes as if praying for patience. "Okay. Thank you. We'll sort out the details before you're done with breakfast."

Tucker waited until Corinne and Omar were done fussing and had returned to their duties before pitching his voice low enough that no one else could hear. "Oh, you're good."

Mama Pearl scowled at him. "Shut up and don't screw this up."

Grinning from ear-to-ear, Tucker said, "Yes ma'am."

"So who is Tucker?" Malika asked in a *Girl, you'd better dish* tone.

Who was he indeed? Friend implied more between them than the casual acquaintance they'd resumed since Corinne started working at the diner. She hadn't expected that from him given her history with him and his friends back in high school. But he'd been one of the few people to be unfailingly nice to her since she came back, which said a lot about the kind of man he was. The fact that he'd volunteered to watch her son so she could go apply for a job certainly went a long way past mere acquaintance.

"I've known him since elementary school." Which didn't quite answer the question, but she didn't know what else to say. *Oh, yeah, he's also my dance partner in this lunatic fundraiser.* Yeah, no, she didn't have the brain to think about that right now.

"Did y'all date?"

"What? No." Tucker McGee had never been part of her entourage of male admirers. "I had a very embarrassing thing for his best friend for most of high school. Why?"

"It's just, after the asshat paid his bill and you went back to the kitchen, Tucker got up in his face about the fact that he'd been rude to you."

"He what?"

"Dickwad insinuated some pretty ugly shit about you, and I'm pretty sure Tucker was about to knock him ass over teakettle before the big crash."

Tucker was defending her? Why would he do that? No one defended her. She was nothing to him.

"Come on. Pretty boy in a suit is all defending your honor and playing stand in babysitter. There must be something to tell."

Corinne pulled into a parking space in the hospital lot and squeezed her eyes shut for a moment as another awful possibility occurred to her. "The only thing there is to tell is that he threatened Jefferson Barksdale, who absolutely *did* have a thing for me in high school and never got past the fact that I wouldn't give him the time of day. His mother is on the hospital board."

"Ooooh. But it was high school. Surely she's not gonna take that out on you at a professional level."

"Wanna bet?"

"Why should something so long ago matter so much?"

"You ever see *Mean Girls?*"

"Yeah."

"I was Regina George." The admission made Corinne want to hide under the seat.

"Shut up! You were not head bitch."

"I really wish I were exaggerating. I was not a nice person in high school." She sighed, thinking back to her biggest shame. "I betrayed my best friend."

"How?"

"When we hit ninth grade, I broke her confidence and publicized some really embarrassing stuff about her. It secured my entry into the in crowd and ensured that she'd be an outcast for the rest of high school." And then Corinne had followed the example of the popular girls above her and continually put her friend down in front of others, because being Queen Bitch had been more important to her than loyalty back then.

"I just can't imagine you doing that."

"I wish I couldn't. I wish I could forget it." She shrugged at the tension lodged in her shoulders. "Anyway, once I left town, I grew up. And once I had Kurt, I *knew* I had to be someone he could be proud of. But coming home...a lot of people haven't forgotten what I used to be like. And they won't let me forget it either."

"I'm sure it can't be that bad."

Corinne could've told her that today's run-in with Jeff Barksdale was par for the course for her work day—at least when Mama Pearl wasn't out front to intimidate people into behaving with the Eyebrow of Doom. But what would be the point? Whining about it wouldn't change anything. She'd behaved badly for a long time. Had even, briefly, fallen back into that ill-fitting role on her return to Wishful before she deliberately gave up all of it. She'd long since accepted she had to pay for that on some level because of karma. "Hope you're right."

They climbed out of Corinne's car and headed up to the hospital. Here, at least, Corinne knew she'd done something of value. She'd done good work during her clinicals. Hard work that had been appreciated. Staff and doctors nodded or waved in greeting as she and Malika made their way to HR. The recognition warmed her. Except for the odd person who'd come in for treatment and who knew her from back in the day, here at the hospital she got to escape the past. She wanted to make it a part of her future.

They stepped into human resources. Wilton Memorial wasn't a huge hospital, but she still didn't know everybody who worked there. Her time here had been spent predominantly on her feet, running from patient to patient, depending on what was needed. She'd meant to swing by and meet the HR staff but it just hadn't happened.

The forty-something woman with ash blonde hair looked up from her computer screen. "Can I help you?"

"Yes ma'am. We're here to fill out applications for the nursing positions posted this morning," Corinne said, a big, confident smile in place.

"Oh, I'd be happy to—"

"Corinne Dawson." From the back of the office, another woman emerged.

Corinne's hard-won confidence faded. Would it be better to pretend ignorance, like she had no idea who this woman was? Or did she own that she remembered exactly who Neva Coffman—and her daughter—was?

"Mrs. Coffman," Corinne replied. This woman was the Chief Nursing Executive on the hospital board. Acknowledgment was really the only option.

Beside her, Malika made like she was watching a tennis match, obviously wondering what the deal was.

"You're applying for a job here?"

"Yes, ma'am, I am."

"How interesting. I thought you were a waitress now." Her expression said she took great delight in the idea of it.

"I've been working at Dinner Belles while I finished nursing school."

"I see." What she saw was clearly that Corinne was nothing more than a bug to be squashed.

"I understand Jana is a human rights lobbyist on Capitol Hill." *There. Proof I know she's made something of herself, while I stand here and humble myself before you.*

Neva's smile spread. The cat who knew the canary was caught and was enjoying the game before it went in for the kill. "She is. Why just last week she attended a black-tie fund-raiser with the good Senator."

There was no telling which senator she meant, and Corinne didn't actually care. "I'm sure she's doing worlds of good." And she probably was. Jana Coffman would've made a far better student body president than Corinne had. She'd been civic-minded and interested in making things better for the school. And Corinne had toppled her with a few well-placed rumors about the sex life Jana hadn't had.

Nausea roiled in her stomach.

The curious receptionist handed over a couple of clipboards without a word.

Corinne murmured thanks and started to turn toward one of the vacant chairs in the reception area.

"There's going to be a lot of competition for these jobs," Neva continued. "*If* you landed it, you'd be stuck at the bottom of the totem pole, emptying bedpans and giving sponge baths. I'd advise you to look elsewhere."

In her position, Neva could easily make that happen. Should she so choose, she could make Corinne's prospective work life here a misery. But instead of bowing to the pressure, Corinne looked the woman right in the eye. "If I were so fortunate as to get the job, I'd be blessed with the honor to serve others. There's no higher calling than that."

Neva blinked.

Corinne did her best to keep her expression neutral and pleasant. "Please give Jana my sincerest congratulations on her success. She absolutely deserves it."

With that, she turned her attention to filling out the application. But even as Neva went on about her business, all hope she'd held about landing the job evaporated. Her past was coming back to bite her in the ass yet again. She was starting to think she might never overcome it. At least not in Wishful. The truth of it made her heart break just a little bit more.

One step at a time, she reminded herself. *One step at a time.*

CHAPTER 4

"SO KURT, HAVE YOU ever played HORSE?" Tucker draped his suit jacket over the bleachers in the community center. He added his tie and began rolling up his shirt sleeves.

"Sure. But my grandma got mad at me for knocking over some stuff with the broom handle."

A kid with an imagination. He liked that. "Not that kind of horse, my little man. The game with a basketball."

The boy shook his head.

"Ever shot a basketball?" He grabbed one off the rack at the side of the gym.

Again with the head shake.

Was Kurt too young for this? Bringing him here for some low-key b-ball was the only thing Tucker could think of to do on a weekday morning in August when it was hot enough to fry an egg on the sidewalk. He needed the AC to ensure he was at least moderately presentable for Judge Carpenter later. Other than the two of them, the place was nearly deserted. A handful of blue-hairs moseyed on the second-floor track surrounding the basketball court.

Taking his position at the free throw line, Tucker lined up the shot and tossed. The ball swished neatly through the net.

"Whoa." Kurt dragged out the exclamation to three syllables, his eyes going gratifyingly wide. "I wanna learn how to do that."

Tucker retrieved the ball and motioned for the boy to join him on the free throw line. He showed Kurt how to hold the ball and described the motion.

"Let's see what you've got."

Kurt heaved the ball into the air. It fell short of the basket by at least ten feet.

"That's okay," Tucker said, jogging after the ball. "Everybody's gotta start somewhere. You've got short people problems."

"Mommy says I'm growing like a weed."

"And one day you won't be short. Meanwhile, let's scoot a bit closer to the basket." Tucker snagged the rack of balls and rolled it out onto the court. Might as well have a bunch to start with.

The kid threw himself into the process with little finesse and a lot of enthusiasm. Best Tucker could tell, he had as much fun chasing the balls as he did trying to hit the basket. But nothing beat the celebration dance when he managed to sink one by flinging it double-handed granny style up from his knees. Laughing, Tucker joined in the boogie, which they finished out with an epic, multi-step high five.

"That was fun!" Kurt declared.

"It was. Wanna do it again?"

"Yeah!"

Since the double handed had worked, Tucker helped him refine his method. Then even that degenerated into silly attempts at trick shots that mostly consisted of flinging the ball as high in the air as they could manage. Tucker had a blast.

Scooping his charge up, he made a sprint forward, boy, ball, and all, dancing around imaginary opponents. "He dodges left, dodges right, making it past the center." He lifted Kurt high so the kid was only a few feet from the basket. "He shoots—" The ball swished through the hoop. "He scores! And the crowd goes wild!"

Tucker boosted him up on one shoulder and they both mimed cheering.

"That was awesome! I wish Mommy could have been here."

Tucker checked his watch. "She ought to be back soon."

"Yeah, but then it'll be back to work."

Not wanting Kurt to lose his happy mood, Tucker flipped him over and held him upside down, giggling.

"Put me down!" Kurt laughed.

Tucker righted him, tugging his t-shirt back in place. "Your mom works a lot, huh?"

Kurt looked at him with an air of imparting Very Serious Information. "A. Lot. I know it's for me and stuff, so we don't always have to live with Grandma, but I just wish she could have some fun."

Out of the mouths of babes. "I'd like to help her with that."

The big dark eyes turned on him like a laser beam. "Why?"

"Because I've seen how hard she works, too, and I think she deserves a chance to play."

"Not everybody gets that luxury."

They both turned to see Corinne in the doorway, subtle lines of strain bracketing her mouth.

How much had she heard?

"Mommy!" Kurt rocketed across the gym, launching himself at her.

She fielded his hug like a pro and only took one step back from the impact. Some of the strain melted away as she wrapped her arms around her son.

"Mommy, you have to see what I can do!" The kid was already dragging her back to the court.

While Kurt showed off his new skills, Tucker went back to the bleachers to retrieve his coat and tie.

"That's great!"

"Can I get a basketball goal?"

"We'll have to see about that."

Tucker knew she wasn't in the kind of financial place for such frivolities.

"In the meantime, I'm sure we can come back here sometime for you to practice."

Slipping the tie under his collar, Tucker crossed over to the two of them. "Got your application in okay?"

"For whatever good it will do."

He arched his brow in question, his fingers fumbling with the tie. Hell, he'd have to wait until he got to a mirror to redo it.

"Some of the board members making the decision are not my biggest fans." She was looking at him in a way she never had before. As if he were some mystery she wasn't sure she wanted to solve. "I...Malika told me what you did with Jeff. Thank you for defending me."

Tucker shrugged, uncomfortable with the praise when he'd accomplished next to nothing. "I wish I could've done more. The guy's a tool."

Corinne sighed with faint exasperation and stepped into him. "Here, let me." She gripped the ends of his tie. "He always was a tool."

Her body was close enough to his that Tucker could feel the heat of her. He had to fight not to reach out and grip her hips. Her fingers moved with a swift surety that left him a bit stunned. He knew next to nothing about her marriage except it was over, but he wondered now what kind of life she'd led away from Wishful.

"But you're not. You never were. Thanks for that." She smoothly slid the freshly-tied knot into place, not too tight, not too loose. Perfect. Her gaze lifted to his and caught.

Those blue eyes weren't wounded now. They were wide and startled, and as Tucker lifted his hand to trace the perfectly shaped Windsor knot, an awareness slid into them that had him wanting to prolong this strange little domestic interlude.

"Thanks."

A faint wash of color stained her cheeks as she realized she still had her hands on him. A pang of regret shot through him as she stepped away. For a second there, it seemed like they'd had a moment.

Corinne shifted behind her son and squeezed his shoulders. "And thanks for this. I hope he wasn't too much trouble."

"Not a bit. We bonded over basketball." Tucker offered his fist for a bump.

Kurt's enthusiastic return teased an almost smile from his mother.

"Afraid it's time for us to go, kiddo," she said.

"Aw man. Tucker, can we play HORSE again sometime?"

"Absolutely."

Corinne seemed surprised at his lack of hesitation. Well, he was just gonna keep racking up the points on the surprise-o-meter.

Tucker slid his jacket back on. "So I'll see you tomorrow?"

Corinne paused, half turned toward the exit. "Tomorrow?"

"The orientation meeting for the competition."

"Right." She didn't look entirely pleased at the reminder. "I'm sorry about the substitution."

"I'm not." He let his own lips curve because he'd gotten what he wanted. "It'll be fun."

AT THE END of her shift, Corinne could no longer put off thinking about the situation she'd landed in. The only thing she'd wanted since she came home was to quietly claw herself out of debt and make a life for her son, while staying as under the radar as possible. She got plenty of looks and snide remarks from people while she worked at the diner. Nobody expected the student body president to wind up a divorced college drop out with a child. She'd been planning on going places, doing things—albeit as part of the fruitless pursuit of her parents' approval. She'd done considerable travel with Lance, but she wasn't about to tell people that. They might think she was bragging or looking for some kind of sympathy for her current lowered circumstances.

And now she was partnered up with one of the town's golden boys, about to be put on display for all to see. How could she possibly get through that? Corinne wanted out. She wanted to find the nearest rock to crawl under, so she could quietly go back to putting one foot in front of the other on the path she'd set for herself.

But she wouldn't let Mama Pearl down. Her boss had given her a job and, more importantly, made her a part of the Dinner Belles family, offering up as much sassy caretaking as she provided her own six children. In the past year and a half, she'd been more of a real mother to Corinne than her own had ever been. So Corinne wouldn't repay her kindness by bailing. No matter how much she wanted to.

But how on Earth was she going to manage to juggle rehearsals for the competition along with work, Kurt, and studying for the NCLEX? The truth was she couldn't. Not without asking for more help from her mother. Marianne would give it, but there'd be a cost. There was always a cost with her. Whatever it was, Corinne resigned herself to paying it.

As she stepped into the house, she put the whole thing out of her mind, calling out for Kurt.

He came rocketing into the kitchen. "Mommy!" His sturdy little body torpedoed into her legs, almost knocking her over as he threw his arms around her.

"There's the droid I was looking for." Corinne scooped him up. Dear God, he'd grown over the summer.

"Do you know what kind of tools a ninja has?" he demanded.

Ninjas were his latest obsession. Because according to Kurt, ninjas were like Jedis. "What kind?"

"They use a gapple hook, a sword, a rope, and a zip line. That's how they fly."

"I believe that's grappling hook."

He looked up at her with eyes as dark as polished walnut. "Will you play ninjas with me, Mommy?"

Corinne's heart simply melted. "Well, we could do that, but I thought we might go to the pool this afternoon."

"Pool! Yay!"

"It's too hot and too bright for the pool," Marianne announced, coming into the room.

Corinne repressed a surge of annoyance as she looked at her nut-brown son. "We've got high SPF sunscreen and it's after three. He'll be fine for an hour. He needs to burn off some energy." She set him down and patted him on the butt. "Go put on your swim trunks and a t-shirt."

With a double fist pump, he raced upstairs. Too bad she couldn't bottle some of that energy and mainline it. It'd make those days she pulled double shifts a lot more doable.

"I figured you'd appreciate some quiet alone time," Corinne said, trying for unperturbed.

"Well, and I won't turn it down. But don't you be blaming me when he gets burned."

"Why would I blame you when I'm the one making the decision?"

Marianne grumbled something unintelligible. Whatever it was, Corinne let it pass.

"I'm going to pick up something to fix for supper tonight, too, since I'm off. Is there anything in particular you'd like?" Might as well play nice.

"Something for the grill. But nothing too heavy."

"I can do that." Corinne started toward the hall, thinking to put off the asking, then changed her mind, opting to get it over with. "Mom, there's something I need to ask you."

With a beleaguered sigh, Marianne settled at the kitchen table with a Diet Coke. "Figured there must be something with all this buttering up."

As if Corinne had never said thank you or done what she could to help around the house, with the cooking, with her son. As if all she ever did was take and never give back. She closed her eyes for a couple of breaths until she had her temper under control again. "Have you heard about the fundraiser Norah Burke has organized for the women's shelter? Dancing With Wishful?"

"Saw something about it in the paper this morning. Why? Were you wanting to go?"

"Well, no. Mama Pearl has asked me to represent the diner as one of the dancers. It wasn't the original plan, but she had a fall at work today and sprained her ankle pretty badly."

"What's that got to do with me?"

"I'm going to need someone to watch Kurt in the evenings while I rehearse."

"Rehearse," Marianne repeated, arching a skeptical brow.

"It'll probably only be for the first week," she rushed to add. "I expect we'll end up cut after the first round." Even if they were technically perfect, and even if Tucker was a town favorite, it wouldn't be enough to override the stigma that stuck to her like stink on a skunk.

Her mother heaved another of those over-dramatic sighs. "I just don't know, Corinne. I'm already doing so much."

"I know. I know, Mama, and I'm so grateful. I wouldn't have chosen this on my own. But Mama Pearl asked, and she's been good to me since I came back. I don't want to let her down."

"And who, exactly, is your partner? That Brody Jensen you wasted all those years chasing after? Because he's getting married."

Shame heated Corinne's cheeks. "Yes, Mama, I know Brody's getting married." She'd been the one to give him the verbal ass kicking he needed to fix things with Tyler when he'd messed up their second chance. "I'm dancing with Tucker McGee."

"Tucker McGee," Marianne drawled. The speculative gleam in

her eye had Corinne wanting to take a step back. "That'd be the one who took Kurt to play basketball this morning. Boy's been chattering about it like a magpie since I picked him up."

"He was helping out so I could get my application in at the hospital ahead of the crowd. The dancing is just business," she warned.

"Might start that way. Doesn't mean it has to finish that way."

"There's nothing between me and Tucker, Mama."

"Won't be with that attitude."

For the love of— She wasn't in this for a man. And she certainly wasn't going to use one of the few people who'd been kind to her since she came back. But it wasn't worth the fight to argue about it.

"Are you willing to watch Kurt so I can rehearse for the competition?"

"I expect the boy and I can keep ourselves occupied. It's for a good cause, after all."

"Thank you, Mama." But as she headed upstairs to change clothes, Corinne had the sense that the fundraiser wasn't the cause her mother was talking about.

CHAPTER 5

"THANKS FOR SPRINGING ME," Piper said. "I swear, since he found out I was pregnant, Myles has about tried to wrap me in cotton and stuff me in a bubble. I had to practically promise to call every five minutes and keep my locater app running on my phone to get him to go on in to the paper to deal with some emergency and let me come out tonight."

Tucker looked over at the now visible baby bump, made more pronounced by the weight she'd dropped the last few months. "You can't blame the guy. You've barely kept any solid food down for the past four months. He's just worried about you. We all have been."

"I'm fine. And I'm stir crazy. Which is why Tyler and Brody are having this cookout. Bless them. Myles is terrified I'll catch something to make me even sicker if I'm out in public."

"He does remember you work at a doctor's office, right?"

"That's what I said. Let it not be said that the new father is in any way, shape, or form rational." But there was amusement in her tone.

"You're happy," Tucker observed.

Piper folded her hands over her belly and gave a blissful sigh.

"I am. This is not where I expected to be six months ago, but it's so much better."

"Even with the preggo nausea?"

"Even with."

That eased Tucker's mind considerably. She and Myles had had a rocky start. Tucker had been Myles' best man in their spontaneous wedding—he hadn't wanted to kick Myles' ass—but Piper was his oldest friend. Womb to tomb. His allegiance would always go to her. Thankfully, she and Myles had found their groove before that had become necessary, and both were ecstatic to be starting a family—even if that had been a fairly epic surprise.

Seeing her now, married and happy, with a baby on the way, gave him an unexpected pang of envy. Tyler and Brody would likely be right behind. Norah and Cam, too, if they could ever clear their work schedules enough to set a date for the wedding. That left him.

He'd been the first of their group to walk down the aisle with his college sweetheart. Everybody had expected him and Laura to be somewhere around 1.5 kids, a picket fence, and a dog by now. Instead, he was still living the single guy's life and feeling every hollow moment of it.

"So, have you started talking names yet?" Tucker pulled into the driveway of the Craftsman-style bungalow Tyler had rehabbed from the inside out.

"We're waiting until we find out the sex of the baby next month. No sense in double the arguing since half the choices wouldn't matter." Piper slid out of the car before he could come around and get her door, then glared at him when he took her elbow at the steps.

"I promised Myles."

She rolled her eyes but didn't fight him.

"May I submit Tucker as a good, fine Southern name?" he continued.

The door swung open. "Oooo, are we talking baby names?" Tyler asked.

"Tucker is." Piper hugged her, then stepped inside, dropping into a crouch to love on Ollie, Tyler's black lab, who stood wagging just inside the threshold. "Who's a sweet boy? He's looking great, Tyler."

A year before, Ollie had suffered a spinal stroke, leaving him paralyzed on one side. Rather than having him put down, Tyler had waited it out, seeing how much he'd heal and spending a small fortune on physical therapy in the process.

She beamed. "Yeah, he's turned into a poster child for the PT department at the MSU vet school. He's not where he used to be, but he's walking again, which is huge. I even caught him trotting after a squirrel the other day when he thought I wasn't looking."

Tucker ruffled Ollie's ears. "Good for you, buddy."

"To return to the baby name discussion, I'm just gonna throw it out there that Tyler would make an excellent, gender neutral choice," Tyler said.

"It is not a discussion. And you're going to have to campaign better than that. I mean, preggo girl foot rubs at *least*," Piper said.

Tyler laughed. "So noted. Come on. Brody's out back manning the grill."

After the traditional back-thumping man hug, Tucker snagged a beer for himself and a gingerale for Piper, then settled in for the visit he'd been craving.

"So, are we gonna talk about the elephant on the patio?" Brody asked.

Tucker stilled, bottle halfway to his lips. Had they already heard the news? "And what elephant would that be?"

"We're all competing against each other," Tyler pointed out.

"Who's started choreographing already?" Piper asked.

"Can't choreograph until we draw our dance," Tucker said.

"When's that happening?" she wanted to know.

"Orientation meeting is tomorrow night," Brody told her. "And I fully expect to get my ass kicked."

Piper plucked a tortilla chip from the bowl on the table. "Who's your partner?"

"Adele Daly."

"But she's graceful."

"Behind the bar, sure. But dancing around and performing tricks with bottles of vodka and whatever is a far cry from this. I've danced with her before. She keeps trying to lead."

"You're just mad we don't get to dance together," Tyler teased.

He snagged her around the waist and planted a firm kiss on her lips. "Damn straight. Anyway, I figure it's gonna come down to you and Cam."

Tucker took another pull on his beer. "My partner and I should give them a run for their money."

Brody quirked a brow. "No offense, bro, but Mama Pearl isn't exactly light on her feet."

"No, she's not. Which is how she ended up falling today and spraining her ankle."

"Oh no! Is she okay?" Piper asked.

"She's fine. Or will be." Tucker still wasn't a hundred percent sure whether she'd actually sprained anything or not. "But she's not dancing, so she assigned a sub."

"Who?" Brody asked.

"Corinne Dawson."

There was a beat of silence. Then another. And another.

Tucker waited for one of them to call him on the deception. After all, he'd faked breaking his own leg in the name of raising Brody from understudy to main man. But nobody went there. Because the idea that he'd do such a thing in the name of partnering with Corinne never even entered their minds.

"You're dancing with Tyler's arch enemy?" Piper demanded.

Here we go. This was exactly why he hadn't wanted to tell them.

"Oh, don't be ridiculous," Tyler said. "I don't have arch enemies."

"Seriously?" Brody asked her. "You're really okay with being around her after all those years she chased me?"

"It hardly matters since I'm the one who caught you, now does it?" Tyler waggled the ring finger on her left hand, showing off the diamond winking in the late afternoon sun. "Besides, I think she's had a rough go of things."

"Karma's a bitch," Piper sang.

"That's not fair," Tucker chided.

"So what? She was awful in high school. Classic mean girl."

That was all you ever saw. All you wanted to see. But he'd seen more. He'd seen that beneath the sharp tongue and bad behavior was a wounded animal, lashing out at everyone around her. Tucker wanted to argue, but that would open up a can of worms he wasn't ready to deal with. There was a reason he'd never made his interest in Corinne known to his friends. Or to anyone, for that matter.

"Well, it's not who she is now," he said. "She grew up. And life has kicked her ass but good. I'd appreciate it if you'd play nice, if only for my sake. If she's stressed out from being around all of you, she won't loosen up enough to dance well. And regardless of past issues, this competition is for a good cause, and we all ought to want to put on a good show. The better the individual performances, the more viewers, the more votes, the more donations."

"Tucker's right," Tyler said. "Norah asked all of us to do this because we're the best dancers in town. We owe her, and the cause, our best efforts, no matter who our partners are."

Shooting Tyler a smile, Tucker raised his drink in a toast. *Solidarity.* If Tyler could get past her issues with Corinne, maybe the rest of them would come around eventually. And maybe by the time they did, he'd have a reason for them to.

∾

CORINNE TURNED down Tucker's offer to pick her up for the orientation meeting. After her mother's reaction to hearing he was her partner, she figured it was best to keep them far apart, lest he get the wrong idea. Or run screaming. But as she stepped into the community center and saw all the people from high school milling about in the lobby, she began to question her decision. At least with him by her side, her presence would've been given some kind of legitimacy. On her own like this, she felt like all eyes were on her, and none of them were friendly.

Near the doors to the gym, she spotted Tyler and Brody. Piper Stewart was with them. Of course the three of them would be here. Tyler and Brody would be dancing, and where they went, Piper was guaranteed to follow. Shame from old humiliation heated her cheeks. She'd wanted so badly to be a part of their group back then. They were tight-knit. Real. She'd wanted everything Tyler had, including Brody. She'd made an utter fool of herself. So. Many. Times. It had all turned out for them in the end. Tyler and Brody were back together, as they should be. And from the looks of things, they were happy. Corinne was glad for them, and if a trace of envy nipped at her heels, she figured that made her human. That kind of happiness didn't exist for people like her. Seeing it in others only highlighted how far off track her life had gone.

With no sign of Tucker, and not yet ready to face the rest of them, Corinne quietly slipped through the crowd and headed for the bathroom. She just...needed a minute to gather herself. In the past year and a half, she'd taken a lot of those minutes. She hadn't expected any kind of fanfare on her return, but neither had she counted on how much hostility and backbiting gossip she'd face. How could she make up for past mistakes if no one would let her? The simple fact was, she couldn't. So she'd learned to keep her head down, take the blows, and not fight back. It was how she'd survived her marriage, after all.

The bathroom door swung open as Corinne reached it. She stepped back. "Oh, excuse me."

The blonde who stepped out was perfectly made up, from the tips of her French manicured nails down to the toes of her designer pumps. Surprise flickered in her dark eyes before a satisfied sneer settled on her pretty face. "Why Corinne Dawson."

Corinne promptly wanted to sink through the floor. Why her? Why now? Of all the people she'd crossed paths with since she came home, she'd managed to avoid this one and regularly thanked God for it. But it seemed her stay of execution was up. It was time to face her worst mistake from Wishful.

"Hello Whitney."

Whitney Edmonds looked her up and down, her smile broadening as she took in Corinne's ripped and faded jeans and the Walmart tennis shoes. "I'd heard you were back in town."

"For a while now." Everything in her urged her to run, but Corinne didn't move. "I heard you got married."

"I did. To Garrett Harrington." Her hand flexed on the strap of her Gucci bag, flashing the huge rock on her left hand.

"Congratulations. Seems like life has been good to you. I'm glad of it." And that was the absolute truth. There was nothing Corinne regretted more than what she'd done to her former best friend when they'd started high school. After the hell Whitney had endured during those years, she deserved something good.

Whitney looked her over again, faux sincerity pasted firmly in place. "Not so good to you, has it?"

I owe her the cheap shot, Corinne reminded herself. She said nothing.

Whitney's smile turned sharper, her words sugar-coated poison. "How does that feel? That no matter what you did in high school, no matter how hard you tried, it's me who has the life you wanted?"

Like justice. But Corinne didn't say that either.

"What's the matter? Cat got that sharp tongue of yours?"

"Look, I'm not here to cause any kind of trouble. We're both here in the name of raising money for a good cause, and I think the meeting is about to start."

Whitney sniffed. "I'll believe it when I see it."

"There you are."

They both turned at the sound of Tucker's voice. He strode down the short hall, an easy smile on his face. But something in his body language telegraphed anger. Corinne tensed as he approached.

"Hey Whitney. I've gotta steal my partner away. We're about to get started." He laid a hand at the small of her back, a gentle touch, at odds with the fury she sensed pumping off him.

Not directed at me. Her limbs went rubbery as relief flooded her system.

"Your partner?" Whitney asked, surprise cracking the mask.

"Corinne's dancing on behalf of the diner. C'mon. I want to get good seats." When he nudged, Corinne moved automatically.

Tucker didn't drop his arm, instead keeping contact with her back to steer her through the thinning crowd. "You okay?" he murmured.

She jolted. He was still pissed...but on her behalf. How long had he been standing there? And why did he even care?

"Fine," she muttered.

They took seats on the second row of bleachers as Norah called everybody to attention.

"I'd like to thank everyone for coming out tonight and for volunteering to make Dancing With Wishful a success. I'd like to introduce you to our dancers. We have Tyler Edison and Cam Crawford as Team Wishful Nursery and Garden Center. Brody Jensen and Adele Daly as Team Mudcat Tavern. Tucker McGee and Corinne Dawson as Team Dinner Belles. Tara Honeycutt and Daniel Palmer as Team Daily Grind, and Charlotte Ballard and Chad Phillips as Team Wilton Memorial Hospital."

Corinne turned her head to peer into the stands. Chad Phillips was the hottie ER doc everyone at the hospital had been buzzing over this year. She wondered if he had an in with the hospital board.

"Now, as we have five couples, we'll have four nights of competition, eliminating one couple each week, until we are left with the grand champions. Winners will be determined by a combination of a judges' panel and popular vote, both by the live audience and online through the competition website. The Babylon is hosting the event and costumes are being provided by Brides and Belles—thanks Babette."

Norah continued to lay out the specifics, but Corinne was only half paying attention. She was too aware of Tucker sitting close enough beside her that she could feel the heat of his thigh alongside hers. There was more than enough room in the stands, so his actions made it seem like he was staking a claim of some kind. Did he even realize what he was doing? He didn't need his reputation tarnished by people believing he was involved with her.

But she didn't edge away. Her nerves were too raw from her encounter with Whitney, and having him sit there, all big and strong and between her and everyone else made her feel...safe for the first time in a long time. Even if it was purely an illusion, she wanted to revel in it. For just a few minutes.

"Okay, now that everybody knows how this is going to work, let's have our dancers come draw their dance out of a hat. Each couple will be performing something different, to the music of their choice."

Norah called them up, one at a time. When Tucker rose to go take his turn, Corinne felt exposed without his body as a shield. He plunged his hand into the top hat and came up with a slip of paper. A broad smile lit up his face as he read what was on it.

"Jive!" He did some kind of step ball change with a hip wiggle that had the crowd hooting. He looked up at her, his expression clearly inviting her to join in his fun.

God, had she ever noticed what an amazing smile he had?

Her own lips curved a little in response because she found she didn't want to disappoint him.

Tucker came back to his seat, rubbing his hands together in nothing less than pure glee. "Now comes the fun part."

"What's that?"

"Practice."

Oh boy.

CHAPTER 6

"*Y*OU ARE COMPLETELY INSANE if you think I can do that." Corinne pointed from herself to the screen of his laptop, where they'd just watched a YouTube video of a jive performance from *Dancing With The Stars*.

"I promise, I'm not certifiable," Tucker told her, shoving back his coffee table to make a bit more floor space in the living room of his apartment. It'd be too small for most of their rehearsals, but for tonight, it would do.

"I'm sorry, Tucker. We're going to get cut right off because there's no way I can do that."

He wondered if he could get a glass of wine into her, loosen her up some. "You were a cheerleader in high school. Y'all did all kinds of complicated choreography for those routines."

"That's different. And a long time ago to boot."

"When was the last time you danced?"

"Like that? Never. At all?" She shoved a hand through her glossy dark hair. "I don't know. Maybe freshman year at college?" Her shoulders slumped. "Mama Pearl made a mistake. I'm not cut out for this. I'm going to disappoint everyone."

"Don't knock it 'til you've tried it, sugar." Tucker wanted to thoroughly beat whoever had put those thoughts into her head. He suspected it'd be a long list of people. Instead, he opened his music and queued up a half dozen songs. As the opening brass sounded for the first number, he held out his hand for hers. "You aren't going to disappoint anybody. You've got me as a partner, and I'm damned good."

With a look of skepticism, she took it. "Were you this cocky in high school?"

"It's not cocky if you're stating the facts." With a quick tug, he had her stumbling against him.

Her breath wooshed out and her breasts pressed against his chest. Half the blood in his head rushed south, and he had to resist the urge to skim his hands up her spine. Instead, he slid one arm around her back, adjusting her posture. "You just need to loosen up a bit, have fun with it."

"Fun," she repeated.

The blank expression on her face absolutely broke his heart. But if he'd learned anything from watching her these past months, it was that Corinne Dawson didn't want pity in any form.

"For the next little while, you need to forget about work, forget about school, forget about your test, forget about being a mom, forget about life. You need to get used to moving with me."

Oh hell, did that actually sound as suggestive as it did in my head?

A flash of something—Awareness? Wariness?—in her eyes told him it probably did.

Slow your roll, McGee. Right now, this is just business.

As Sinatra crooned that he wouldn't dance, Tucker stepped into her, enjoying the press of her body against his before she stepped haltingly back. Even stiff as a board, she felt amazing. She tried to look down at her feet.

"Relax. Eyes on mine. You're thinking too hard about what you're doing."

"I told you I'd be terrible at this."

"You're not terrible. You haven't stepped on my feet once. Norah would've broken three toes by now."

The corner of her mouth twitched. "Seriously?"

"God's truth. I love her to death, but the woman can't dance to save her soul. Admittedly, she did try to warn me."

"Was that before or after she and Cam got together?"

He considered. "Mmm, well, before they told anybody they were together, anyway. Details are rather sketchy as to when they actually coupled up. Now Cam, he's got some rhythm. He and Tyler will be our big competition."

"I figure everybody will be big competition. And what's with the easy jazz? Jive is more upbeat than this, isn't it?"

"It is, but you've gotta crawl before you can walk. I need to get a sense of how you move. How well you can follow direction."

She stumbled again and made a growling noise before breaking away to pace across his living room. "I suck."

"Were you able to balance at the top of the pyramid your first day as cheerleader?"

"No."

"Okay then. You learned that, and you'll learn this. Come here."

Sinatra rolled into Dean Martin.

Corinne sighed and took his hand again.

"It's hard to trust a partner you don't know. So why don't we do a little Q and A?"

"Okay." But she drew the word out, as if she wasn't sure what he'd ask.

"What is your favorite food?"

She relaxed a fraction. Had she really thought he was going to go somewhere deeply personal right off the bat?

"Fried calamari."

"Seriously? Squid?"

"Don't knock it 'til you've tried it," she shot back.

"Touché. I'm a bit more prosaic. Pizza. In every possible form. It is the world's perfect food."

"Kurt would be inclined to agree with you. My turn. You've always been into dance and theater. I remember from back in school. Why? What's the draw?"

"Well, apart from the fact that it's fun, and the fact that I knew how to dance meant I never had to worry about getting a date for stuff, I guess I love it because it makes me feel good. Dancing always made me smile."

"Didn't the jocks hassle you?"

"That's two for you, little missy. But I'll answer anyway. No, they mostly didn't. And that was on Brody. Playing football, he straddled both worlds, so I guess that bought me a pass." He ignored how she stiffened again at Brody's name. Brody was a part of his world, and she'd just have to get used to it. "Okay, let's see. What were your favorite movies as a kid? The ones you could quote all the way through?"

Her answer was instant. "*Footloose.*"

"Reaaaaally?" he drawled. An idea was forming in his head. "What did you love about it?"

"I appreciated that Ariel ultimately bucked her restrictive parents. Plus, it's fun."

Lot of identification there. But he didn't want to bring it up because she'd finally stopped thinking about what her feet were doing and was actually following his lead.

"I'm more of a *Singing In The Rain* kinda guy."

She eyed him. "I can see that. You've got a bit of Gene Kelly air about you."

"Why, Miss Dawson, am I to understand you like old movies?"

"I do. I used to watch them with my grandparents, before they passed. My grandma adored Gene Kelly and Fred Astaire."

Tucker spun her out, then back again. "Looks like you've got a bit of Ginger to go with my Fred."

Surprised pleasure flickered over her features. "I did it."

He grinned. "You did indeed."

"Then I concede. You're very good. I suppose the cockiness is justified."

"Helps that you're a natural. You've got good rhythm and good awareness of your body." He had a good awareness of her body, too. With a spin and a dip, he finished the dance and stepped away before she gained too good an awareness of certain parts of his. "I can absolutely work with that."

Striding over to the fridge, he grabbed a couple of bottles of water, tossed her one.

"Thanks for being a patient teacher," she said.

"Thanks for being a good student." He took a long pull of water. "Can I ask you something?"

"Oh, are we still playing Q and A?"

"Why didn't you fight back when Whitney got in your face?" Tucker regretted the question the moment it fell from his lips because the light that had sparked in her eyes went out.

Corinne shrugged. "Whitney's not wrong."

"You're not that girl anymore."

Her gaze tracked to his. "You're the only one who believes that. Why?"

"I've got eyes. Give them time. They'll see."

"I appreciate your optimism," she said dryly.

In the awkward silence, he cursed his big mouth.

Corinne stepped into the breach. "So, do you have any ideas on music? I'll bow to you on this."

"Yeah, I've got some thoughts. I'll let you know for sure tomorrow. I made a few calls, got us in to the fellowship hall at the Methodist Church. We'll need more floor space to practice than we've got up here. What time works for you?"

"I need to work around my shifts at the diner and studying for the exam, not to mention spending time with Kurt. I've seen so little of him this past semester."

Tucker could see how the guilt weighed on her. And he realized rehearsal time would likely cut into much needed work hours for her at the diner.

They settled on a practice time for the next day. "I promise I'll have some choreography ready, and we can play the rest by ear."

"That's fine with me. Despite your ability to channel Gene Kelly, it's probably only going to be for the next week anyway. I don't quite have the same faith you do."

He tapped his half empty water bottle against hers in a toast. "Then I guess I'll have to have enough faith for the both of us."

FOR ONE BLESSED hour between 9:30 and 10:30 on Monday morning, after the breakfast rush was past and before the early lunch crowd trickled in, Corinne finally got a chance to slide into the booth across from Malika and study for her licensure exam. She hadn't looked at the material since Friday, splitting her weekend between Kurt and rehearsal with Tucker. This wasn't going to cut it. That she'd been studying her ass off for a year didn't matter. She needed to have this material down cold, which meant finding more study time. Somewhere. She could make do with four hours of sleep. She'd done it before.

Corinne squinted at the list of practice questions and read the next one off. "To facilitate drainage of oral secretions in a child who had cleft lip repair, the nurse should place the child in what position? Supine, Side-lying, Trendelenburg, or High-Fowler's?"

"Side-lying," Malika said.

"Correct."

"When communicating with children, what most important factor should the nurse take into consideration?"

Cracking a yawn, Corinne answered without hearing the choices. "Coffee. How much coffee she's had."

Malika laughed. "I thought you were supposed to have more time for sleep since clinicals were over."

"I was delusional."

Mama Pearl set down a tray carrying three cups and a pot of coffee before sliding into the opposite side of the booth with a sigh that had Corinne wondering if she'd been on her feet more than she'd claimed. "Drink up."

"Bless you. But I could've done that." She reached for the pot, expertly pouring a cup for each of them. "How's your ankle?"

"Fine."

Which had been her stock answer since the incident had happened.

"So, what's the plan for this here test?"

"I'm waiting on the school to send transcripts to the testing center so I can register." And there went a couple hundred bucks she didn't really have to spare. She couldn't afford to screw up this first attempt. "Meanwhile, we're studying."

Mama Pearl took a slow sip of coffee. "Can't have much time for that, while pulling double shifts and practicing for the competition."

She'd hit the nail on the head, so Corinne didn't argue with her. What was there to say?

"Competition?" Malika asked.

"I'm the diner's representative for a local fundraiser."

"I'm pulling you off second shift," Mama Pearl continued.

"What?" No. She needed the money, needed to make up for the hours she hadn't been able to work during the semester. "But Mama Pearl, I—"

The older woman waved a hand. "Hush now. I'm not finished. I'm the one got you into this competition. It's for the diner, so it counts as work. I'll be paying you for all the time you're putting into it."

Corinne bristled. Had Tucker said something? He knew how worried she was about fitting everything in.

"I don't want a handout."

Mama Pearl sniffed. "It's no such thing. I'll get more mileage out of this competition than a whole passel of newspaper or radio ads. I want the publicity, which means I want my team to win. Which means y'all need time to practice. So hush yo' mouth and deal with it."

There was no arguing with The Tone. Greater men and women than she had tried and failed.

"'Sides, you need to be spendin' some time with your youngin. I got no intention of taking you away from him any more than you already are."

Corinne's throat went thick with gratitude. Mama Pearl Buckley was the other person who'd been unfailingly kind to her since she'd come home. Direct and prone to sharing hard truths, maybe, but at the root, always kind. She'd given Corinne a chance to show she was no longer the misguided girl she'd been. And Corinne had to believe that eventually, hopefully, others would follow her example.

"I don't know what to say."

"Ain't nothin' to say. You just put your all into this competition. I got a side bet with Cassie over at The Grind and I want bragging rights, damn it."

Corinne huffed a laugh. The coffee shop was the other primary gossip center in town. The owner, Cassie Callister, was in a permanent competition with Mama Pearl for the crown of Gossip Queen. "Yes, ma'am. Thank you."

Mama Pearl shoved to her feet and picked up her coffee. "I'll let y'all get back to your studying."

Corinne watched her shuffle back toward the counter and realized she wasn't limping. At all. "Your ankle."

"It's better."

At that level of improvement, Corinne wondered if it had been sprained at all in the first place. Had she been played? "Then you could dance."

"Child, these old bones cain't move the way they need to to win this competition. Yours can."

Realization slammed into her like a freight train. "You set me up!"

"I ain't confirming or denying." Which was as good as a confession.

"Why didn't you just ask me?"

Mama Pearl turned knowing eyes in her direction. "Would you have said yes?"

No. No, she'd have found some way to get out of it because she already had a million things on her plate.

"That's what I thought." Mama Pearl nodded to herself, as if confirming the wisdom of her actions. "Now you're in it. The officially registered representative of the diner. And you finish what you start. So go dance and do us proud."

She would. Of course she would. But... "Why me?"

"I told you—"

"I know what you said about Darlene and Cindy. But really, why me?"

"Two reasons. First, you've been hidin' long enough, lettin' folks pick and poke at you for what amounts to ancient history. It's time you got out there as who you are now and held your head up high. You're making a life for yourself and your little boy, and that's something to be proud of."

Her throat went thick again. "And the other?"

Mama Pearl winked. "Because you could do with a little fun, and Tucker McGee offers that in spades."

Corinne was still gaping as her boss swung through the door into the kitchen.

This was a *matchmaking* attempt? It was one thing to get such a thing from her mother. Marianne would look at Tucker and see nothing but his position in local society, his success as an attorney. But Mama Pearl?

"Tucker McGee? The hot attorney who was all defending your honor last week?" Malika shoved her books aside and leaned forward on both elbows. "Tell me all."

"There's nothing to tell."

One brow winged up. "Am I gonna have to get the scoop from Mama Pearl?"

"We're only dance partners."

"Right, because Mama Pearl thinks you could use a little fun. Which, by the way, I am in full agreement with."

"I don't have time for 'a little fun', the euphemistic kind or otherwise." And seriously, calling Tucker "a little fun" was like saying Godzilla was a little lizard. She'd laughed more during their rehearsals this weekend than the last three months combined. Tucker was... He was... Charming. Funny. He'd grown into the gawky, long limbs she remembered from their youth. And that smile...

She wondered why she'd never noticed him in high school. She'd seen him, of course. Known who he was. They'd been on student council together. He'd been the class treasurer. But she'd never really *seen* him. Probably because he was usually attached to Brody, and when Brody was around, she'd never been able to see anyone else.

"And yet you're about to be paid to have it." Malika's teeth flashed in a delighted smile.

"She's barking up the wrong tree."

"Why?"

Corinne blew out an exasperated breath. "Because even if I had time for something—which we have established I don't—he's out of my league. He's not interested in me. Why would he be? A college drop out. A single mom with a less than pristine past. Nobody wants that package."

Malika's expression darkened. "Don't make me come across this table and kick your ass. That's my friend you're talking about. Who is an awesome mom to an even awesomer little boy and who just finished one of the most rigorous nursing programs in the state, while working full-time. You set out on your own to start over after life blew up on you. That makes you one of the bravest people I know. So make all the excuses you want about not having time, but don't you dare act like you're not worth his attention."

One corner of Corinne's mouth twitched. "I'll consider my ass kicked. I love you."

"Love you back."

But as she turned back to her textbooks, Corinne couldn't help but think that dancing with him made her remember she was still a woman, not merely a mother. She hadn't expected that and wasn't entirely sure she liked the reminder.

Forget it, she ordered herself.

After the competition was over, however long they lasted, Tucker McGee would go back to being entirely out of her league. And that was fine because she had more important life stuff to focus on. Like passing the NCLEX and taking care of her son.

Mind made up, she turned to the next page of questions. "A nurse caring for a client with a platelet count of 60,000 should observe for which initial finding…"

CHAPTER 7

"WE'RE GOING *FIRST?*" CORINNE'S voice rose to a squeak. "How did that happen?"

"Luck of the draw," Tucker told her.

She wrapped her arms tight around her ribs and paced a small circle in the "backstage" holding area The Babylon was providing for the dancers. Her breathing was too shallow for his taste. Around them, the other competitors talked quietly as event volunteers moved in and out of the room, carrying on last minute prep for the show.

"It's no big deal. Think of it like a pep rally. You ought to be used to being the first to hype people up."

She stopped pacing and glared at him. "At a pep rally, I had a full squad of other cheerleaders."

Wanting to put her mind at ease, Tucker crossed over and took her by the shoulders. "Don't worry. You absolutely nailed this routine in practice."

"No one was watching in practice." Her teeth worried at that full bottom lip.

Tucker wanted to kiss it to soothe the hurt. Shaking his mind away from that idea—whenever he *did* kiss her, it wouldn't be in front of an audience—he rubbed his hands down her arms in a gesture he hoped was comforting and kept his voice low, for her ears only. "I've got this. I've got you. Trust me."

Her head canted to the side, awareness flickering in those pretty, sky blue eyes, along with a hefty dose of confusion and uncertainty. Because they both knew he wasn't just talking about the dance. And this was so *not* how he'd planned to approach all this.

"Mommy!"

At the sound of the happy shriek, Corinne turned away from him, her face lighting up like Christmas morning. "Kurt!" She opened her arms and her three-foot firecracker flew into them. "Hi baby."

Kurt pulled back. "Grandma brought me to see you!"

"I see that!" Corinne looked up as her mother approached. "Thanks for bringing my cheering section, Mama."

Tucker had seen Marianne Dawson around town over the years. In a town the size of Wishful, how could he not? But he hadn't actually interacted with her since high school. She was an older, harsher version of her daughter.

"Past his bedtime, so we'll go after you're through," she said. Not a word of actual encouragement. Which was pretty consistent with how he remembered her treating Corinne back then. He suspected nothing had changed in that department.

"Well, that works out because we're up first."

Tucker recognized the fake it 'til you make it smile Corinne pasted on.

"Hey Tucker!" Kurt lifted his hand and, to Tucker's surprise, flawlessly executed the complicated fist bump they'd come up with the day they'd played HORSE.

"Good to see you, buddy. We appreciate the support, Mrs. Dawson," he added.

Marianne looked him up and down. "Well, didn't you grow up fine? You were such a gangly thing in high school."

"Hit college and filled out," he said easily, despite the fact that he recognized a cougar survey when he saw one. *Yeah, that's not creepy at all.*

"You look pretty, Mommy."

The false smile turned real as Corinne looked down at her son. "Thanks, kiddo."

Kurt's attention shifted over to him. "You look like that guy in that movie."

Depending on which movie, that was a pretty dead on assessment, Tucker decided.

"Hey there, little man." He crouched down, pointing at the Chewbacca doll Kurt had clutched in one arm. "I see you brought part of the Rebel Alliance to cheer us on."

Kurt's eyes got round as saucers. "You know *Star Wars?*"

He nodded gravely. "I do."

"I'm gonna be a Jedi when I grow up."

Tucker grinned. "Best job ever!" He offered his fist for a knuckle bump. The boy bumped his fist with enthusiasm and a matching grin. No wonder he was the center of Corinne's world. He was a great kid.

"Are you a Jedi?"

"I'm a lawyer."

"What's a lawyer?"

"Uh." How did one explain that to a five-year-old?

Corinne scooped him up. "There are different kinds, but a lawyer is someone who fights for what is right and to make sure people are getting what's fair according to the law."

"Jedis fight for what's right."

"That's right, they do. But instead of lightsabers, lawyers use words," Corinne told him.

Kurt pondered for a minute. "I'd rather have a lightsaber."

Tucker laughed. "Me too, kid. Me too."

One of the volunteers tapped him on the shoulder. "Five minutes to start."

"Thanks." Tucker smiled at Kurt. "It was nice to see you again, Kurt. You and your grandma need to go find your seats."

Kurt gave his mother a smacking kiss. "Good luck, Mommy."

She squeezed him. "Thanks, baby."

Marianne held out her hand for her grandson's. She divided a look between Corinne and Tucker. "Don't screw this up."

What a fucked up way to say 'Good luck'.

As the pair of them walked away, Tyler came over. "Was that your Kurt?"

Corinne looked startled. "Yes, it was."

"My goodness, he's grown since I saw him last year! And I remember him being so shy." Tyler smiled at her.

After a brief hesitation Corinne answered. "That phase has officially ended. He talks pretty much from the moment he gets out of bed until his head hits the pillow. And sometimes in his sleep, too."

Tucker reached for her hand. "We've gotta get in position."

"Break a leg, you two!"

"That's theater speak for 'good luck'," he reminded Corinne.

She blinked a moment. "Thank you."

Tucker mouthed his own "Thanks" back at Tyler before following the waiting staffer to the doors leading into the ballroom.

"Oh my God. It's *packed*," Corinne whispered.

"Norah organized it. Of course it's packed. She doesn't do anything halfway."

From inside the ballroom, the emcee's voice boomed over the sound system. "Welcome to Dancing With Wishful!"

Corinne's hand tightened in his as the announcer went through the opening spiel, talking about sponsors, introducing judges, and explaining to those watching at home how they could cast their vote online. And then it was time.

"Without further ado, let's give a warm, Wishful welcome to

our first dancers of the night, Team Dinner Belles' Tucker McGee and Corinne Dawson, performing the jive."

He could feel her nerves telegraphing up his arm as they walked out to the center of the ballroom. They'd have to split. The routine began with him at one end and her at the other. Before they parted, he bent his head to her ear. "Remember to breathe and look at me. It's just us. We're here to have fun."

"Fun," she repeated.

Tucker let her go and took his position.

CORINNE'S DANCE shoes echoed in the weighty silence as she took her position. Her heart fluttered madly in her throat.

Breathe, she reminded herself.

Pivoting to face her partner, she took a long, deep breath. He pointed to her with two fingers and flicked them up to his eyes.

Okay. Just watch Tucker. It's just me and Tucker. She nodded at him, taking in his maroon dinner jacket and bow tie and grinning, despite the nerves. He'd picked this for her, and she loved that. So, when the opening bars of "Footloose" rolled out of the speakers, Corinne did as he'd asked. She had fun.

He made it easy. Everything, it seemed, was easy with Tucker. Corinne matched him step-for-step. She relaxed into the music and let him throw her around like a rag doll. Their kicks were high and in sync, their footwork perfect. When it came time for the back flip, she mirrored him—and damn if she didn't nail it, even in dance shoes. A thrill of triumph shot through her. She felt a bigger one when she successfully sank into the splits before him on the last note and the applause thundered around them.

Tucker lifted her to her feet. They grinned at each other like loons and took their bows.

"Tucker McGee, ladies and gentlemen. Proving he's still every girl's favorite prom date. Let's give him and Corinne another round of applause while the judges calculate their scores."

He slid his arm around her waist. "We did it!"

"Yes, we damn well did," she agreed, giving him a squeeze.

"Let's hear from our judges."

They shifted toward the raised dais, where the three judges all lifted their paddles.

"Team Dinner Belles earned an eight, a nine, and another eight. An admirable performance to kick us off on this first night of competition here at Dancing With Wishful."

Corinne and Tucker walked off the floor, waving to the crowd. "I see why you like the applause."

"Awesome, isn't it?"

She caught sight of Whitney at one of the tables they passed. Whitney leaned over to speak to a well-dressed man beside her. "Somebody should remember she's not in high school anymore and doesn't have the body to pull off that dress."

Corinne's pleasure dimmed.

As soon as they cleared the crowd, they were surrounded by well wishers, all clamoring to speak to Tucker. She turned to him and forced a smile. "I'll be back in a minute. I want to step out for some air."

He shot her a questioning look as she pulled free. Corinne gave him an *I'm fine* wave and made a beeline for the elevator. She punched the button for the roof and didn't take a proper breath until the doors closed.

Of course she wasn't in high school anymore. Being a mom, she absolutely didn't have the body she'd had at eighteen. Is that really what people thought? That she was out there pretending she was still in high school? Reliving some kind of glory days?

When the doors slid open, Corinne moved quickly through the small vestibule and pushed through the glass doors leading out to the lush rooftop gardens that gave the hotel its name. No one was up here. She was pitifully grateful for that as she sank down on one of the stone benches. She didn't need anyone else to slap her in the face with reality.

It had been so lovely, for that few minutes, to escape her reality. To not feel like a pariah or a screw up.

All good dreams come to an end.

"Is this bench taken?"

Corinne jolted at the sound of Tucker's voice. She hadn't heard him follow her up.

He didn't wait for an invitation before wedging himself beside her on the bench and sliding an arm around her shoulders.

"We busted our asses for tonight and it paid off. You were dynamite out there, and you look goddamned amazing. Don't let the words of one bitter, angry woman ruin everything we've worked for."

Of course he'd heard. Her cheeks heated and she dropped her gaze to her lap, ashamed, though of what, exactly, she wasn't sure.

Tucker cupped her cheek, forced her to face him. His usually jovial face was serious. "Stop letting the opinions of assholes be your truth. You are a talented, beautiful, hardworking woman. It's time you started believing that."

Corinne stared at him, this lovely, kind man, who couldn't possibly be more different from Lance. He took the time to build her up instead of tearing her down. Had she ever truly had someone like that in her life?

"You're sweet, Tucker." He'd made her feel better, and she hadn't expected that. She tipped her face up and brushed her lips lightly over his in gratitude.

But as she pulled back, his hand slid deeper into her hair, trapping her. She had time for one, brief pulse of surprise and awareness before his mouth covered hers. And her mind simply emptied. Sweet? She'd thought him sweet? His kiss rocketed from zero to explosive in less than a second, sparking something inside her long since dormant. She leaned into him, wanting more, sliding her hand into the short strands of his hair, holding him to her. His tongue traced the seam of her lips, and she opened to him, enjoying his taste as it seeped into her. Someone groaned. Him? Her? She didn't know. But he gentled the kiss, stroking his hands lightly up and down her spine before easing back.

They sat on the stone bench in the pretty garden, surrounded by the scents of honeysuckle and jasmine, breathing hard and staring at each other.

Corinne's brain was struggling to come back online and failing. "That was...I..." What did a girl say when she'd just had her mind blown by an unexpected kiss?

"I'd apologize, but I'd be lying. I've been wanting to do that for nearly fifteen years."

Surprised pleasure slid through her, almost as seductive as the taste of his lips. "Seriously?" She couldn't even imagine.

Tucker took a deep breath and offered a self-deprecatory smile. "Confession time: I had the biggest crush on you in high school."

"Why? I was horrible. And I kept throwing myself at your best friend." As soon as the words were out of her mouth, she wished she could take them back.

"Everybody's allowed at least one crush to make a fool of themselves over."

"And who was yours?"

"You."

"Me?"

"Remember all those notes in your locker senior year?"

For months after homecoming, she'd had daily notes and the occasional tiny gifts left in her locker. Flowers. Candy. Never anything extravagant. The gifts had been nice, but it was the regular messages reminding her she was someone special that had touched her. She'd cherished those notes. They'd gotten her through some dark days. And she'd never known who left them.

"That was you?" she whispered. Even as he gave a sheepish

shrug, she knew it had been. Because he was still the guy who made an effort to build her up.

"Why?"

"Because sometimes the cheerleader needs cheerleading."

Knowing it had been him made the anonymous gesture from back then feel suddenly intimate. Corinne didn't even know how to feel about that right now. She gave a half laugh. "Maybe that's why she did it."

"Why who did what?"

"Mama Pearl faked her sprained ankle. She said I needed a little fun in my life. Evidently you're the poster boy." She looked up at him as a sinking sort of suspicion wormed its way into her brain. "Were you in on it? Is this whole thing about living out some kind of...I don't know, latent high school fantasy?"

"No. I wasn't in on Mama Pearl's plan, though I figured it out quickly enough. This isn't about a high school fantasy. Or at least, not entirely." He skimmed a thumb over her cheek and she shivered. "I know you're not the same girl. I liked the girl. But I'm a helluva lot more attracted to the woman. Have been since you walked back into town."

He'd made her speechless again. She wanted so desperately to see herself as he saw her. What did that even look like? Was she willing to risk testing the waters here for the chance to find out?

"Tucker, my life is really complicated."

He smiled. "I know. No pressure. Just wanted to put it out there." Rising, he pulled her to her feet. "Why don't we head on back down and watch the rest of the competition for the night?"

So she filed away this new information to think about later, when she was alone and had more than two brain cells to rub together, and followed him back to the ballroom.

CHAPTER 8

"TO SURVIVING THE FIRST round of competition!"

Tucker lifted his beer automatically in response to Brody's toast, but he was only half listening.

She's not coming.

When he'd texted Corinne earlier with an invite to a celebration for the victors of Round 1 of Dancing With Wishful, she'd said she'd stop by after work if she could. But after half an hour of watching the door to Speakeasy, while trying not to look like he was watching, she was a no show. And that disappointed him more than he wanted to admit. He worried it was more than her just bailing to study. Maybe he'd pushed her too far with the kiss. That explosive, amazing, better than all of his high school dreams combined kiss that he hadn't been able to stop thinking about. She'd been right there with him on that rooftop. But maybe she'd talked herself out of taking a risk to see where things went. And that would be a damned shame.

"What'd y'all draw this next go round?" Cam asked.

"The Charleston." Another glance at the door and his pulse leapt. There she was, standing inside the entryway, hands twisting the strap of her purse as she scanned the room.

"We got salsa. I am not at all sure my hips can do—"

Tucker stood up. "Be back."

By the time he made it to the front, she was out on the side-walk. She'd almost made the corner when he bolted outside.

"Corinne!"

She stopped in her tracks, shoulders tensing.

Caught.

"Hey Tucker. I was just…I thought I'd have time to stop by, but I really need to be getting home to study. I haven't put in enough hours this week, with rehearsal and everything." Again with the twisting of the purse strap, and she wouldn't quite meet his eyes.

He ducked down so he could look into hers. "You came over here just to walk away?"

She was going to lie, to blow him off. He could see it in her face. So he reached for her hand, the one not squeezing the life out of her purse strap. She looked down at their twined fingers.

"Why are you really running away?" he asked quietly.

Corinne lifted her head to look at him then, and he could see what it cost her. "Because going in there and hanging out with all your friends is about the scariest thing I can imagine for a social situation."

Everything in him wanted to gather her up, to soothe that worry away. But he ordered himself to keep things easy between them, so he settled for stroking his thumb on the back of her hand. "Is this about not wanting to face them? Or me?"

Her voice was small as she admitted, "Some of both."

Tucker untangled her other hand so he had them both, because he needed to touch her. Needed to make this better. "I wasn't trying to scare you."

Her hands flexed in his and she let out an irritated huff. "I'm not scared. I've been scared. This is—I don't know what this is. It makes me nervous. You make me nervous."

I make her nervous? Nervous meant she felt something. More than a little something, he was guessing. Tucker liked that a bit too much and wanted to use the information to tease a smile out of her. But he knew she wasn't in the right frame of mind, so he held in the cocky grin and kept his voice gentle. "You've earned the chance to celebrate. This is your achievement, too. Come inside. Just for a little while."

She bit the lip he hadn't stopped fantasizing about. "I don't know, Tucker."

"C'mon. For me?" He squeezed her hands. "I've got you."

She hesitated. "Well, Kurt's already had supper. I guess I could come in for one slice."

"That's a girl."

Tucker kept her hand in his until they got through the door, then switched to nudging her at the small of her back. He was aware of his friends' curiosity as they approached the table, cognizant of the need to walk the line between behaving like he and Corinne were a couple—which they weren't—but still making it clear to his friends she was with him and they'd damned well better behave. Back at the big table there was a beat or three of silence, a few raised eyebrows.

Then Norah—bless her—offered a broad smile and said, "That back flip's been the talk of the town! How on *Earth* did you pull it off? In *dance shoes*, no less?"

"I was, um, a cheerleader all through high school."

"Head cheerleader," Tucker added.

When Corinne began to twist the purse strap again, he tugged it from her shoulder and looped it over the chair he'd pulled out for her. With a quick, almost panicked look in his direction, she sank into the chair. He dropped back into his beside her and reached for one of the hands trying to white knuckle the chair edge.

"What'll it be?" asked Tyler. "Pepperoni? Vegetarian? Supreme? I'd offer meat lover's but it's already been wiped out."

"Oh, I—a slice of supreme, please. Thanks."

"I still can't get over those acrobatics," Norah continued. "If I tried to do any of that, my partner would be taking his life into his hands."

Corinne's lips twitched as she glanced at Tucker. "I did hear something to that effect."

Norah laughed. "Hand to God, I have no skill in that department."

"You've got a multitude of other skills, Wonder Woman." Cam leaned over to punctuate the statement with a kiss.

"Get a room," Brody called.

"Better yet, get a wedding date," Tucker added.

"We're working on it. Every time we think we have one nailed down, something comes up," she said.

"If you'd acknowledge the fact that someone other than you could run this town for a week or two, you'd probably get a lot further," Piper pointed out.

As banter picked back up around them, Corinne unbent a little. She ate her slice of pizza in small, neat bites, observing his friends, occasionally contributing to the conversation. And the world didn't end. Better yet, everybody made an effort to include her. Tucker considered the evening a success when Corinne snagged a second slice of pizza as she chatted with Tyler about some project or other she'd found on Pinterest.

Eventually, she checked her watch, eyes widening. "Oh, good Lord. I need to get on home or I'll miss Kurt's bedtime story."

"Yeah? What're you reading?" Myles asked.

"*Captain Underpants* for possibly the hundredth time."

Myles nudged Piper. "Obviously we need to add that to the library for the Peanut."

Tucker rose as Corinne did. "I'll walk you out to your car."

She flashed him a puzzled smile. "That's not necessary. I'm all the way over by the diner."

"All the more reason for an escort, as it's after dark."

Her mouth opened, then closed again. "All right. Just let me run to the restroom right quick."

As soon as she was out of earshot, the table erupted with questions.

"What's going on?" Tyler asked.

"Corinne Dawson? Seriously?" Piper put in.

"What exactly was that?" Brody asked.

"*That*," Tucker said, "is a hardworking, single mom, who's scared to death of the lot of you, and too afraid to ask for a second chance, lest y'all judge her like everybody else in this town for mistakes that are ancient history."

Well that shut up any replies they might've made.

As he spotted Corinne coming back, he leaned down to Piper. "I've got a favor to ask of you. I'll call you about it later."

She cut her eyes toward Corinne, then back to him. "Okay."

Everybody made polite farewells. Tucker found himself grateful to step out into the hot, sticky night, if only to escape the interrogation he knew was brewing.

"I'd say that went better than you expected. Seems like you maybe enjoyed yourself a little."

"Do you want a cookie for being right?"

He liked the sass in her tone and grinned at her as he took her hand. "Well now, a smart man never turns down a cookie. Especially not a cookie from a pretty woman."

"How is it I never knew you were charming?"

"I never had a chance to charm you back in the old days. Besides, I've improved with age."

She looked down at their joined hands as they crossed the town green. "You're taking your reputation in your hands, you know. Risking being seen like this with the likes of me."

At the side of the fountain, he stopped, used momentum to pull her in. "Oh yeah. Tucker McGee finally wised up and decided to go after that pretty brunette he's been eying for more than a year. Took him long enough."

"That's not what they'd be saying." But she slid her arms around his waist.

"Well, they should be." He dipped his head to within an inch of hers.

"I like your version better," she whispered, tipping her lips up until only the barest hint of breath separated them.

"Me too," he murmured.

They met on a sigh. And oh yeah. He'd been wanting this pretty much from the moment he'd stopped on the roof. She melted into him. That slow, gradual release of tension was the best kind of victory. Heat licked in his blood, but he held it in check. This wasn't the time or the place. So he kept it easy, sweet. The kind of kiss he'd imagined giving her years ago. The kind of kiss that said he had all the time in the world to savor her. That she was worth savoring.

She swayed a bit in his arms when he pulled back. That was gratifying, too.

"I'm thinking charm isn't the only area where you improved with age," she said, still a trifle breathless. "If you'd kissed like that in high school, I'd have heard about it."

Tucker laughed. "I was a lot more talk and a lot less action back then."

"I like action. God, I'd forgotten I like action."

His body was a hundred percent on board with that plan.

She took a breath and blew it out. "But this is...I'm not... I wasn't expecting this, Tucker. And I certainly wasn't looking for it."

"Not a fan of surprises?" he said lightly, working to ratchet down his own reaction.

"It's not that, I just don't know what to do with this. My life is a mess."

"Seems to me you've been doing a damned good job of straightening out that mess since you came home."

"I've got a long way to go, yet."

He stroked a hand through her hair, then took her hand and began strolling again. He hoped it was toward Dinner Belles because he was rattled, too. "There's no time clock on this. No expiration date. I'm not in a hurry. I just want to see where this goes. That's all I'm asking for. A shot."

"I'm a package deal."

"It's a pretty great package. Kurt's an awesome kid."

"Easy to say on a morning's acquaintance."

"Sometimes a morning is all you need. I like you Corinne. And I like your son. He's not a problem for me."

As they reached her car, she turned to him. "You're one in a million, Tucker McGee."

"Does that mean I'm getting a shot?"

"I suppose it does, if only to satisfy my curiosity about what on Earth you see in me."

He opened her car door to keep from pulling her in again. "I'll take great pleasure in showing you."

She shook her head at him, as if he was a complete puzzle to her, then climbed into the car.

"See you at rehearsal, Ginger," he told her.

That teased out the smile he'd been looking for. "Until rehearsal, Fred."

"WATCHED you and Tucker on the live feed Friday night. My word, it was incredible!"

Corinne couldn't stop the smile on her face as Mamie Landon beamed about the performance. "Thank you, Mrs. Landon. We worked really hard on it."

"Well, and it showed. I can't believe that back flip. I was telling Loretta how impressed I was and how we should get tickets for all the future shows. What are y'all doing this week?"

"The Charleston. I'm meeting Tucker in a little while to go over choreography."

"You can bet I'm gonna be there Friday night."

"We appreciate the support. Can I top off that tea for you?"

As she went through the routine of taking orders and serving, Corinne found she held her head higher, actually looked customers in the eye. People were enthusiastic about the competition and impressed with what they'd seen. Even some of her former classmates, who'd given her the cold shoulder since her return, had admitted to watching and enjoying the performance. She wasn't under any delusion that all was forgiven and she was suddenly accepted, but maybe it was a step in the right direction.

Maybe Tucker was right. Maybe it just takes time.

Or maybe they'd started to accept her because he did.

She couldn't account for it, but she'd somehow snared the interest of a smart, interesting, funny, kind, and—she had to admit—sexy man. And that made her feel good. When was the last time she'd felt truly *good* about herself? She couldn't remember. And that was probably pretty damned sad. Corinne didn't want to be sad. Not anymore. She knew this couldn't go anywhere, but right now, she wanted to enjoy Tucker, enjoy his interest, and ride out this flirtation as long as it lasted. So when she left at the end of her shift, she was loaded with takeout containers of all his diner favorites.

The murmur of voices greeted her as she swung through the doors and into the fellowship hall that had become their designated practice space.

"I brought dinner!" she called.

The babble stopped in an instant. Corinne's smile slipped a few notches as she noticed Piper perched on a table beside Tucker. If the hurried silence hadn't been a big enough clue, the side eye Piper shot her made it absolutely certain they'd been talking about her.

Corinne hesitated.

Tucker broke away, all smiles. "Do I smell onion rings?"

"And a bacon, mushroom, and Swiss burger."

"Somebody's been paying attention." He lifted the bag from her hand and opened it for a good sniff and a groan.

"It's all you ever order for lunch, so it wasn't hard. You'd mentioned you had a long day in court, so I thought you might want something before we got into the routine." Corinne shot a look at Piper, who hadn't moved. "I'm sorry, I didn't bring anything for you. I didn't realize you'd be here." It had been a stupid impulse to bring dinner. Stupid to act like this was anything more than what it was: rehearsal.

Piper waved that off. "I've already eaten. The only thing this baby's tolerating right now is breakfast. I swear, it's going to come out clucking like a chicken and oinking like a pig for all the bacon and eggs I'm eating."

"At least it's staying down now," Tucker pointed out.

"Thank God. It's a pitiful thing to be smaller at the end of your first trimester than you were at the start."

"When I had morning sickness with Kurt, there was this citrus drink I'd make. Fresh lemons and limes—a blend of them, maybe a dozen—with a simple syrup to sweeten it up some. It helped when nothing much did. And without the chemicals in soft drinks."

"I still get a twinge most mornings, so I'll try it." Piper rubbed her baby bump and didn't move.

Corinne couldn't imagine why she was sticking around. "Are you helping out with choreography tonight?"

Tucker looked up from where he was pulling food out of the bag. "No, she's here to help you study."

Her head snapped around. "What?"

He handed over her grilled chicken sandwich and snatched one of her fries. "I know you're worried about your licensure exam and feel like you don't have near enough time to put into it, so I asked Piper to help. We're going to kill two birds with one stone. Piper's going to drill you while we dance." He said it so casually, as if him thinking to do this, trying to lighten her load a bit, alleviate a worry, was par for the course.

The whole thing made her chest tighten. She looked over at Piper. "You're...really?"

Piper shrugged. "Been there, done that. I've got some general advice for how to take the test, in addition to quizzing."

"That's really kind of you. I appreciate it." And she did, no matter what Piper had been saying before she walked in. "But I'm not sure if I can do that *and* learn choreography."

"Sure you can. You dance better when you're thinking about something else." Tucker scarfed an onion ring and made nomming noises. "This is awesome. Glad you thought of it. I was gonna try to talk you into swinging by the Mudcat when we were done. This is better."

"If you want, I can get started with the quizzing while you eat," Piper offered.

Corinne glanced at Tucker. "How strong is your stomach?"

"Cast iron."

"You lie," Piper accused. She looked at Corinne with a conspiratorial twinkle in her eye. "He can't stand the smell of blood."

"It was *one time*," Tucker protested. "And the blood was coming *out* of me at the time."

"Your own fault for walking old man Whitehead's fenceline to start."

"I was *eight*. And you were right there with me, thank you very much."

"Good thing, too. Tyler freaked out. I was the one who figured out how to use your belt for a tourniquet." Piper looked at Corinne. "He fell and wound up with a nasty gash to his leg. Just barely nicked the femoral artery. Bled like a stuck pig. I was fascinated. I think that's when I decided to go into medicine."

"Your bedside manner has improved some over the years," Tucker said.

They kept on like that for a few more minutes, poking at each other with the ease of long-time friends. They went back, Corinne knew. Way, way back. And that made it a little bit easier to accept the side eye and whatever concerns Piper might have about her. Piper was an absolute tigress when it came to protecting her friends. But if she'd agreed to this study session, she had to be giving Corinne the benefit of the doubt. It was more than Corinne had expected.

"Okay, let's get started. What is the priority nursing action after a subtotal thyroidectomy? A) Airway obstruction, B) Hemorrhage, C) Tetany, D) Edema?"

Corinne unwrapped her sandwich. "Airway obstruction."

"Good." They continued drilling for several minutes, until Corinne and Tucker had finished their dinner and her chest had eased.

"Okay, pause for a bit. It's time for the unveiling of the music." He punched some buttons on his phone and music blasted out of a Bluetooth speaker.

Corinne listened for several moments. A laugh burbled up as she recognized the tune. "Seriously? 'The Cantina Theme' from *Star Wars*?"

"Yeah. We'll dress you up in a white dress with the bagel bun hair, and I'll do Han. Or maybe Luke, depending on what Babette can help me come up with for costumes. It's got a great beat for the Charleston, and I thought Kurt would get a kick out of it. I even got us lightsabers." Tucker produced a pair of them, switching something on the hilts so the blades glowed green. "He can have them when we're done."

Corinne stared at him. He'd knocked her legs right out from under her. She couldn't quite get her breath. "You did all this for Kurt?"

"Sure. Kid's got good taste in sci-fi. Which he gets from his mother. Don't think I don't remember your love of *Star Wars* novels back in high school."

He did? Now Corinne and Piper were both staring at him.

"Anyway, I felt like letting my geek flag fly, and I figured we'll get pop culture votes from the online crowd."

He'd sought to take care of her and entertain her baby. And he remembered something about her that *no one* in high school had known. Oh, he was playing it off, but he'd put thought into this. For both of them. No one had ever done that before. Certainly not Lance.

Something inside her warmed and shifted, and this unexpected thing between them slid right on past a simple flirtation and into something more.

As he put his hands on her, began to demonstrate the basic steps of the dance, all she could think was, *Uh oh.*

CHAPTER 9

"OKAY, I'M CALLING IT. I can't possibly cram in any more questions or choreography tonight."

"Sure?" Tucker asked, whipping her into a spin.

Corinne stumbled, lost her footing, and ended up plastered up against his chest, her arms clutching his shoulders. Exactly what he'd intended.

"Whoa there. I've got you."

She blinked up at him, her pupils blown wide. One corner of her mouth quirked as she regained her footing and stepped away from him, bracing her hands on her thighs as she worked to catch her breath. He could pretend it was from more than the dancing, right?

Tucker handed over a bottle of water and chugged one of his own. "It's a good start. You've got all the components. We just need to work on putting them all together. And it sounds like you're better prepared for your test than you thought. I might even be able to answer a fair chunk of that test now."

"Keep dreaming, Tuck," Piper laughed. "Seriously, though, you're in good shape, Corinne. We can do this again, if you like. When is your exam?"

"A week from Monday. I'll be so relieved when it's over. And yes, I'd love to do this again, if you don't mind."

"I'll dig through my stuff at home. I know I've got more test materials stuffed in a box somewhere."

"Thank you." Corinne capped her water. "I should be getting home to Kurt. It's nearly time for bed, and we have another installment of *Captain Underpants* to cover."

"Same time tomorrow night?" Tucker asked.

"Yeah, I can do that." She smiled down at the lightsaber. "Kurt is seriously going to love this. Thanks for thinking of it."

It was such a small thing and a fun thing. He'd just wanted to see the kid light up. But the way his mother looked at him as she handed the toy back over, as if he were her own personal superhero, made his chest swell with pride. Yeah, he could get used to that.

"You gonna tell him?"

"Oh no. He'd want to come to all the rehearsals and then we wouldn't get anything done. This should be a surprise. Mama Pearl's bringing him to the show."

"Somebody will have to be sure to get a picture of his face when he sees," Tucker said.

"It'll be pure magic." She grinned at him, and that, too, was pure magic.

The moment stretched out between them, full of things unsaid, gestures not made because they were both aware of their audience. They'd turned a corner, and he wasn't quite sure how or what it meant. But there'd be time enough to figure that out later.

At last, Corinne scooped up her purse. "I'll see you tomorrow, Tucker."

"Tomorrow."

"Thanks again for the study session," she added, with a wave at Piper.

"No problem."

They both watched as she walked out of the fellowship hall.

Tucker turned back to his Bluetooth speaker and made a bit of a production of turning it off, stowing it in the case.

"You know, I thought, at first, when you asked me to come drill her that this was about the competition and you helping out so you could get the most practice time. But you like her."

"She's been a good partner." Tucker shrugged, putting off the inevitable for a few moments longer.

"No, I mean you *like* her like her." Piper's words came out more like an accusation.

The tone made him bristle. But he bit back the irritation and fell back on sarcasm. "What is this, high school?"

"Tucker." A plea this time.

He sighed, knowing the jig was up. "Fine. Yes, I like her."

"You legitimately like Corinne Dawson," Piper clarified. "The woman who spent all of high school and at least a year of college shamelessly throwing herself at one of your best friends and trying to torpedo his relationship with Tyler."

Temper stirred again. "That's what she *did*. It's not who she is and that's never who she was."

"You're just gonna excuse all the bad behavior?"

"I'm accepting it's in the past. Why the hell does everyone insist on punishing her for something that was over and done a decade ago?"

"I'm not punishing her, Tucker."

"You would have happily run her through on Tyler's behalf when Brody came back last year."

"Only because I thought she upset Tyler."

"She didn't. At least not deliberately. Tyler seems perfectly willing and able to get past their history now that she and Brody are engaged, so why can't you?"

"I haven't had a reason to before now. Look, Tucker, I'm not trying to be difficult here, I'm just trying to understand where this is coming from. You know as well as I do that performing together can create a false sense of attraction and intimacy."

"This isn't new," he interrupted. "This isn't because we're dancing together. I've been wanting to ask her out for more than a year."

Piper gaped at him. "A *year?* Tucker, I know you haven't really dated anyone seriously since Laura, and maybe that's left you feeling kind of lonely, especially since all of us are coupled up now, but *Corinne?* She's all wrong for you."

"Oh, because the one who was perfect for me on paper turned out so well?"

"I'm not saying you should find someone else like Laura, I just think you should find someone..."

"Who isn't Corinne?" he finished flatly. "It's not your call to make, Piper. And you're hardly the poster child for making rational relationship decisions. You and Myles decided to get *married* before you'd even dated."

She flinched, her hand going automatically to her belly, and Tucker felt like an asshole.

He sucked in a breath, striving for calm. "I'm not proposing. I'm not making any rash decisions. But I like her." What the hell? Might as well go for broke. "I've always liked her. Had things been different, I'd have asked her out in high school."

"But why? She was such a mean girl."

"That's all you ever saw. All you wanted to see."

"Oh, like you knew her so well?"

He remembered what he'd seen after she'd been crowned Homecoming Queen, when her parents hadn't even congratulated her. Instead they'd laid into her about what she hadn't done, highlighting what they perceived as her failures. He'd watched them walk away from her and seen the tears streaking her makeup as they absolutely ruined her night. "I knew better what was driving her behavior."

"And what exactly was that? What could possibly excuse how she treated people back then?"

"It's not my story to tell. And it doesn't excuse it. I'm not saying it does. She made some mistakes. And she's more than aware of it. Since she came back to Wishful, she's been working hard to make up for them. But that's really hard when everybody keeps shoving her back in that box, acting like she still expects some kind of respect because of her former accomplishments. Newsflash: She doesn't expect anything from anybody. She's just trying to get by and make a better life for her son. I admire that. I admire what she's done, what she's trying to do. All I'm asking is for you and everybody else to give her the chance to do that without giving her more grief."

"If I was interested in giving her grief, Tucker, I wouldn't have been here tonight. I'm perfectly willing to concede she's not as I remember her. And I'm sorry if I'm having some trouble wrapping my brain around all this. It just took me by surprise, is all." Piper slid off the table and crossed to take his face in her hands. "I love you, and I want you to be happy. I know you wouldn't be investing the time in her if you didn't believe she was worth it. So I promise, I'll work on getting past our history, okay?"

It wasn't exactly the wholesale endorsement he'd hoped for, but under the circumstances, it was probably the best he'd get for now. He'd been right when he told Corinne it would take time for people to see her as who she was now.

Dropping a kiss on her cheek he said, "Thanks. Buy you and the Peanut a hot fudge sundae before Lickety Split closes for the night?"

She looped her arm through his and laid a hand over her belly. "We'd love that."

SOMETHING bright and buoyant filled Corinne's chest as she headed toward home. High on the successful rehearsal and study session, she felt lucky and grateful and—dare she admit it?—hopeful for the first time in...maybe ever. This improbable, surprising thing between her and Tucker might just be the start of a legitimate something. Maybe. That was both wonderful and terrifying. But every time the fear started to creep through her buzz, she thought about all those tiny moments over the past three weeks.

I've got you.

She believed him. And she'd learned never to believe in men. Maybe she could believe him because, for some reason, he believed in her. That was something she could quickly get addicted to. If there was a part of her counseling caution, for tonight she wanted to silence that voice and bask.

Her good mood carried her through the back door and up the stairs, where she pinned Kurt with a tickle attack post bath and gloried in his freshly-scrubbed little boy smell, before curling up on his narrow bed to read the latest chapter in *Captain Underpants.* Because she'd missed him, she made it two chapters before finally getting him settled in for the night.

Feeling a few aches from practice and deciding she'd earned a good soak, Corinne made her way down the hall to the bathroom. She was humming as she switched on the water, dug out some scented bath salts.

"Somebody's in a good mood."

Corinne looked up to see her mother leaning in the doorway, her lips curved into a smile that seemed just a little smug around the edges.

"Had a good day."

"Yeah? How's that?"

What did she say to that? It wasn't as if she'd actually confided in her mother about the problems she'd had since she came home. Not after the first time she'd come home from work, in tears because someone had scrawled an ugly note on the check instead of leaving a tip. Marianne's response had been, "Well, what did you expect?" As if she hadn't been the one driving Corinne to climb the social ladder in high school, no matter who she had to step on to do it. The ends justify the means had been one of her favorite sayings.

"It was a good day. Lots of folks talking about the competition. People enjoyed Friday's performance." God knew, it was nice to have them talking about something positive that was in the now instead of a history from a lifetime ago. A lifetime she'd rather forget.

"You did good there."

Surprised by the compliment, Corinne said, "Thanks, Mama. We worked really hard."

"Don't suppose that good mood has something to do with the dance partner you were seen locking lips with by the fountain the other night."

Corinne's cheeks heated, so she leaned over the tub to stir in the bath salts. It was Wishful. Of course someone had seen them. But she'd hoped she'd get the chance to enjoy the newness of what was between them for a while longer without commentary from the peanut gallery.

"He might have something to do with it," she admitted. Too late to deny that. "It's been a long time since I was kissed."

Marianne came further into the room, hopping up on the vanity. "Tell me everything."

Where was this buddy-buddy girlfriend thing coming from? They didn't do this. Had never done this.

"There's nothing much to tell. We kissed. That's it." No reason to mention the rooftop garden at The Babylon or all the reasons that thoughts of him had her going soft inside.

"Nonsense. That can't be everything. One kiss wouldn't put that look on your face."

"What look?" Corinne resisted the urge to check her expression in the mirror. Did she have *In serious like with a wonderful guy* tattooed on her forehead?

"That dreamy-eyed school girl expression. You like him."

She was *not* dreamy-eyed. Was she? "Of course, I like him. He's a nice man. Thoughtful. Funny."

Marianne nodded in approval. "Good lookin', too. Sure did fill out nice for being so lanky in high school."

He did, indeed. But she felt weird discussing it with her mom. "He grew up. Happens to everybody."

"Not everybody has a backside you can bounce a quarter off of."

"Mama!"

She waved a dismissive hand. "Oh, don't look so scandalized. I'm divorced, not dead. So are you two dating now?"

Corinne didn't know what they were. Not yet. And she wasn't in an all-fired hurry to define it. She'd rushed into a serious relationship with Lance and that had been a disaster of epic proportions. Not that she believed Tucker was anything like her ex-husband. But she couldn't afford to be impulsive and foolish. She had a child to consider. "I don't have time to date. Not on top of rehearsals." And Tucker had seemed fine with the idea of going slow, letting her set the pace.

"Rehearsals." The tone put Corinne's back up. "You wanna keep a man like him, you best be rehearsing something other than choreography. Leastwise the vertical kind."

Corinne switched off the water and pivoted to face her mother. "Excuse me?"

"I'm just saying, he's a good looking, successful attorney. You've gotta lock that in while you can."

"Lock what in, exactly?"

"Don't be dense, Corinne. He'd be a good provider and a helluva step up from where you are now. It's time you stopped wallowing and did something about it."

"Wallowing?" she repeated. Sheer disbelief was the only thing keeping her from shouting. "Is that what you think I've been doing?"

"You've gone a year and a half with no man at all. What else do you call it?"

"Prioritizing," Corinne snapped. "I've been working and going to school and doing everything I can to make life better for Kurt. To get us to a place where we're no longer a burden to you."

Some small part of her hoped Marianne would jump in and correct her. Say they weren't a burden. But, of course, that didn't happen.

"Be a lot quicker to find a new husband."

Because she really wanted to hurl the jar of bath salts, Corinne curled her hands around the edge of the tub. "Do you not understand what I came from, Mama? Do you not realize exactly what kind of marriage I had? And you really think I'm in any kind of a hurry to find another man after that?"

"You picked wrong the first time. Figured you'd learned better. No question, Tucker McGee is a better man than Lance."

"That's the first thing you've said that I agree with."

"Then what's the problem? You like him. He seems to like you." Her expression implied *Though God knows why.* "Why not better things for yourself?"

Appalled, insulted, Corinne rose to her feet, mustering as much pride as she could manage. "Because I'm no longer in the business of using people to get what I want. Now please step out. I want a bath."

Marianne sniffed. "You don't have to get all huffy about it."

"Just go. Please, go."

"Fine."

As soon as her mother was out of the room, Corinne locked the door. Then she sagged against the counter.

God. Was that what people would think of her with Tucker? That she was out to use him? Planning to sink in her claws and drain him like some kind of parasite?

Of course they would. Because she'd done it before. Because no one cared that she wasn't that girl anymore. No one would let her be someone else. And who would possibly believe a man like Tucker could legitimately be interested in someone like her? Who could blame them? She didn't understand his interest herself.

The gossip was inevitable. She knew that. She'd come to expect it about her and resigned herself to enduring it. But she wouldn't repay Tucker's kindness by painting a target on his back. She simply couldn't put him through that.

He'd be angry and say it didn't matter. But what did he know? He'd never been at the center of the shitstorm of public opinion. He didn't understand what that was like. And even if he stood by her, it wouldn't last. Couldn't. No one would willingly subject themselves to that. Not for the likes of her. It would change how he saw her, whatever he thought he felt for her. He would walk away, and she'd lose the only good thing to happen to her since she came back home.

She'd already endured so much. She didn't think she could go through that. She couldn't stand to have him look at her like everyone else. As if she were less. As if she'd brought all her misfortunes on herself in some kind of epic karmic smackdown.

There was only one thing to do. She had to walk away before either of them got in any deeper.

Decided, she slipped into the water and sank, feeling the bright light of hope wink out.

CHAPTER 10

SOMEHOW, SOMEWHERE, TUCKER HAD made a serious misstep.

It wasn't the kiss. Either of them. Corinne had been on board both times. He didn't think it had anything to do with hanging out with his friends. She'd made it through the experience like a champ and even enjoyed herself. It wasn't last night's rehearsal either. No question she'd been grateful for the drill session on her exam material. And she'd gone downright misty-eyed on finding out he'd picked *Star Wars* music for Kurt. Their rehearsal had gone well, with Corinne picking up the components of the routine without a problem. They weren't quite polished yet, but with most of a week left until the performance, he wasn't worried there.

But he'd woken up to a text this morning saying she had to cancel rehearsal tonight. His first thought was that something had happened to Kurt, and he'd asked as much. But after assuring him Kurt was fine, Corinne had gone radio silent.

It might be nothing. He might simply be paranoid. But all Tucker's instincts were telling him he'd screwed something up. Corinne was distancing herself, when he'd expected another step closer. He needed to see her, to get to the bottom of this, and waiting until tomorrow, giving her longer to think whatever she was thinking seemed like a tactical error. Which was why he was driving all the way out to Hope Springs to the women's shelter, where he happened to know she was volunteering today.

Thank you, Mama Pearl.

Corinne's old, gray Toyota was still in the drive when he pulled up. He'd brought actual business with him to legitimize the trip either way, but he was relieved he hadn't missed her. Grabbing his briefcase, he trotted up the front steps. The door swung open before he could knock. Lily Mae Pollard filled the doorway, hands on her generous hips, her silver streaked blonde hair pulled back in a thick braid.

"Wasn't expecting you today, Tucker. Something going on?" Her manner was easy and friendly, but Tucker knew she could turn hellcat fierce if one of her charges needed protection. Her reputation as a former sharp-shooting champion was widely known around town.

"No ma'am. Got some paperwork for Cassidy to sign is all." He made a show of looking back at the Toyota. "Is that Corinne's car?"

Lily Mae's lips twitched. "It is. She'd probably appreciate a rescue. Come on in."

"A rescue?" *From what?*

"You'll see."

Lily Mae led him back to the great room, which had a wide bank of windows overlooking the water. An enormous sectional dominated the space, surrounded by bean bags and giant pillows for lounging. Corinne sat in the middle of a crowd of women, looking like she wanted to bolt but was too polite.

"What about his hands? He looks like he has great hands," one woman sighed.

Tucker held one out, examining his palm with interest. "I don't know. Long fingers, a little calloused, kinda knobby at the knuckles."

There were a couple of shrieks, and one woman dove behind the chaise at the end of the sofa. Corinne closed her eyes, with less a look of relief so much as *Just perfect.*

Because he didn't know what else to do, Tucker fixed on his trademark smile. "Sorry to interrupt, ladies."

"What are you doing here?" Corinne asked.

He lifted the briefcase again. "Business."

"Hope you gave yourself plenty of time. We have a fan club."

"Yeah?" He grinned again, delighted by the idea.

Corinne looked less than amused as she rose. "Ladies, you can transfer all your questions to him now. It's time for me to go."

A chorus of disappointment rose up.

Tucker took a step to block her path. "Actually, can I talk to you for a bit before you do?"

She hesitated, her gaze skimming over their audience.

"It'll only take a few minutes. Outside," he added.

"Okay."

"Be right back, y'all." Tucker set down his briefcase and followed Corinne out of the house. When she veered toward her car, he snagged her hand and tugged. "Let's go down by the water."

She looked down at their joined hands and frowned, pulling away before heading toward the bank. "Make it quick. I have to get to work."

Definite confirmation he'd screwed something up.

Tucker fell into step beside her, saying nothing until they'd reached the shoreline and were therefore out of earshot of the house. "What happened?"

"Nothing happened."

"Then why won't you look at me?"

In defiance, she lifted her head and met his gaze straight on. Tucker searched her face, looking for some hint, some clue as to what had changed between them. But her expression was blank. The same kind of mask he'd seen her wear when someone was rude to her at work and she couldn't afford to show her upset.

"I can't fix it if I don't know what I did wrong."

A muscle jumped in her jaw. "You didn't do anything wrong, Tucker."

"Well, you know, I didn't think I had. I was under the impression things were going well and we were on the same page with each other. And then you threw up a wall. You backed out of tonight's rehearsal and you're doing your damnedest to freeze me out right now. So I'm forced to concede I've done *something*, but damn if I can figure out what it is."

She crossed her arms, the mask cracking enough to reveal exasperation. "You didn't do anything," she repeated.

Tucker sighed and shoved a hand through his hair, looking out at the lake to try to gather his thoughts. "Look, Corinne, if I pushed too hard or said something or whatever the hell and you want me to back off, I'll do it. It sucks for me because I really like you, but that's absolutely your call. Just say the word. But I have this sense I hurt you somehow, and I never intended that. I can't apologize properly if I don't understand what I did."

Her eyes closed and she shook her head, those arms going from barricade to holding something in. "It's for the best. I'm trying to protect you."

Whatever he'd expected her to say, it wasn't that. "From what?"

"Ridicule. Gossip. All the complete bullshit being involved with me would bring down on your head. I don't want people to think I'm using you."

"Using me? Who thinks that?"

"It's what people think I do. Use people to get ahead. God knows it's exactly what my mother thinks I should be doing here."

It took him a full thirty seconds to rein in his temper. "Okay there's absolutely nothing I can say about your mother that doesn't violate everything I believe in as a gentleman, so we'll set that aside for now. You don't use people. Maybe at one time you did. You were under a lot of pressure from your parents to do exactly that. But you're not that scared girl anymore, trying to win their approval."

She gave a bitter laugh. "Tucker, I'm scared all the time. I'm scared I'll fail my test. I'm scared I won't get the job at the hospital. I'm scared I'll have to uproot my son again to find a decent paying nursing job. I'm scared I'll do something to completely screw Kurt up because I wasn't good enough or smart enough or strong enough. I'm scared if I stay here, I'll never ever move beyond this image of who I used to be."

"You are moving beyond it. Every day you're proving them wrong."

"You're the only one who sees that. And I'm not going to subject you to the backlash because of it."

So she decided for both of them without consulting him or giving him a say in the matter? Oh hell no.

"Look, I appreciate the thought, but I'm a big boy and it should be my decision to make. I'm not afraid of some gossip from people whose opinions I don't give a damn about."

She was shaking her head. "You can't know that. You don't know what it's like. No one walks into that willingly and just endures it. You'd walk away eventually. If not because of that then because you finally figure out I'm not this idealized picture you're painting. And I can't take that. I can't take it if you start looking at me like everyone else."

"Bullshit," Tucker snapped. He took her by the shoulders, turning her to face him. "Don't put that on me. I'm not your ex. I'm not your parents. And it's a goddamned insult to act like I am."

Corinne flinched, the color draining out of her face, her body going rigid and still, as if braced for a blow. That had him want to start swearing all over again, this time at himself for not recognizing the signs sooner. But he said nothing, gentling his hold, stroking his thumbs along her shoulders.

"You're not," she choked out. "God, I know you're not. It's just…"

"Just what?"

"You're not real," she whispered.

"What?"

"You can't be real. You're this smart, funny, attractive guy. You pay attention to the small things, the things no one else notices or thinks about. You reminded Mama Pearl that I'd be missing work to rehearse with you, so she's paying me as if I'm still on shift. Don't think I didn't realize. You know I'm stressed out about studying for my exam, so you somehow convinced one of your best friends—who doesn't even like me—to come help me study. And you picked music my child is going to go gaga over, just because you thought he'd get a kick out of it. You do all this stuff that puts other people first, trying to make their lives better, easier. And I can't find the angle, I can't find the motivation for why you'd do any of it for me. That makes you too good to be true, and my life has taught me never to trust anything that comes easy."

"So…what? You'd be more okay with this if I were acting like a self-absorbed dick?"

She huffed out a laugh without an ounce of humor. "That, at least, I'd understand."

"That's not who I am, Corinne."

"I know. Believe me, I have ample experience with self-absorbed dicks to know the difference. But I don't feel like I'm on even footing with you."

"Why?"

"You're successful and talented, well-liked. You can do so much better than a divorced, single mom, college drop out."

"Stop it," he snapped, fighting not to shake her as his temper flared at every person who'd ever put her down or made her feel small and stupid. "You were a National Merit Finalist, for God's sake. You're smart and beautiful and resilient. That didn't change just because you didn't end up taking the traditional college path. You've put yourself through nursing school, while working a full-time job and being a single parent. Do you have any idea how many people would've crumbled under a weight like that? But you didn't. Then Mama Pearl and I put something else on your plate, something you didn't have time for. And you did it anyway because you didn't want to let anyone down. So I tried to do a few things to make that a little easier on you. It's not a big deal."

"But it is. You do these things, things that are effortless to you that mean everything to me." One hand fisted over her heart and she looked up, those wounded eyes that had first pulled him boring into his. "It makes me feel things, Tucker, and that scares the shit out of me."

For the first time since the argument began, the clamp around his own heart loosened. Tucker gentled his voice as he ran his hands down her arms to lace his fingers with hers. "Well join the damned club. I've been off balance and feeling things for you for almost a year. But I'm not running from it. If you need some time to settle, to get used to the idea, fine. But don't throw up road blocks just because you're scared. We're too good together."

Corinne looked down at their hands. "I was all set to walk away from you. To get out of this before you had the power to hurt me." She blew out a breath. "Too late."

He stepped into her. "Do you still want to walk?"

She looked up at him, those blue eyes bright and searching. "No," she whispered. "I never *wanted* to walk. I was just—"

"Afraid. I get it. I'm going to stick, Corinne. Until you believe it. However long it takes."

She didn't believe him. He could see it in her face. But she wasn't running, so that had to count for something.

"I can't promise I won't freak out again. I've got issues, Tucker."

He snaked his arms around her waist. "We'll work through them together."

Her hands slid up to his shoulders. "You're a remarkably steady man, Counselor."

"That a good thing?"

"From where I'm standing, absolutely."

"Good." He tipped forward, intending to kiss her.

"Don't."

"Why?"

"Because we have an audience."

Tucker turned his head to look back toward the house. Sure enough, nearly a dozen faces were pressed against the glass.

"They're shipping us anyway. We might as well give them something worth watching." And he took her mouth with his.

"THAT. WAS. *AWESOME!*" Kurt's enthusiastic endorsement of their performance meant more to Corinne than the thundering applause that had barely died down from the ballroom. "You even have the bagel hair!"

She laughed. "Yes, yes I do." And had that been a challenge to execute. But absolutely worth it for the look of total enchantment on her son's face. "You know, Tucker picked the music special for you."

Kurt swung toward him, dark eyes big and round in surprise. *"Really?"*

"Really." Tucker ruffled his hair, crouching down in the short, Episode IV style tunic Luke had worn. Corinne had been privately disappointed he hadn't gone with Han Solo. With his swagger, he'd have made a great scoundrel. But he'd made the reasonable argument that Han had never carried a lightsaber, so Babette from Brides and Belles had fashioned costumes in matching white.

Mama Pearl beamed her approval. "I'm bettin' that's another winner of a performance. No way you're gettin' cut tonight."

Corinne agreed but figured it was bad luck to say it out loud. "Well, we'll see."

"Either way, since the performance is done, we won't be needing these anymore." Tucker held up his lightsaber. Dropping to one knee, he presented it to Kurt. "For you, young padawan."

Kurt gasped, his eyes going impossibly wider. "For me?" He reached out a tentative hand toward the hilt, but didn't quite touch it. He turned instead toward her, face questioning, as if he were afraid he was being punked.

"For you," Corinne assured him. "But," she added as his hand darted to pick up the saber, "these are *not* for playing with inside Grandma's house."

"What about here?" Tucker asked, his eyes sparking with amusement.

"Yeah, what about here, Mommy?"

They both looked at her, the two men in her life, desperate intention written clear on their faces. She glanced around the wide, empty lobby of The Babylon. "Don't go near anything breakable."

"Yes!" Kurt snatched up the lightsaber, immediately turning it on with whooshing laser noises.

Tucker held out his hand for her saber. "If I may, Princess?"

Corinne handed it over without question. The pair of them launched into an epic duel, as if they'd been fencing together for years. Her heart squeezed hard at the identical, delighted grins. How had she gotten so lucky?

"Some men are born to be daddies," Mama Pearl observed.

The idea of it kicked her hard in the gut. She wasn't thinking along those lines. Or hadn't been until Mama Pearl said it. After divorcing Lance, she'd had no intention of marrying again. At least, not for a good long while. That would require dating, which would require time and trust she didn't have. Except she'd made time, and Tucker had consistently worked to earn her trust.

Too much, too soon. She needed to dial back to the simple, where they were still easing their way along. They weren't even actually *dating* yet.

Still, it was impossible to deny Tucker was great with Kurt. He'd make a good father. Someday.

"That's rather putting the cart before the horse, don't you think?" She was saying it as much to herself as her boss.

"Not rushing things to know the kind of man you're letting into your life. Into your son's life. I'd expect it's a comfort to know, should things head in that direction."

"It's something," she agreed, throat thick with an emotion she didn't want to name. "Anyway, it's a comfort to know he's got your stamp of approval. Even if you did do everything but lock us in a room together and throw away the key." Corinne shot her a knowing look.

Mama Pearl appeared completely unaffected by the accusation. "Been watchin' that boy watchin' you since you came back. All I did's nudge you to look back."

I'm certainly looking now. And she definitely liked what she saw.

From across the lobby, Tucker's eyes met hers, warm and sure. Until Kurt almost ran him through with a lightsaber, forcing him to break eye contact as he danced back and executed some fancy footwork on the stairs.

Even as Corinne laughed, the fullness came back in her chest. It was stupid, really, to feel this much over the two of them horsing around. But she just needed a minute. "Can you make sure they don't get too rowdy? I need to run to the ladies' room."

"Raised six. I can handle two."

Corinne made her way past the huge curving staircase and down the hall toward the bathrooms. They were blessedly empty, so she had the opportunity to collect herself before she did something completely sappy and bawled because her son and her... whatever Tucker was...legitimately enjoyed one another. Kurt's own father had rarely looked at their son with anything more than annoyance. He'd given up all his parental rights last year without a qualm, already moving on to her replacement. Couldn't have a rugrat messing with that, now could he? Kurt hadn't had a male role model in his life since then, and Corinne hadn't worried too much about it, what with all the more practical worries. But it would be good for him to have a truly good man to look up to as an example. Right now, she couldn't think of a better one than Tucker.

She'd have to give some thought to that. Kurt was primed to get attached and if things didn't work out between the two of them, she didn't want her son to be an inadvertent casualty. Tucker would be annoyed she kept looking for the end of things when they'd barely gotten started.

More cart before horse, Corinne.

As she was wrestling her costume back into place after taking care of business, the door opened. She stilled as she heard someone come inside.

"—I know you're upset but—"

Corinne couldn't make out the words of the person on the other end of the phone, but she could detect the furious tone well enough.

"I know you asked me to—"

Corinne recognized the apologetic tone and she tensed with memory.

Pacify. Diffuse. Redirect.

Staying silent, she shifted until she could see through the thin crack in the tall door at the front of the stall. A delicate, long-fingered hand rested on the edge of the marble vanity. Even from this distance, she saw it shook.

"I know I should've asked you, but Norah needed an answer—"

The woman's shoulders hunched and her voice got smaller as the guy on the other side continued to talk.

"I thought I could make some good contacts for your campaign. Political wives are supposed to be involved and volunteer. This is a good cause, Garrett."

Garrett? Corrine tipped her head and caught a flash of blonde hair. *Whitney.*

"I understand. Yes, I'll—" The French tipped nails tapped a nervous tattoo on the counter. "But I'm on the tear down committee. I—No. No, I didn't think about your schedule." Whitney seemed to draw in on herself.

God, Corinne knew that feeling so well.

"No, I don't need to see the rest of the performances. I'm sorry. I'll find Norah and make some excuse. A family emergency or something. I promise I'll be home as soon as I can."

The man on the other end continued to berate her.

"I'm sorry your dinner isn't waiting. No, you're right, I should have—Okay. I'll be there soon."

Whitney clicked off. The shuddering breath she took was edged with tears. "Stupid," the woman muttered. "God, you're so stupid."

Corinne stood frozen in the stall. She knew that kind of self-talk. She'd engaged in it herself for more years than she cared to admit.

This is why she's so harsh with me, because she's dealing with someone who makes her feel like less, like she has to cater to his every whim.

Something was unzipped and Corinne heard the sounds of plastic compacts and brushes being brought out. Through the whole careful retouching of makeup, she wrestled with herself.

She knew what it was to go through this, what it was to be isolated from others, to be desperate to do anything and everything to please him. Everything in her wanted to help, to do something to make up for being so hateful in high school. But because of that history, Whitney would hear nothing she said and would, more than likely, lash out.

Think. Think.

Whitney had volunteered to work on a fundraiser for the women's shelter. Maybe that was her first step. Maybe she wasn't making contacts for her husband but for herself. This could be the first part of a plan to escape. If Corinne stepped out and revealed herself or tried to say anything, it could destroy Whitney's courage and set her back weeks or months.

Better to stay put and say nothing. Wait and see how it all played out. Then, if nothing happened, she could notify Lily Mae or someone else from the shelter. Whitney would take the talk better coming from anybody else but Corinne.

Decided, she stayed put until Whitney vacated the bathroom. She was still a mite shaky herself when she rejoined Tucker, Kurt, and Mama Pearl in the hotel lobby.

Catching sight of her face, Tucker frowned and slid his arms around her. "You okay?"

"Fine. Just tired." She tipped her head against his shoulder, grateful to feel his solid strength and to know he'd use that strength to protect her, not against her.

With every fiber of her being she wished that for Whitney. If there was any kind of a just God, her former friend would find it, too.

CHAPTER 11

"YOU'VE BEEN AVOIDING US."

Tucker looked up from the brief he'd been staring at for the past forty-five minutes to find Tyler in the doorway of his office. He automatically saved the file and rose to come around the desk for a hug. "I've been busy."

"We've all been busy with our respective rehearsals, but nobody's seen hide nor hair of you since your talk with Piper last week."

Which implied everyone else had gotten together without him and discussed the nature of that talk. Super.

"I'm not avoiding you." *Liar, liar, pants on fire.*

Tyler dropped into one of the club chairs. "I can see the smoke coming off your ass, Tuck."

He rolled his eyes and kicked back against the front of his desk. "I've just been focused on the competition."

"Right." Evidently deciding to drop the subject, she relaxed back into the chair. "Y'all's Charleston was spot on."

"Wish I could've said the same about Brody and Adele's tango."

Tyler laughed. "Brody did say she kept trying to lead. I think he's relieved to be done."

"He doesn't like dancing with anybody but you."

"True enough. There's nothing quite like dancing with a partner who gets you." She fixed him with a Look. "You and Corinne get each other. It shows. And not just to us."

He didn't know which part of that statement to respond to first. "What are you talking about?"

"Haven't you been following the town blog about the competition?"

"No, why?"

"There's a poll about whether you and Corinne will get together."

Tucker stared at her. "You're kidding."

"Nope." She circled around his desk, fingers flying over the keys for a moment before pivoting the monitor toward him and pointing. "After that second performance, the 'Yes' vote is up to 66%."

Right there on the screen was a close up of him and Corinne during their jive performance, eyes locked, with a helluva lot more than focus shimmering between them. He felt it every time he looked at her, but it was a whole other thing to actually see it right there in living color and know it was out there for everybody else to see.

"People are actually voting on our theoretical love life?"

"Everybody loves love. And honestly, you two are the only possible couple who could come out of this competition. Well, I guess Charlotte and Chad, but they didn't stay in long enough for it to matter. But you and Corinne? You're going to the finals. And there's a sizable chunk of the town who are absolutely shipping you both."

Tucker scrubbed a hand down his face. "Corinne definitely hasn't seen this."

"How do you know?"

"Because she'd panic and bolt. Being the center of attention has been hard on her."

"How are things going with you two?"

"What? I'm just supposed to tell you? What if you're in on the pool at Dinner Belles?" he joked.

Tyler brightened. "There's a pool?"

"I don't actually know, but c'mon. There's always a pool."

"I'll have to stop by and put in my bet."

"I wouldn't bother. Mama Pearl did the setting up here. She's got the inside track."

"Oh, *did* she? Because Norah told me what you said when you agreed to participate and that had a Tucker McGee setup written all over it."

He spread his hands. "I will neither confirm nor deny my original intent. But I will say Mama Pearl apparently did *not* sprain her ankle."

Tyler leaned across the desk to pop him on the arm. "You stinker, you."

"What? I had nothing to do with it. Can I help it if she took inspiration from my noble sacrifice in the name of saving *your* love life?"

"If you're expecting another thank you for that, you'll get it at our wedding. Now are you actually going to give a straight answer about how things are with you and Corinne or do I need to pull out my pliers?"

Long experience had taught him she wouldn't drop it, so he caved. "Things are good. Accepting I really am interested and this isn't some kind of cosmic joke where somebody's going to pull the rug out from under her and yell, 'Pysch!' has taken her some time. But I think we're finally on the same page of there actually being an us. The beginnings of one, anyway."

He cut a glance in her direction, trying to peg whether Tyler was okay with there being a him and Corinne. Too tired for analyzing subtext, he decided to flat out ask. "Are you okay with this? Because Piper wasn't."

"Piper was surprised. There's a difference. She's working her way around to the idea."

"She thinks I'm deliberately going for someone the opposite of Laura."

"Are you?"

"None of this has anything to do with my ex-wife."

"Are you ever going to tell everyone else the truth about her?"

That the divorce hadn't been a mutual decision? That she'd up and left him less than a year after they'd said their vows? "Not anytime soon." And he was beginning to question the wisdom of having told Tyler years ago when he'd been in the thick of it. But of all of them, she knew what it was to be left behind. Without a choice, without a word. It's what Brody had done to her—or so they'd all believed for the better part of a decade.

Tyler sighed. "You can't get mad at them when they're operating on false information."

"What happened with Laura has nothing to do with their reactions to my being interested in Corinne. They're clinging to the past instead of looking at the now. If you can let go of what happened back then, why can't they? Or am I wrong that you have?"

She came back around the desk to sit beside him. "I've made my peace with Corinne. Brody and I are together, and we're happy. Whatever happened in the past is the past."

Something in Tucker's chest loosened. "I guess it was probably something of a surprise to you, too."

"Actually, I wasn't surprised. Not after I gave it some thought."

"Why?" he asked.

"For one, she isn't like Laura. Now don't get your dander up about it. I know that's not the only appeal, but it's a component. Laura was too easy and you were bored. The two of you were like a matched set of golden retrievers, all set to make perfect little golden retriever babies."

Tucker lifted a brow. "I'm trying to decide if I'm supposed to be offended that you're comparing me to a dog."

"My point is, you went into this postcard perfect life. It's what everybody expected for you and so it was what you thought you wanted. You went along with it because it was the easy thing, the logical thing. Because everything in your life to that point had been easy and logical. Laura walking out was your wakeup call to the truth—that you don't actually want easy and logical."

She wasn't wrong, but that didn't make it any easier to listen to this reductivist accounting of his marriage.

"Nothing about Corinne is easy or logical. But besides all that, you, my dearest, darling boy, have always had a soft spot for broken things." Her arm linked through his and she hesitated. "And I'm pretty sure Corinne fits that category."

Tucker leveled his gaze on her and waited.

"I think she was abused."

"Why?"

"Something she said when she came into the store last year, before she told me Brody was back. And I've watched her some since then. She's not the same ball buster she was back in high school. I think somebody's spent a good chunk of time tearing her down."

He loosed a breath, needing to talk about his suspicions. "And maybe knocking her down."

Tyler straightened. "Is she in trouble?"

"No." But God bless Tyler for her instant desire to help if she was. "And she hasn't said a word to me about it. I just... I knew she'd been verbally abused. That started way before the asshole ex. But last week we got into a fight."

He told her what had happened out at Hope Springs. "She mostly doesn't show those kinds of reactions, but every now and then something slips out. I don't know if that's because she's great at hiding them or if it's because she's mostly worked her way through whatever trauma is there and sometimes stuff sneaks up on her. So I'm being very, very careful because I don't want to do anything to scare her off."

"Have you looked into her divorce? To see if there were any charges or restraining orders anything?"

"Thought about it. Had to stop myself several times. I want to know, but I want it to come from her. Anything else feels like a violation of her privacy."

Tyler's voice was gentle. "And you want her to trust you enough to tell you."

"That too."

"Think she'll get there?"

"Eventually. I'm a patient man. I know how to play the long game."

She went silent for several long moments. "Is that what this is with her? The long game?"

Tucker looked down at his friend. "That a problem?"

"Not if she makes you happy at the end of it."

"Then yeah, this is the long game."

CORINNE WASN'T in the right mood for rehearsal tonight. But as they hadn't been cut in Round 2, she still had an obligation to put her all into this competition. Not that spending one-on-one time with Tucker was an obligation. Far from it. But after the day she'd had, her brain wasn't in any condition to absorb choreography. Still, she pasted on a smile as he pulled open the door to his apartment.

"Hey, Ginger." His grin and obvious pleasure at seeing her went a little ways toward making up for her mood. He leaned in and bussed her cheek as she came inside.

Corinne scanned the apartment, noting the absence of her study buddy. "What? No Piper tonight?"

"Not tonight. Not for this dance. I need you paying attention for this one." Tucker shut the door behind her. "And I get the sense you aren't all here. What's wrong?"

She frowned as she tossed down her purse, irritated at being read so well. "Nothing."

He drew her in, already circling her to the music spilling out of his stereo. "Corinne." In someone else, the tone might have been a warning. In Tucker, it was a simple acknowledgment that he knew something was wrong and he wanted to help.

She instinctively matched his easy rhythm and a few more knots unraveled. He was so good at this. Not just the dancing, but the uncomplicated caring. At making her feel like she could tell him anything. She blew out a breath.

"Okay, there's nothing wrong. I'm having a bit of a moment, is all. Kurt started kindergarten today."

"Ah. And how did that go?"

Because the whole thing wanted to spill out, she didn't quite meet his eyes. "You don't want to hear about this."

"Sure I do."

"Lance never did."

"Lance was an asshole." He kept his voice conversational and easy, as if remarking on the chances of the Bulldogs in the College World Series. "I thought we'd already well established that point. And the fact that I am not."

Corinne did look at him then, analyzing with the part of her able to read moods and body language in an instant. He wasn't angry with her for making assumptions again, though she recognized the low burn of temper and his desire to beat the shit out of Lance for how he'd treated her. And he didn't know the full story.

"You're right, Counselor. We did. I apologize to the court."

The golden boy smile flashed. "So, how did it go?"

"For Kurt? Great. He was so excited. He actually tried to take his lightsaber to school."

"Gotta establish yourself as one of the cool kids right off."

His *well duh* tone made her smile. "Is that how it's done?"

"It's how I'd have done it if I could have."

"Yeah, well, I managed to convince him that since it didn't fit in his backpack, it wouldn't fit in his cubby at school either and said he could maybe bring it for show and tell."

"Good compromise."

"Toddler and pre-school parenting is all about compromise. Anyway, when he got home, he was full of talk about his teacher and his classmates and the stuff they got to do. I thought maybe he'd be nervous for me to leave him with all the new people, but he was absolutely fearless." And that had been a double-edged sword. She didn't want her baby afraid of the world, so the fact that he'd jumped right in without problem made her proud. But couldn't he have clung to her a little bit?

"And how did it go for you?" he asked gently.

"I dropped him off this morning. He waved goodbye and dove in to a game of blocks with another couple of kids. Didn't even notice I'd left. I cried like a baby as soon as he was out of sight."

"Aw." Tucker cuddled her closer. "Baby boy is growing up."

"I'm not ready for that." She laid her head against his shoulder and it felt just exactly right. Having him to share this with felt even better. And that was skirting dangerous territory. Territory involving long-term feelings and expectations. She wasn't ready for that either.

"It's good he was comfortable enough for that. You gave him that foundation."

"I wish I was steadier on mine."

He tightened his hold. "I'm right here to lean on until you are."

Corinne lifted her head to study him, taking in the unwavering focus and patience, the sheer *goodness* of this man. And she knew, ready or not, those feelings and expectations had already taken root. "I believe you actually mean that."

"I do."

"It's my knee-jerk response to want to discount it. But right now, I don't want to question it. I just want..."

He tucked a lock of her hair behind one ear. "What do you want?"

You. As simple and complicated as that. She wanted him. All of him.

But wanting was a dangerous thing, and Corinne had learned long ago it was safer to take what came without wanting more. What she had right now was so very good, and she didn't want to do anything to mess it up. She sighed, letting go of that want—for now. But at the question in his eyes, she gave him a smile. "You know, right now, in this moment, I have everything I want."

"Yeah?"

"My kid is happy, and I'm spending yet another evening with an attractive, interesting man, who knows how to dance."

Tucker twirled her. "A woman of simple tastes."

"I didn't used to be, but I've learned to appreciate simple."

"Simple is good. Simple is why Brody and Adele got cut in Round 2."

"How's that?"

"Because a tango is simple and he forgot that. He was more concerned with showboating his skills than honing in on the soul of the dance."

Corinne laughed. "Nothing I saw in the video you emailed me looked simple."

He put on a face of mock affront. "Have I led you astray yet?"

Feeling better than she'd expected when she got here, Corinne relaxed into the flirtation. "No. No you haven't. Educate me, kind sir."

"I've always thought of tango as a story." He stepped back, nodding for her to mirror his position, until they stood an armspan away. "Man sees woman, is attracted." Tucker looked her up and down, and the heat simmering in his gaze fired her blood. "Woman decides she's attracted back."

So much for letting go of that want. Corinne's gaze scraped up and down, lingering on his chest, caressing him with her eyes.

He moved into her, wrapping an arm around her waist until they stood hip to opposite hip. "And the dance tells the whole tale of their courtship, from the first hot blush of interest, through all the ups and downs." When he shifted, so did she, responding to his slightest touch as he led her through the slow, basic steps of the dance. With every touch, she imagined satin sheets, a night of sighs and single-minded purpose.

"All that give and take." He traced the outline of her body, his hand skimming close enough she could feel his heat but not quite touching. Desire denied. When he spoke again, his voice was rough. "But in the end, it's only about one thing." He spun her out and back, until their mouths were but a heartbeat apart.

"What's that?" Her whisper came out breathy, even to her own ears.

"Seduction."

Oh, yes please. Because she wanted to melt into a puddle of lust at his feet, she made a bid for humor. "Hence the change in practice venue?"

"Well, it did seem a little awkward to be doing in the church fellowship hall." She could tell Tucker had to work to keep his tone light. But there was nothing light about the look in his eyes or the feel of his hands.

She wanted those hands to touch her. Wanted to feel him moving over her, in her. And so, wanting, accepted her decision was already made. She stroked her hand up his arm and reached to skim a finger down his cheek. "Fair enough. I'd just as soon there be no prospective audience for this myself."

His body gave a perfectly satisfactory response to that remark. She closed that whisper of distance between their mouths. The hands that had teased slid down over her hips, pulling her closer against the erection straining his pants. With a groan of approval, she slid her leg up the outside of his, fitting him more perfectly against her.

Tucker shuddered, breaking the kiss to rest his brow against hers. "Have dinner with me," he gasped.

Corinne blinked, her hand resting against the thundering pulse in his throat. "What?"

"Have dinner with me."

Her gaze slid over to the box on the counter. As they'd planned, he grabbed a pizza from Speakeasy on his way home, intending to heat it up for them later.

"No, not take out. Dinner. Real food somebody else cooks and serves us. Out. A real date."

"Why?"

"Because I have no business thinking the thoughts I'm thinking right now if we haven't even had our first date. And if we stay here and keep rehearsing, I'll try to talk you into bed, and we're not there yet."

Her lips twitched. "I'm pretty sure it wouldn't take more than a dozen steps. Only four to the sofa." She'd been calculating for the last few minutes.

Tucker looked heavenward, as if that might give him strength. "Part of me really wants to take you up on that right now."

"I noticed." She rotated her hips, still pressed against his and he groaned.

"But I'm not going to rush this. I'm not going to rush you into something you might regret." She sensed his struggle, but he stepped away from her. "So, we're going to go to dinner and have a proper date. Then I'm going to drop you home with a goodnight kiss that'll ensure you'll dream of me, and I'll come back here and take the coldest shower known to man."

This wasn't what she wanted—at all. But even so, he was so *earnest,* it was hard not to be charmed. "You are charmingly old-fashioned, Tucker."

"And believe me, it's killing me." He scrubbed a hand over his face. "How long will it take you to go home and get ready?"

"What? Now?" He was really serious about this?

"Now. Tonight."

She blinked, considered. "If it were only me, thirty minutes. Kurt will still be up, so probably closer to an hour. But I can meet you—"

"I'm picking you up."

She grimaced imagining the interrogation Marianne would put him through. "My mother—"

"I can handle your mother. I'm picking you up at home. Let's make it an hour."

"What about rehearsal?"

"Later. I think it'll be better later." He said it like a prayer, as if maybe later he'd have himself under better control. "Let's do this right."

Right?

Now that he'd woken her long dormant girlie parts, they had an entirely different idea of what would be right at the moment. She considered saying it outright. He'd fought for her when she would've walked away. He made her feel worthy, and that wasn't something she had a lot of experience with. That was all she'd needed to know. But this part of the process was important to him. If he needed to feel like they'd checked off steps like some kind of items on a list—or if he thought she needed it—who was she to argue?

"Okay." Amused, she scooped up her purse and strode to the door.

"And Corinne?"

She looked over her shoulder.

"When I do take you to bed, I won't rush that either."

The amusement faded and her breath went short. Maybe they were on the same page after all. "I'm counting on it."

CHAPTER 12

SHE'D DRESSED TO KILL him.

As Corinne shifted to cross her legs in the passenger seat beside him, Tucker caught a glimpse of long, toned leg and tightened his grip on the steering wheel. He'd thought getting out of the apartment, going on a proper date would help him reset his priorities, let him focus on something other than getting her naked. But he'd absolutely underestimated her.

Corinne had always been beautiful. But since she came back to Wishful, she usually dressed more for function than fashion. Nothing she'd done, short of the costuming for their performances, had been intended to draw any attention to herself. Tucker liked the minimalist look on her. No muss, no fuss, no artifice. Just her.

Tonight, though. God. The dress reminded him of Marilyn Monroe, except instead of the trademark white, this one was fire engine red. The halter neck left bare those shoulders and arms toned from long hours hauling heavy trays. She wasn't wearing her old pageant queen style makeup, but she'd done something smoky with her eyes that made the blue dark and mysterious, and her lips were glossy, pink, and utterly kissable. This was the

Homecoming Queen all grown up. She was all his. And tonight, everybody in town was going to know it.

Tucker wasn't at all sure she was okay with that. She'd been tense as a bow string when he'd picked her up, which he'd attributed to her mother. No telling what garbage she'd been filling Corinne's head with in the time it took her to get ready. But he'd charmed them both with flowers and had a quick and impassioned discussion with Kurt about how it really *did* make more sense for the preacher to say "May the Force be with you" instead of "May the peace be with you" at church on Sundays. He'd expected the tension to lessen once they'd gotten away, but she'd stayed silent on the drive out to Hope Springs, the leg-crossing more a product of fidgeting in discomfort than a deliberate attempt to seduce. Where was her head?

The parking lot of The Spring House was packed, even for a Saturday night.

"Crowded tonight," she observed. "Are you sure we'll be able to get in?"

"We've got a reservation."

"The Spring House doesn't do reservations."

He flashed her his trademark grin. "They do when the owner owes you a favor." Before she could say anything else, he'd skirted the hood of the car and was there with a hand as she opened the door.

"Ooo, calling in your chips on my account. I feel special," she teased.

One long leg extended from the car, drawing his eyes down to the strappy heels that made her almost as tall as him. He couldn't help but imagine her in nothing but the shoes.

"That's certainly the goal."

Because he wanted to and because he wanted to gauge how she was feeling, Tucker drew her up and out of the car, into his arms. He loved how they fit together, loved that he could surround her with his bigger frame. His mouth brushed hers, once, twice. A hum resonated in the back of her throat as she curled her fingers into his shirtfront and drew him in for more. Yeah, they both needed this. Tucker sank deeper, enjoying the lazy stroll of a kiss, until her limbs went fluid as candle wax on a hot July day and he sensed her nerves melting away.

Feeling the shift in her mood, he edged back, gratified by the slightly dazed expression on her face. "Thought we'd start with dessert first."

Her lips curved in a languid, feline smile that went along with the seduction of her dress. "I'm hoping that's just the appetizer."

How long until the main course?

Reminding himself patience was a virtue, even if it did lead to blue balls, Tucker stepped back and escorted her up the steps to the door, subtly adjusting his pants. The vestibule of the converted antebellum house was standing room only. Taking a firm grip on Corinne's hand, he began shouldering his way toward the hostess station.

"Tucker McGee!"

No. Oh no. Let it be anybody but the Casserole Patrol.

"Oh look, Delia! They're here together," Miss Betty cried. "I need to update my vote."

Tucker closed his eyes and prayed for patience as the trio of devils in granny's clothes converged on them. "Ladies."

Miss Betty was furiously tapping at the screen of a smartphone.

Lord, preserve us all.

"So is it true?" Miss Delia asked.

"Is what true?" Tucker was no dummy. The only way to even hope to curtail gossip was to admit to nothing.

Miss Maudie Bell took a long look at his hand linked with Corinne's. "Reckon you won't be one of those bachelors at the auction now."

Before he could try shifting the subject by asking if they'd finally talked Norah into it—surely, he'd have heard if she had—

Corinne stepped into him. One arm slid around his waist, her fingers curling in his belt loop, her head tipping against his shoulder. "I'm delighted to say that he won't."

She spoke easily, her expression relaxed, her posture straight and tall. No prevarication, no trying to hide. With this move, she publicly proclaimed that they were together in a manner as efficient as taking out a billboard on Main Street.

Miss Delia popped Miss Betty's arm with the back of her hand. "I wonder who won the pool?"

Corinne laughed. Outright *laughed*. And her smile, as she answered, was radiant. "That'd be Mama Pearl. But I'd say she had the inside track since she more or less set us up, so she might've recused herself."

"There was a pool?" he asked.

Her smile flashed again. "Of course there was a pool. It's Omar. He can't resist."

Where was this confidence coming from? And it was true confidence. He knew her well enough now to see the difference between the fake-it-til-you-make-it kind she'd used in high school. He'd spent so long watching her wallflower routine, he'd almost forgotten how vivacious she could be when she wanted. It was sexy as hell. *She* was sexy as hell.

"Tucker! So glad you could make it."

Grateful for the reprieve from his less than G-rated thoughts, Tucker turned to shake the hand of their host. "Tom. I'd like you to meet my date, Corinne Dawson. Corinne, Tom Thatcher. He's Miss Mattie's grandson and the current owner of The Spring House."

Any eyes that hadn't already been on them turned in their direction.

Corinne didn't flinch, didn't shrink. She flashed her Homecoming Queen smile and took the hand Tom offered. "So nice to meet you."

"If you'll both come this way. I've got something special put together, just for you."

Tucker laced his fingers with hers again and they followed Tom through the labyrinth of rooms making up the restaurant. At all the attention they gathered, Corinne kept her head held high, no hurry. Everything about her said *I am with Tucker McGee* and defied them all to make issue of it.

He loved every second.

Tom led them out the back and into the tiny greenhouse. A single table was set up in the center of all the lush greenery. Wide-bladed fans stirred the air.

"Oh, this is lovely," Corinne said as they stepped into a private oasis.

"Isn't it? We haven't officially opened it to the public yet. We'll use it for small events, receptions and the like. But for tonight, it'll be for you. I thought perhaps you'd like to escape all the speculation."

Tucker braced himself for the shock, but Corinne merely sank into the chair he held out for her.

"I expect we've added to it now," she said. "But the quiet's appreciated. Thank you."

Tucker circled around to his own chair.

Tom handed over a couple of menus. "I'll let you two look over these."

He retreated, leaving them alone.

"I feel like I owe you a round of applause."

"Why?" she asked. "For finding my spine?"

The self-deprecatory tone rubbed him the wrong way. "You have plenty of spine on any given day. I was just thinking confidence looks good on you." His gaze skimmed over her again. "Right now, everything looks good on you."

Corinne set the menu aside and leaned back, crossing those long legs again. "It's easy to be confident when you know what you want."

"Yeah? And what's that?"

"You."

She'd never been indifferent to him, and he'd known during their failed tango rehearsal that she was willing. But hearing her boldly state her interest, knowing he was the root of that new confidence made Tucker feel about ten feet tall and bulletproof.

Corinne's gaze stayed steady on his, no signs of timidity or embarrassment or fear of rejection. "I'm done waffling, done worrying, done wondering what I did to deserve you. At the end of the day, at the end of the night, I want you. Now, we can stick to your original plan if that's what you really want, but if you're hanging out in the slow lane because you think it's what I need, let me assure you, it's not."

There was absolutely nothing slow about what was going through his mind as she reached across the table to lay her hand over his.

"You've given me everything I need. You gave me kindness and friendship, and you made me feel like a person with value for the first time in I don't know how long."

His heart gave a hard, painful lurch, both happy he'd managed that and aching that it had been necessary. "Corinne." Tucker turned his hand over to curl around hers.

"Let me finish." She wasn't so blasé now, and he could feel the faint trembling through their linked fingers. "I don't know if it's forever or just for now, and I'm okay with that. But I'm tired of standing still. I want to move forward. With you."

CORINNE WAITED, her heart in her throat, as Tucker stared at her, dumbstruck. And why shouldn't he? He was the consummate Southern gentleman and she'd essentially propositioned him. As the silence spun out between them, her hard-won confidence slowly evaporated.

His throat worked. She knew him well enough to understand he was considering his words carefully.

Had she disappointed him? Shocked him? Did he prefer the meek version of her that needed saving?

"Tom went to a lot of trouble tonight. I can't just ask for the check, throw you over my shoulder, and run."

The relieved laugh burst out. "I hadn't actually intended to bring it up quite yet. It seemed an appropriate topic for dessert."

"I have never wanted to start a meal with dessert so much in my life."

The fear that had crept in slid away at the hunger in his eyes. "I was afraid we weren't on the same page."

"Believe me, I've been reading way ahead. But I didn't want to give away any spoilers in case we weren't actually reading the same book."

Where did his version of their story end? Tucker McGee wasn't a casual fling sort of guy. She'd never been a casual fling kind of girl. As much as she was ready to do this, she wasn't to the point of imagining puppies, rainbows, and white picket fences. She'd known too much harsh reality for that. But she'd meant what she'd said. Forever or for now, she wanted him. After so long spent merely surviving, tonight, she wanted to live.

Tom came back to take their orders.

Somehow, despite the heat crackling between them, they both managed to relax into some semblance of normalcy. They had the proper date he'd wanted, enjoying excellent food and adult conversation. He talked of law school and theater, filling in the gaps since they'd graduated high school. She told him of her elopement and surprised him with all the world travels in the years before her marriage had turned into a prison. Beneath it all, desire simmered at a low hum.

When her wine glass was empty and the check paid, Tucker offered his hand. "Still want dessert?"

Corinne laid her hand in his. "Dessert and a dance seems like the perfect end to a perfect evening."

They said little on the drive back to his place. His thumb stroked the side of hers and the heat seemed to build between their palms. She wanted those palms on her skin. He pulled into the private lot behind the building housing his law office and led her upstairs to his apartment. Shutting the door behind them, he turned into her, pressing her back into the door, his hands curving around her hips as he took her mouth in a kiss that hid nothing of his carnal intent. All the civility melted away, and she pressed into him, her hand fisting in his shirt to drag him closer. The bed could wait. She was completely good with the door.

When he broke off, she whimpered in protest.

"Be right back."

He stepped away. Corinne stayed where she was, blindly setting her clutch on the entry table as he moved around the apartment, lighting candles. Candles. He was a man who could incinerate her with a kiss against a door, and he kept candles. He moved to the stereo. Of course there'd be music for this. It seemed Tucker was always surrounded by music. He liked to set the scene. And tonight's scene would be romance. She hadn't counted on that, and her heart hitched because he would take the time to do it. For her.

Tucker came back and took both her hands in his, drawing her into the room. "Want wine?"

She shook her head, eyes on his.

Music spilled out of the speakers, dark, throbbing strings that made her heart ache with longing. He pulled her into his arms, into the dance. Corinne realized that here, now, there'd be no eroding that endless patience of his. This would be no quick, mindless meeting of bodies. This wouldn't be simple. He wasn't simple.

Pulse thick in her throat, she followed where he led, her body responding to the press of his as if she'd just been waiting for him to flip the switch to bring her back to life. His hands skimmed over her, lighting little fires in their wake. She lost herself to the music, to sensation as he bent his head, pressing his lips to her bare shoulder. The contrast of hunger and care unraveled her. It wasn't until his hands stroked up her back, to the knot at the neck of her dress that she realized they'd made it into the bedroom.

His eyes met hers, dark with desire. Corinne pressed her lips to his, threading her fingers into the hair at his nape as he worked the knot free. The fabric slithered down her shoulders, the dress held up now only by the press of his body to hers, and nerves jittered. She'd been with no one since Lance. She'd had a child. Her body wasn't what it had been.

Tucker's hands came up to frame her face as he eased back. The dress slid down, catching on her hips, baring her breasts. Feeling exposed, Corinne flexed her fingers in the fabric of his shirt and fought the urge to press against him and hide. Stretch marks and mommy tummy were not attractive.

He kept his gaze on hers, one thumb stroking her bottom lip. "Let me look at you." His voice was a rough whisper.

Sucking in a breath, with the last shreds of her courage, she reached down to nudge the dress past her hips and to the floor. Ever the gentleman, he helped her step free of the puddle of fabric, then kept her hand in his as he drank her in.

"Goddamn, you're so fucking beautiful."

The harsh words did more to relieve the tension than a dozen assurances. Emboldened, Corinne stepped into him, running both hands up his chest and over his shoulders. "Show me," she ordered.

Capturing her mouth, he bore them both down to the mattress. As heartbreaking strings transitioned to sensual jazz, he worshiped every neglected inch. She came alive again beneath his hands, his mouth, body coiling with unbearable pleasure until she shot over the first brutal peak with his name on her lips.

She was still shuddering as he stretched out over her, finally, deliciously naked. God, the weight of him felt so good, so right, and when he shifted, nudging her core, Corinne tipped her mouth to his and wrapped around him, welcoming.

He slid home and stilled, waiting as her body adjusted to his fullness. "Okay?"

"So okay," she moaned.

He retreated a scant inch and pushed back in. Corinne drew her knees back, hooking her feet around his waist. With each slow stroke, he thrust in deeper, filling spaces of aching emptiness that had been her constant companion for years. Throat tight, she closed her eyes.

"Stay with me, Corinne."

She opened her eyes, focusing on his face. He lowered his chest to hers, lacing their fingers, and began to move again, driving her relentlessly up. She chased the high, matching his rhythm, wanting the exquisite friction to last forever, yet yearning for release. Her skin slicked with sweat and her vision blurred until all she could see was his eyes, darkly green, staring into hers.

"Stay with me," he growled.

"I'm with you." She drew his mouth to hers and murmured against his lips, "I'm with you, Tucker."

And at last that infinite control snapped. He picked up the pace, plundering her mouth as he plunged into her. His eyes went blind as he lost himself in her, and the sight of his pleasure catapulted her over the edge. She bowed up, wrapping around him and seating him deep as he spasmed, finding his own release.

They clung together trembling from aftershocks. His bigger body draped over hers, his cock still twitching inside her. Corinne decided she'd never been quite so completely, wonderfully used. If she could pause this moment for a year or three, she'd be good with that.

"I'm crushing you."

Before she could protest, he'd rolled off, disappearing to the bathroom to take care of the condom. A chill spread through her that had nothing to do with the temperature. Would that be it, then? Would he expect her to go ahead and get dressed so he could drop her home?

The mattress dipped as he came back, hauling her against him.

"Whatever you're thinking right now, don't."

"What?"

"You looked like you were about to panic." He brushed a kiss over her brow. "Regrets already?"

"No. Absolutely not." Because it was there, because she could, she pressed a kiss to the underside of his jaw. "I'm not good at this part."

"Which part?"

"The after." Lance hadn't been one for cuddling or talking. Sex hadn't been about them, it had been about him. Tucker wasn't Lance. Why did she keep having to remind herself of that? "It's… been a long time for me."

"Since the divorce?"

She nodded.

His fingers traced patterns on her back. Closing her eyes, she enjoyed the sensation. She hadn't realized exactly how badly she'd needed to be touched. Yet again, Tucker had given her exactly what she needed. He'd made her feel desired and beautiful. And his pleasure had been in giving her hers.

"It's been a while for me, too. Since a certain sad-eyed brunette walked back into town."

Her eyes popped open. "Seriously?"

Tucker searched her face, his lips curving. "Not so sad now."

"Have you been waiting for me?"

"I don't know as I was actively campaigning to get here in the beginning. I wasn't interested in anybody else, and I'm not the scratching an itch sort. But for the last six or eight months…yeah. And if you hadn't had the stupendous idea of crossing this line tonight, I'd have waited longer. I'm a patient man, and I know how to play the long game." His grin widened. "I'm damned grateful I didn't have to."

"God, so am I." Wanting to lighten the mood, Corinne smoothed her hands down the flat plane of his abs. "You know, you're in amazing shape for a guy who works in a suit."

Tucker laughed. "I spend a fair amount of time in the gym. A good bit more since you came back to town. Had to work off all the pie I ate in the name of seeing you."

"Really?" The idea that he'd come more for her than the pie delighted her because Mama Pearl's pie was a reason unto itself. She ran her hands over his perfect ass. "I don't think the pie's hurting you any."

He flopped backward, arms open wide. "Feel free to examine the rest of me to confirm."

Pressing a kiss to his pec, Corinne snuggled into him, loving the closeness of skin to skin. "I would like nothing better. But..."

"But you can't stay."

"I can't stay," she confirmed. "I wish I didn't have to get back to real life. I wish I could just stay here, in your bed."

"Someday you'll be able to stay. You'll wake up with me, and I'll wow you with my French toast for breakfast. After sating us both with stupendous morning sex."

That he looked so far ahead, saw a future where that could be a reality warmed her down to her toes. Corinne propped herself on his chest so she could look into his face. "I've had a serious dry spell, Tucker. Sating me might take a while."

His smile was unapologetically male. "I believe I'm up to the challenge."

Evidence of that fact stood cheerfully in her peripheral vision. His smug grin turned into a groan as she wrapped her hand around him. "You've effectively proved you're a skilled and thorough lover. How about presenting evidence to the court that you can pull off a quickie?"

"Challenge accepted."

She was still laughing as he slipped inside her again.

The verdict was a resounding oh yes.

CHAPTER 13

"*W*HAT'S WRONG WITH YOU?" Corinne whispered. "You're jumpier than a cat in a room full of rocking chairs."

Tucker laced his fingers with hers and squeezed. "Nothing. I'm fine."

She smiled and leaned into him. "I think you're more nervous than I am. I've never seen you nervous before."

"I'm not nervous." Was that smoke coming from the grill or his ass?

Corinne leveled him with what he thought of as her Mama-can-smell-the-stink-of-that-lie-from-a-mile-away-so-you-want-to-try-that-again look. He bet it had Kurt spilling his guts.

"What do you have to be anxious about? They're your friends."

From Tucker's perspective, he had plenty to be anxious about. He and Corinne were truly together now, and everybody knew it. He ought to be pleased that Tyler had organized a couples' cookout for everyone and included Corinne, but the only thing he could think about was all the ways this could go wrong. They'd been the last to arrive. That hadn't been the plan, but he'd had an impromptu lightsaber battle with Kurt, while Corinne had thrown together her tomato and sweet corn salad for the occasion, and he'd lost track of time.

Tyler and Cam had been fine. They'd both made an effort. Norah and Myles, too since they'd been outsiders to this whole thing. But Brody was an unknown quantity. And though Piper had promised she'd work on accepting things, he didn't fully trust her not to stick her foot in it.

Discussion thus far had largely centered around the competition and the current level of fundraising. With two performances to go—both already sold out—they were slated to exceed their goal. At the moment, Cam and Brody manned the grill, while Norah, Piper, and Myles clustered around the patio table. He and Corinne had taken a quick tour of the backyard, admiring the landscaping Brody and Cam had put in.

To put Corinne at ease and to soothe himself, he lifted her hand to his lips and mustered a smile. "It's been a long time since I brought a girlfriend into the mix." They hadn't actually had that discussion, but he hoped it might distract her from his real concern.

"And you're worried because that girlfriend is me and there's...history between most of us."

So much for distraction.

"No argument on the girlfriend thing?"

One dark brow arched.

"Look, I just want you to be comfortable. I know how difficult it is for you to hang out with them. It means a lot you were willing to come."

"You want this to work. So do I. Part of that is making peace with your friends." She stepped away from him, shoulders straightening, head tipping up as she moved with purpose up the deck steps. Tucker hurried after her.

As Tyler came out of the house with a platter for the burgers about to come off the grill, Corinne spoke. "I'd like to say something, if y'all don't mind."

"What are you doing?" Tucker asked.

"What I should've done a long time ago."

He knew in an instant that she was about to rip the Band-aid off every wound this group carried from high school. "You don't have to do this."

Conversation around them muted, and Tucker could all but feel the spotlight of attention turning their way.

"Yes, I do. Part of coming back here has been about me owning my mistakes. They were some of my biggest, and they have every right to say whatever they need to to me. And you're going to let them."

He scowled. "The hell I will."

"Tucker, hush." She didn't raise her voice, but the command in her tone was unmistakable. "You need to give all of us a little more credit."

"It's not about—"

Corinne laid a finger over his lips. "Stop. This needs to be done to clear the air so you don't keep trying to crawl out of your skin every time we're all in the same room together because you're waiting for the other shoe to drop."

Maybe she was right. Maybe if she reopened these wounds, they'd finally run clean.

"All right."

She cupped his cheek, then nudged him toward a chair. "Now sit down and stop glowering like some kind of attack dog. I don't need you to protect me from this."

But he still wanted to. That need to save her from any more pain rose up, had him wanting to argue. One more look from her, though, and he sank into a chair.

With a bracing breath, she took a step away from him—deliberately separating, he thought, so she stood alone. She didn't have the stage training he, Brody, Piper, or Tyler had, didn't have Norah's professional poise or Cam's comfort with addressing crowds. But Corinne held their attention as she squared her shoulders and braced, as if for a firing squad.

"First off, I'd like to thank you for inviting me tonight. It means a lot to Tucker and to me. Now, maybe this isn't the perfect time to bring all of this up, but I'm not sure there is a good time, and I think—hope—we'll all be better for having cleared the air."

Her hands knit together, the only outward sign of her agitation. "You're all good, kind people. You opened up your circle to me simply because Tucker asked you to, even though I'm sure some of you don't think I deserve it. *I* don't think I deserve it."

Tucker opened his mouth, but she laid a hand on his shoulder and squeezed.

"At least not the me I used to be. Norah, Myles, this really doesn't impact you at all, as neither of you knew me until recently. But to the rest of you—I'd like to offer my sincerest apologies. I behaved badly in high school. Probably for longer than that. I won't offer any reasons or excuses. Whatever they are don't matter, and they don't change that I said and did things to all of you, at one point or another, that were intended to hurt you. I hurt a lot of people back then. I'm not proud of it. Any of it. But I own that I was wrong. I've had a lot of years to reflect on that, and I carry around a lot of regrets, a lot of things I'd be ashamed to admit to my son."

Her gaze skimmed over the table. "But that's not who I am anymore. I'd like to think I'm a better person now, and I'm working on being the kind of person who's worthy of Tucker's good opinion, and yours. But that kind of thing takes time. Trust takes time to build. So if any of you needs to say anything to clear the air, now's your chance. Because whether I deserve him or not, I'm with Tucker, and I will be as long as he'll have me. So we might as well get it on out there so we can all move past it."

She'd laid herself bare to them, stood quietly waiting for their attack or their judgment. It was one of the bravest damned things Tucker had ever seen. Pride shone through him like a beacon. He started to rise, to go to her, but a subtle shake of her head had him sinking back into his chair. She was determined to do this on her own, come hell or high water.

Tyler spoke first. "It takes a lot of guts to stand up and admit when you're wrong. It takes more to strike out on your own as a single parent to make a life for yourself and your child. I, for one, accept your apology and say everything else is water under the bridge."

Corinne angled her head in acknowledgment, murmuring a soft, "Thank you."

Brody crossed his arms. "I'm fairly sure we're close to even after you kicked my ass for fucking things up with Tyler again last year."

That got Tucker's attention. "She what?"

Corinne's attention stayed on Brody—actually looked at him, instead of off to the side or at his feet. "I just gave him a needed dose of honesty at the right time."

"I'm where I'm supposed to be because of it." Brody wrapped his arm around Tyler. "So I'll say thank you and that makes up for all the rest."

Her cheeks colored. "If we could maybe never mention the rest ever again, that would be *awesome.*"

Cam kicked back. "I've got no beef with you. I was always peripheral to that drama."

"So was I, but I've had plenty of beef," Piper said.

"Piper—" Tucker began.

"No, let her speak," Corinne insisted. "The whole point of this is to air grievances."

"I spent a lot of time hating you. I hated how you treated people, how you kept trying to poach Brody, how you fought dirty to get what you wanted. When you came back to town, it was easy to fall back into that."

Tucker ground his teeth.

Corinne didn't even flinch. "I can't blame you for any of that. I deserve all of it."

Piper sighed. "No, you don't. Not anymore. And if you're strong enough to stand there waiting to be flogged, I'm strong enough to admit when I'm wrong, too. And that if not for Tucker, I probably wouldn't have taken the time to revise my opinion based on who you grew up to be. But he pressed us all to look beyond the past, to give you another chance. I've known him all my life, and he's a damned good judge of character. Maybe we don't see yet what he sees—and I kinda get the impression you don't either—but what *is* obvious is you *did* grow up, you *did* become a better person. You're going to make a damned fine nurse. And I'm not the kind of asshat who won't take that into account. So I'll say the past is past and we're on a clean slate."

Corinne's throat worked. "Thank you. All of you."

Christ, what did it say that she could take a verbal punch without so much as blinking, but a compliment had her near tears? Unable to sit any longer, Tucker sprang up and pulled her into his arms. This time she didn't resist, burrowing in, and he could feel the trembling she'd held back.

He glared over her head at his friends. "Is everybody good now?"

"No," Brody said. "I'm with Corinne. You should've given all of us a little more credit. Assuming the worst of us was a dick move."

"Then it was a dick move. Blame it on the day job. I see the worst of people all the time. And all too often Corinne bears the brunt of it."

"Simmer down," she murmured. "It's over and done. We talked about it and the Earth didn't shatter."

Didn't mean he had to like it.

"I've gotta admire your moxie," Piper admitted. "Laura would never have done that. She'd have gone right on pretending the world was perfect and hoping the bad stuff would go away."

Corinne lifted her head. "Who's Laura?"

Shit.

In the silence, Tucker knew there was no avoiding an answer. "My ex-wife."

"Your—" She cut herself off. "I didn't realize you'd been married." Her face smoothed out into the polite mask he knew she used when she was upset. She stepped back.

Tucker wanted to swear. "For about five minutes my first year of law school. It was a long time ago."

"I see."

No, she didn't. Tucker could tell in the absence of the facts, she was drawing her own conclusions. Probably all of them were wrong. But now wasn't the time to get into it.

When she smiled, the edges were brittle. "It seems we have some things to discuss. But later. I believe those burgers should be about finished."

Brody rescued the burgers from burning and everybody made a valiant effort to rescue the conversation, steering toward safer topics. Corinne was a good actress, pretending everything was fine. Tucker didn't like thinking about why that was the case. He had to employ some of his own skills to get through the rest of the dinner, not that he thought any of his friends believed him.

Shit was very definitely not okay.

As soon as they got into the car to head home he said, "It's not what you think."

"You can't possibly know what I think, Tucker." Her voice was maddeningly calm.

"It's not a big deal."

"That you were married at all, no. That you and I are supposed to be together and I didn't know about it? That is a big deal. That's a pretty major omission."

Tucker thought of all the omissions she'd made, everything she hadn't told him about her marriage. But he wasn't interested in starting a full-blown fight right now.

"I wasn't deliberately keeping it a secret. I just…don't ever talk about her. We were college sweethearts. Got married straight out of undergrad and divorced before the end of my first year of law school. It was over and done six years ago."

"And how hard would it have been to say exactly that when we were at dinner the other night?" A rare hint of temper underscored the question.

"I avoided talking about it for the same reason you avoided talking about your divorce. That night was about us and no one else." He laced his fingers with hers. "Look, I'm sorry you got caught by surprise. I don't know why Piper even mentioned it. They don't talk about her either. The fact is, there's still a ton we don't know about each other. That's the whole point of being in a relationship—having the time to learn those things. Once the competition is finished, we'll have the time to sit down for whole damned infodump marathons of biographical information to fill in those holes. I'll tell you anything you want." *And you can do the same.*

Corinne sighed. "You're right. I'm sorry. It just blindsided me. Tonight took a lot out of me to begin with and not knowing something that huge was just...embarrassing."

"I'm sorry. That was never my intention." He pulled into her driveway. "For what it's worth most of town doesn't know I was married."

Which was the only way anything could stay a secret in Wishful.

"That's an impressive feat. How'd you manage it?"

"Laura's from the west coast. The wedding was out there. It was over and done before I came home. And then the gossip factory seemed a lot more interested in my single status."

"And now they're talking about your *not* single status."

"Damn skippy." He walked her to the door. "I'm really proud of you."

Her lips curved. "I'm pretty damned proud of myself, as it

happens. I don't think we're all going to magically be buddy buddy, but this was a step in the right direction."

"And Friday night's performance will be the next. We're going to tango our way to a win."

She raised her lips to his. "Damn skippy."

TUCKER'S HANDS curved around Corinne's hips. "Are you ready for this?"

She leaned back into him, tipping her face toward his and keeping her voice low as they watched Tara and Daniel finish up their paso doble. "Ready to dance in front of half the town and God knows how many viewers online to the song we first made love to?"

"It'll keep us in the proper mood," he murmured.

"I've been in the proper mood for a week." Not that she'd been able to get away long enough to act on it. What hours weren't filled with work or rehearsals were bookended with Kurt and textbooks.

"There's time after this before you have to get home."

She opened her mouth to protest. With her NCLEX exam on Monday, she needed to spend every last second studying.

"You'll think more clearly without the sexual haze."

He was probably right. God knew she couldn't concentrate when she got home from rehearsals because she was too busy imagining him naked.

"We'll see what time we get out of here." Maybe she could steal a little time. As aroused as she was likely to be when this tango was over, it wouldn't take much.

From the ballroom proper, the emcee announced Tara and Daniel's scores—straight nines from the judges.

"Tough to beat," Corinne said.

"We can do it."

They awaited their signal from the competition staff, walking out at the emcee's introduction and the audience's applause. Corinne ignored them all, keeping all her focus on her partner as she took her position. The X Ambassadors' lead singer began to croon the opening bars to "Unsteady" and her heart began to beat slow and thick against her breast. The ballroom, their audience, all of it melted away as Tucker lifted and spun, dragging her across the floor. They flowed into the dance, one mind, one desire. The scent of him stoked her senses, the feel of his hands fired her blood. And as the music faded, she was left only with want, her mouth a breath from his.

As the crowd cheered, Tucker said, "Come home with me tonight."

"Yes. God, yes."

The emcee's voice boomed over the speakers. "Wowza! Tucker and Corinne, Team Dinner Belles, ladies and gentlemen. If you haven't already put in your bet in the pool, I'd say that ship has sailed."

They pried themselves apart and turned, hand-in-hand, to face the dais.

"Let's see what the judges' scores are for that stupendous Argentine tango."

The first paddle went up. "Nine." The second paddle. "Ten! Our first ten of the night. And the final score?" The last paddle rose. "Another ten! Ladies and gentlemen, give Team Dinner Belles a round of applause for a fantastic performance."

Tucker whooped and Corinne found herself tugged into a fierce celebratory kiss. The crowd went nuts. Corinne's head was still spinning as he released her to wave at the audience, towing her off the floor. His friends were waiting, offering high fives and congratulations to them both. And amid all the hubbub, she saw Malika fighting toward her. She'd hardly spent any time with her friend since the start of the competition.

"Be back," she told Tucker, and wove her way through the crowd.

"Girl, that was amazing!" Malika wrapped her in a tight hug. "I been watching online up to now, but da-yum—emphasis on the yum. Please tell me you're keepin' him."

Corinne laughed. "Seems I am."

"I knew he was into you! Good for you. Mama Pearl was right. You absolutely needed some fun." She almost had to shout to be heard over the noise of the crowd during the brief intermission.

"Come on. Let's go somewhere quieter."

They left the ballroom.

"It's so good to see you. I'm sorry I haven't been available to study more."

"It's okay. I can study on my own just fine. What about you? Have you actually had time to do much?"

Wincing, Corinne admitted, "Not as much as I'd like. But then, I'm not sure I'll ever feel like any amount of studying is enough until the test is over."

"Three more days."

"Don't remind me."

Malika mimed zipping her lips. "So how is the hottie lawyer?"

"He's fine. Pumped about our scores. They're our first tens."

The other woman rolled her eyes. "No, how *is* he?" She added an eyebrow waggle for clarification.

Blood heated Corinne's cheeks. "I'm not one to kiss and tell."

"Come on now, I'm ridin' the single train at the moment. Have some pity and spill."

She wasn't ready to share all the amazing details of her night with Tucker. Before she could think of some way to deflect, Corinne caught sight of Whitney being dragged across the lobby from the ballroom. The man who had her arm in a vice grip was more than a head taller and twice as broad as her. Whitney struggled to keep up with his longer strides, stumbling on her heels.

Corinne was moving before she realized, trailing the couple down the corridor toward the bathrooms.

Malika fell into step beside her. "Oh, I get it. You want some more privacy."

"No, I... Something's wrong." Every inner alarm she had was blaring.

Malika clued in to her tone, followed her gaze to the couple well ahead of them. "You know them?"

"I know her."

They'd stopped at the far end of the hall, well away from the crowds. He had Whitney by both arms now, his head dropped close to hers. But there was nothing loving or romantic about the gesture. Whitney's face twisted with pain and no small amount of fear. The man, presumably her husband, Garrett, said something in a low, menacing tone.

"I...I'm sorry. I won't—"

"Is everything okay here?" Corinne demanded.

Both of them shifted their attention to her. And she suddenly remembered Garrett Harrington. He'd been a few years ahead of them in school, one of the golden boys of Wishful High Athletics. He'd gone on to college on a football scholarship. Those big hands were still curled around Whitney's arms, hard enough to bruise.

Surprise and embarrassment flickered over Whitney's face. "Everything's fine."

"This is no concern of yours," Garrett said.

Remembering how it felt being caught in such a punishing grip, Corinne fisted her own hands and took a step closer, conscious of Malika flanking her. "Take your hands off her."

Garrett released Whitney at once, lifting his hands palm up in the universal gesture of mean no harm. She saw the mask slip into place, the genial guy everyone liked, hiding the monster beneath. "There's no problem here. Is there, honey?"

"No problem," Whitney repeated dutifully. "I'll be right along home as soon as the competition is over for the night."

That wasn't what he wanted to hear. Garrett's face rippled as he tried to control his reaction in front of an audience. "I thought you'd ride with me."

"No sense in that. My car's here. We'd just have to come back and get it later, and you've got too much going on tomorrow to have to mess with it." Placate. De-escalate.

Clearly sensing he'd lost this battle for the moment, Garrett nodded. "Right after the competition is done. I need your help packing."

"Of course. It sounds like the next performance is starting now, so it shouldn't be long."

Faint sounds of the emcee rousing the crowd floated down the hall.

With one last look at his wife, Garrett plastered on a smile that might pass as charming to those who didn't know better and headed toward the lobby.

Silent, Corinne watched him go, not relaxing until he'd rounded the corner.

"What the hell is wrong with you?" Whitney demanded.

Corinne turned back to her. "He was hurting you."

"Why on Earth should you care?"

"No man has the right to manhandle his wife."

"He wasn't manhandling me."

"Then why are you wearing long sleeves in August?"

Whitney reflexively reached for her forearm, before she fixed her sneer back in place. "Oh, because you're in such a position to be handing out fashion advice."

"Lashing out at me is not going to work, Whitney. I know his type. You don't have to stay with him."

"He's my husband."

"He's a bully. And if he hasn't escalated to full on violence yet, he will. Let me help you." Corinne stepped toward her.

"I don't want anything from you."

"Look, Whitney, I know we have a bad history but trust me

when I say—"

"Trust you? Trust *you*? Why the hell would I make that mistake again? I trusted you once, and you turned on me. You were hateful and horrible, tearing me down at every turn, exactly like your mother."

The words hit Corinne like a blow, so hard she almost stumbled back. Like her mother?

"You act all innocent and contrite now that you're back, but nobody believes it. You're still the same vicious harpy you were in high school. And one of these days, Tucker will figure it out and drop you, exactly like you deserve. You're not worth his time."

"Look, lady—" Malika started, but Corinne put a hand on her arm.

Reeling, she struggled to find the right words to salvage whatever she could of this situation. "You don't have to get help from me. You don't ever have to speak to me again, Whitney. But get help from someone. Before it's too late."

Whitney squinted at her as if trying to reconcile the woman standing in front of her with the girl she remembered. Then, without another word, she turned and fled.

Malika laid a hand on Corinne's arm. "Honey, are you okay?"

Abuse always started somewhere. Not fighting back was a learned behavior. And for Whitney, it had started in high school, with Corrine. She'd done this. She'd made her former friend into this. Into a woman who was too afraid to fight, too afraid to leave. This was on her.

Heartsick, horrified, Corinne said, "I need to find Tucker."

$\mathcal{A}$S TYLER AND CAM took the floor for their rumba, Tucker looked around for Corinne. She'd gone off with Malika quite a while ago. Maybe they'd gotten caught up talking test or catching up, but it seemed odd that she'd miss this last performance. They usually preferred to deconstruct their competition's performance after the fact.

Beside him, Myles leaned in. "You know, the Babylon has a pretty epic romance package."

Tucker arched a brow.

"I'm just sayin'. Eliminating the drive saves some time." He only grinned as Tucker glared at him.

"He's not wrong," Piper added, not taking her eyes off Tyler and Cam.

"I really don't need to hear about your honeymoon," Tucker said. But now that the idea had been planted, it began to take root. They wouldn't have all night—he knew that—but if he could get a room, have the hotel set something up while they finished up down here, he could give Corinne some romance. She'd had little enough of that. The more he thought about it, the more he liked the idea. Champagne, some music, maybe flowers. And maybe he could sweet talk her into trying out the swank bathroom with a bubble bath or shower for two. Either way, it'd be some pampering she wouldn't get otherwise.

As the judges raised their paddles—two tens and a nine, exactly as he and Corinne had earned—Tucker slipped away to the front desk. The desk clerk, Jenny, had a gooshy, romantic heart and put a rush on things, assuring him everything could be ready in fifteen minutes. Tucker slipped the key card into his pocket and went in search of his lady.

It took nearly the full fifteen minutes to find her amid the mass exodus of the audience. She and her friend were in the staging area. Catching sight of him, the unusually serious Malika pointed in his direction. Corinne turned. The corners of her mouth tipped up, but there was something wrong with her smile.

Tucker hurried over, sliding an arm around her. "I was starting to think I'd lost you."

She leaned into him, and that quieted the alarm that had begun to sound when he'd seen her. "Just been talking about the test. Three days left. Less, really. Today's mostly over."

He rubbed at the tension knotted in her shoulders. That hadn't been there during their performance. First order of business up in the room would be easing the stiffness out of her.

"You'll do great. You've been studying your butt off for weeks."

"Y'all did great tonight," Malika told him.

"We did, thanks," Tucker agreed with a grin. "Helps to have an amazing partner."

Her dark eyes flicked from him to Corinne and back again.

Something there.

"You take good care of her now, you hear?"

The spurt of protectiveness from her friend pleased him. Corinne needed someone looking out for her besides him. "Oh, you can count on it."

Evidently satisfied with his answer, Malika gave Corinne another quick hug and made her farewells.

"You ready?" he asked.

"Yeah." Her tone was off, and she didn't quite look at him.

"Corinne? You okay?"

She mustered another of those not quite right smiles. "Tired. All the adrenaline's worn off."

"Well, I've got just the thing to help with that. A little surprise for you."

"A surprise?"

Instead of answering, he ushered her across the lobby. He'd debated whether she'd worry about being seen getting into the elevator with him, but ultimately decided to save them both the effort of climbing four flights of stairs. They stepped into the car, and he pushed the button for the correct floor.

As the doors slid shut she asked, "We're not going up to the roof?"

"Nope."

Corinne frowned. "What are you up to?"

"You'll see." Yeah, she absolutely needed to relax. She'd sleep better and be able to focus more when she settled in to study tomorrow.

She stayed silent as they stepped into the plush and silent hall. Something was off with her mood, but her hand still held tight to his as he led her to the room. Was she nervous about this? Worried about being with him again?

Tucker slid the key into the slot and opened the door. "Milady."

She took a few hesitant steps inside, not letting go of his hand. He followed, kicking the door shut behind them. Jenny had been as good as her word. A bucket of champagne chilled to the side of the massive king size bed. Two plush bathrobes were laid out on the bedspread, and the whole thing was accented by a scatter of red rose petals.

"What is this?"

"Your surprise."

"Tucker—"

"I know you can't stay the night. But you can absolutely do with some pampering. Champagne. A bubble bath for two. My bathroom's not big enough, and I think you need to relax for an hour or two." Longer, if he could coax her. As it was a performance night, she wasn't expected home for bedtime tuck in.

"I don't know what to say."

Tucker drew her in, cupping her head and bringing her lips to his. "You don't have to say anything."

Her stiff posture relaxed, degree-by-degree, as he kissed her, slow and deep.

Better, he thought, and slid his hands down the length of her spine, fingers probing for a zipper on her dress. Failing to find one, he broke off. "Did Babette paint this thing on you?"

"I—it's a side zipper." She stepped back, turning away toward the champagne bucket and reaching for the bottle.

Reminding himself to slow down, even if they did only have an hour or two, he took the bottle from her and popped the cork, pouring into the two waiting flutes. He handed her one. Before he could lift his in a toast, she'd drained hers.

Okay, something was definitely wrong.

Tucker set his glass aside and reached for her, gently tugging her toward him. "You're upset about something."

Corinne looked down at his hands on her forearms. "I can't do this," she whispered.

"What?"

When she looked up, her eyes were sheened with tears. "I'm sorry, I can't do this."

"It's okay. I just sprang this on you without asking. I can take you on home. We'll do this some other time. It's not a big deal." He reached out to stroke her cheek and she flinched back.

"No not all this. I'm sorry about all this, too. That makes it worse."

"Makes what worse? Corinne, tell me what's wrong."

She stepped fully back from him, squaring her shoulders. "I can't do this. Us. This is over. We're over."

"What? Why?" He took a step toward her, arm outstretched, and she evaded in a move so instinctive, it left him cold.

"I just can't."

"That's not an answer, Corinne. You were fine forty-five minutes ago. We were on the same page. What the hell happened between then and now? Did Malika say something to you?" He couldn't imagine what, but who else had she seen?

She shook her head. "No, it's not—I... This has to be finished, Tucker. It just has to. I'm sorry."

Without another word, she turned and fled.

"Corinne!" Tucker started after her.

"Don't!" The panic in her voice stopped him. "Just don't."

So he let her go. As the door snicked shut behind her, he reached for the open bottle of champagne, tipping it up for a long pull and wondering exactly how things had gone so sideways on one of the best nights of his life.

CORINNE MANAGED to pull it together by the time she got home. She knew better than to show weakness. Her mother would pounce on it, and right now, Corinne couldn't handle that. She couldn't take anything else. But Marianne wasn't up. With pitiful gratitude for the reprieve, Corinne made it up the steps and into the privacy of her room before the tears started in earnest.

She took care with the dress. After a trip to the cleaners, it would be going back to Babette at Brides and Belles. She considered having a shower and curling up in her robe, but that only reminded her of the gift she'd walked away from and made her cry harder. A text came in as she slipped straight into pajamas.

Tucker: **At least let me know you made it home okay.**

God. She'd just broken up with him and he was still That Guy.

Corinne thumbed back a one word reply: **Home**.

She fell to the bed, pressing her face into the pillow. Makeup would stain the pillowcase, but she didn't care right now. Not when her heart was cracking right in two. But she deserved the pain—all of it and more—for having ever put Whitney in a position to fall into this kind of life. She'd broken her best friend. Destroyed Whitney's self-worth as her own self-worth had been eroded over years. And for what? A false popularity in high school? The approval she'd never won from her parents?

Rolling over, she tugged open her nightstand drawer and pulled out the pencil box. Drawing herself up, she flipped open the metal lid and removed the stack of notes, neatly bound in thin blue ribbon. Six months' worth of inspirational quotes and personalized messages scrawled out on 3x5 index cards small enough to fit through the vent in her locker. She'd read them so often over her senior year and afterward, she'd had them memorized at one point. After finding out Tucker had been the one to send them, she'd unearthed them again, rereading them with that knowledge to see if there'd been any clue.

She'd never have seen it in high school. She hadn't known him then, hadn't understood him. But God, he'd understood her. Rereading them now, Corinne's heart bled a little more with every card. She wasn't worth his good opinion. Not then. Not now. Breaking things off was the only logical choice. The only decent choice.

Tucker would want an explanation. He deserved one. But she simply couldn't cope with seeing his view of her change, couldn't handle him recognizing that the version of her he saw was a lie. That she really was the mean girl. He deserved someone nice. Someone as sweet and solid and wonderful as he was. Corinne wasn't that girl. She was saving them both before they got in any deeper.

She'd considered staying. Of taking the gift he'd offered her. Giving them both a last goodbye. But she didn't deserve to be pampered, didn't deserve to relax. And if she'd made love with him again, she wasn't sure she'd have been able to walk away. Even if she had, it would've hurt him more because he wouldn't have known the night for the goodbye it would have been. No, it was better she left at the start.

Maybe someday she'd actually believe it.

"Well, you screwed things up with him, didn't you?"

Corinne lifted her tear-streaked face to find her mother in the doorway. She hadn't heard the door inch open over her tears.

Marianne evidently interpreted her silence as agreement. She stepped inside with a sigh. "You can't get anything right, can you?" She shook her head in that oh-so-familiar way conveying pity and disappointment.

Raw and wounded, the tenuous tether on her temper snapped. "Nothing is ever good enough for you."

"I just want what's best for you."

Corinne gave a bitter laugh. "Bullshit. Nothing is ever good enough. Not with me. Not with Dad. Your expectations drove him away. He's happy now. Did you know that? Do you even know what that is? You've never, ever been satisfied with anything in your life."

Her mother's mouth thinned. "We're not talking about me. You're the one who let a prize like Tucker McGee get away."

"Tucker isn't a prize. He isn't some kind of trophy. He's a good person. A good man. And I let him go because I don't deserve him, because he sure as hell deserves someone better than me."

Marianne gaped at her. "Is that really what you think?"

"What was I supposed to think, Mom? I tried my hardest. I was a horrible person, clawing my way to be what I thought you wanted. And it was never enough for you."

"That's not true. I—"

"Don't," Corinne snapped. She didn't want to hear her mothers' denials. It was never enough and it never *would* be enough. The realization trickled through her, making her straighten her spine and square her shoulders as she slid off the bed and stalked toward her mother. "Well I'm done doing anything for you. I only live my life for one person now. Kurt. And I'm going to do everything in my power to be supportive of him, as you never were of me."

"How can you say I wasn't supportive? I've put a roof over your head, haven't I? I've helped with the boy."

"Yes. Yes you have, and I've thanked you for that until I'm blue in the face, though you always make me feel like that's never enough either. But I'm not an impressionable teenage girl anymore, Mom. I'm not going to live my life by your principles. Because I don't believe people are tools to be used just to get ahead. And I'm ashamed of everything I ever did to support that. I'll be raising my son better. And I'll be doing it somewhere else as soon as I can scrape together first and last months' rent and a nursing job."

"You're leaving town?" Was that a thread of panic in her mother's voice?

Corinne hadn't actually meant leaving Wishful, only this house. But maybe she should leave town. Could she really stay here where she'd inevitably run into Tucker every week? Could she really serve him at the diner and pretend like everything was fine? Could she watch him eventually find someone else, fall in love, and make a life? After everything she'd been through, everything she'd survived, Corinne was pretty sure that would break her for good.

"I'll start applying for jobs as soon as I finish my test on Monday. Now get out. I need to go to bed."

CHAPTER 15

*T*UCKER WAS NOT A man accustomed to sitting around doing nothing. Yet for two days, he'd done exactly that. Well, not nothing. He'd reviewed every moment of the past few weeks with Corinne, analyzing and rehashing and wondering what he was missing. Other than confirming she'd gotten home okay, she wasn't answering his texts or calls.

He wanted an explanation. Needed one. Because this whole silent treatment was far too redolent of his ex-wife. Except Laura hadn't been in tears when she walked out of his life. The fact that those tears made him feel better made him a sick son of a bitch. But surely tears meant she hadn't wanted to walk, right? She hadn't wanted to walk that day at Hope Springs. That meant something else was at play. There had to be because Tucker couldn't think of a damned thing he'd done wrong. Then again, he hadn't been able to think of a thing he'd done wrong in his marriage either and Laura had still left him.

The only thing stopping him from going over to Corinne's house and banging on the door was that he didn't want to scare Kurt, and he didn't want to upset Corinne any more than she already was before her test. Which meant, for another twenty-four hours, his hands were tied. He'd been filling them with shots of Jameson.

The knock on his apartment door was far too brisk and business-like to be Corinne. Tucker dragged himself from the sofa and opened the door. Brody, Cam, and Myles spilled inside, each carrying some form of alcohol.

"What do you want?"

"After a breakup, it is our God-given duty to commiserate and attempt to cheer you up. Failing that, we're here to help you get shit-faced." Brody took a look at the glass in his hand. "Guess you already got started on that portion of the program."

Deliberately, Tucker took a swallow of whiskey. "We didn't break up."

His friends exchanged a look.

"So you just had a fight?" Cam asked.

Tucker didn't know what the hell they'd had because she hadn't told him jack shit except it was over. "Things are up in the air, at the moment." He had to believe that. Had to believe that after the test, he could corner her, sit her down, and get to the bottom of what exactly had upset her. "How did you know something was up?"

"Y'all didn't leave together after the performance the other night. People noticed." Brody shrugged.

Perfect. People were already gossiping about them and the demise of their relationship. Which had to be how these knuckleheads had heard because Tucker hadn't breathed a word to anyone.

He pinched the bridge of his nose. "What are people saying?"

Another long pause and exchange of significant looks.

"What. Are. They. Saying?" he demanded.

"A bunch of stupid speculation," Cam hedged, ever the local politician.

"That you finally wised up and cut your losses," Brody said flatly.

Tucker swore. "I did nothing of the kind. She's the one who walked out."

Myles clapped him on the shoulder. "Brother, she was seen practically running from the hotel in tears, and the grand gesture I foolishly talked you into went to waste. I'm sorry about that, by the way. If y'all didn't break up, what was she so upset about?"

"I don't know." The admission stung. "We were fine after our performance. Then she went off with a friend while I was getting everything arranged."

"She was gone a while, wasn't she? Missed Cam and Tyler's performance," Myles noted.

"Yeah. I didn't ask where she went. I assumed she was visiting. But when she came back, she was...off somehow. I thought she'd just gotten tense worrying about taking more time away from studying." Maybe that was an avenue to explore. Tracking down Malika and finding out exactly what they'd talked about. Except he didn't know her last name, and he was pretty sure if the other woman thought he'd hurt Corinne, she'd be happy to castrate him.

"What exactly did she say?" Cam asked.

"Nothing. Just that she couldn't do it. Couldn't do us anymore." Again with the looks.

"That sounds like a breakup to me," Brody said carefully.

"It's not," Tucker insisted. "She's just upset." About something. "She always pulls back when she's upset."

"What's she got to be upset about?" Myles asked.

"I don't fucking know!" Tucker slapped the low-ball glass on the counter and shoved both hands through his hair.

"There has to be something. Women always have a reason, even if it doesn't make sense to us," Myles reasoned.

No, they didn't. Laura hadn't had a reason. At least not one she'd ever told him.

"Look, have you considered maybe this is for the best? I mean, you two are awfully different," Brody said.

"Because same worked out so well for me the first time?" Tucker reached for the whiskey again.

"You and Laura wanted different things," Cam said. "You said it was easy as that."

"I lied."

They stared at him.

Tucker tipped the bottle to splash another two fingers of amber liquid into the glass. "The divorce wasn't a mutual decision. Laura left me. For her high school sweetheart back in California. No explanation. Not a goddamned word. She had divorce papers delivered to the house and didn't even come home to pack up her things. Hired a service."

"Dude," Myles said, and the word held a wealth of sympathy that made Tucker's shoulders hunch.

"Why didn't you tell us?" Brody asked.

Because I'm the guy not worth fighting for. The one women can simply walk away from. His hands clenched around the glass.

"Because it was fucking humiliating. We were supposed to be this perfect couple. On paper it all added up. In reality, we made no fucking sense at all. I didn't tell anyone because I didn't want the questions or looks of pity. I just wanted to move on." And he hadn't managed that. Not until Corinne.

"So, what? You decided to try someone who was her polar opposite in almost every way?" Brody asked.

"It wasn't like that. *Isn't,*" he corrected.

"Still, I'd think taking on an insta-family would be a pretty big—"

Brody didn't manage to finish the sentence before Tucker propelled him into the wall. "I love that kid and I love her. I'd be a lucky bastard if I got to make them my family."

Brody made no move to defend himself, instead staring into Tucker's face, as if deciding exactly how serious he was. "I didn't know you were in love with her."

Tucker released him and picked up the glass again. "Neither

did I until she walked away and ripped my heart out of my chest."

They fell to silence.

"Well," Myles said, finally, "commiserating and cheering up are an epic fail. Getting shitfaced is the only option left. Pull out some more glasses and somebody order pizza."

"Praise Jesus, it's over!" Malika announced as they burst out of the testing center. "This calls for a celebration."

Celebrating was the absolute last thing Corinne wanted to do. The certainty that she'd failed the NCLEX settled into her bones like an ache. She couldn't afford to waste the $200 testing fee, especially not now that she'd started a ticking time clock on getting out of her mother's house. But was it really any surprise? She'd barely slept since Friday night, barely eaten. All she could think about was Whitney. *Exactly like your mother.* And when it wasn't Whitney's recriminations ringing in her ears, it was Tucker and the look of utter betrayal on his face.

"I'm not much in the mood for ice cream, Mal."

"Well, if not ice cream, how about drinks? It's five o'clock somewhere."

The temptation to drown all this heartache in alcohol was too great to follow through on. The only thing she hadn't irreparably screwed up yet was her son. She couldn't afford to crawl into a bottle. She might not crawl back out.

"I don't feel like I have anything to celebrate."

"Oh now, are you gonna have your panties all in a wad until you actually get the results back?"

"Probably." Meanwhile, she needed to pick up some extra shifts. First and last months' rent and all the utility deposits on a little place for her and Kurt wouldn't be cheap. And she'd need another $200 to take the test again. Plus, moving expenses because having failed the exam meant she wouldn't be licensed soon enough to be considered for the job at Wilton Memorial, despite the fact that her interview was tomorrow. Not that she believed they'd seriously look at her as a contender.

Malika swung an arm around her. "Okay, you officially need to go spend some time with your man to unwind. You're too tense."

"That's not an option," Corinne managed. The tears wanted to start up again. She'd barely managed to stop sobbing long enough to take the damned test.

"Why? Is he working late?"

"He's not mine anymore."

Malika stopped in her tracks halfway across the parking lot. "What? What happened?" The younger woman's eyes glinted dangerously.

"I broke up with him."

"You did what? Why? And aren't you two still in the competition?"

Yeah, they were. She hadn't really given it a lot of thought at the time. Both the final performances were freestyle, so Tucker and Tyler would both be choreographing something from scratch. Unless she wanted to bail and let Mama Pearl, the ticketholders, and all the women out at the shelter down, she'd have to face him and soon. They wouldn't win. There was simply no way they'd be able to maintain that chemistry on the floor after what she'd done. But she didn't want to add to her list of failures.

"Did he do something?" Malika demanded.

"No." Corinne started walking again.

"Then why?"

"I don't want to talk about it."

Tucker would ask the same question. She owed him some kind of answer, but what could she say that he'd accept?

"Corinne." The deep male voice carried across the last few rows of cars.

Her heart leapt into her throat as a tall figure straightened from beside her Toyota. But it wasn't Tucker. It was Brody.

She hesitated, but there was no sense in trying to avoid him. She had to face the music sometime, and if she had to start with him, so be it. "What are you doing here?"

"Wanted to talk to you."

"You came all the way to Tupelo to talk to me?" It took a special level of pissed off to follow her ninety miles from Wishful to rip her a new one. At least if he did it here, it wouldn't be as bad as making a scene at home where everyone could hear.

Brody nodded. "Buy you a cup of coffee?"

Corinne frowned. Why would he buy her coffee? "All right."

He jerked his head. "My truck's over here."

Malika put a hand on Corinne's arm. "You don't have to go with him."

Brody might be angry with her, but she knew without a doubt he wouldn't actually hurt her. Corinne squeezed Malika's hand. "It's fine. Brody and I go way back." She turned back to him. "But I'll drive myself, if it's all the same to you."

"I'm stayin' in town. You call me if you need me," Malika said.

"Thank you, but it's fine," Corinne repeated. *If you say something often enough, you start to believe it, right?*

She followed him to a nearby Starbucks. Neither of them said a word as they stood in line. Taking their coffees—plain black for both of them—they settled at a table in a back corner, away from the few patrons scattered through the place. Corinne wrapped her hands around the cup, trying to find some comfort in the heat between her palms.

"I don't know what your deal is. I don't know why you decided to break things off with Tucker, and I don't need to know. That isn't my business. But you hurt him, and that is my business."

She wanted to drop her head in shame. Instead, she held Brody's gaze, waiting for whatever judgment he was handing out. "Say what you need to say."

"Last year you gave me some pretty frank advice, and you

saved me from making a huge mistake. I'm here to return the favor."

It was so far from the accusations she'd expected, Corinne could only stare at him.

"I was all set to give you a piece of my mind when I got here, but you look as bad as he does, so I can tell you're hurting, too."

She felt like she'd been bleeding from a mortal wound since Friday night.

"The fact is, Corinne, you told me once you wanted somebody to look at you the way I look at Tyler. Tucker does."

Her throat slammed closed and all her efforts had to go toward not bursting into tears again right here in the middle of the coffee shop.

"Now I don't know if you can't see that or if you don't believe it. But as one of his best friends, let me tell you, you're making a huge mistake cutting him off. He's crazy about you. And your son. The point is, if something is wrong between you and Tucker, you have to fix it. You can't let the gift of that kind of relationship go just because stuff got hard."

Hearing the advice she'd given him thrown back at her made her want to curl into a ball. "That wasn't why."

"I don't much care about the why. Do you love him?"

"I'm not good for him."

"I disagree, and that's not what I asked you. Do you love him?"

She had to swallow several times before she managed to get the word out. "Yes."

Brody nodded and shoved back from the table. "Then don't let go. Talk to him. Work out your shit. You owe it to both of you."

He walked out without another word.

Corinne stayed where she was, paper cup clutched between shaking hands.

It couldn't be that simple. She couldn't just go to Tucker with the knowledge of what she'd done so stark in her mind. She couldn't allow herself to chase after happiness, not when Whitney was caught in her own private hell.

What if you got Whitney out?

Even as the question popped into her head, she knew Whitney would never listen. She'd made it perfectly clear that she'd never trust Corinne again. And yet... If Corinne could find a way to convince her to leave, to get out before Garrett snapped—if he hadn't already—that might go a little ways toward redemption. If she could get Whitney out of her abusive marriage, maybe she could actually live with herself again. And maybe, just maybe, she'd feel like the kind of woman who deserved the love of a man like Tucker McGee.

CHAPTER 16

COURT HADN'T GONE WELL. Tucker had been so argumentative, Judge Carpenter had threatened to charge him with contempt. If he'd had his way, he'd have asked for a continuance until he had his head screwed on straight, but that wasn't an option for this particular case. At least they hadn't lost. After a long-ass afternoon of deliberation, the jury had finally come back in favor of his client. Instead of celebrating, he'd be holed up in his office, catching up on paperwork because he wasn't fit for human company right now.

A scuffle sounded down the hall from his office. The voice of his legal secretary, Margaret Prescott, came floating back. "—can't let you—"

The door swung open and Malika barged in, hand balled on her hip. "I need to talk to you."

Behind her, Mrs. Prescott pressed her coral-coated lips together. "I'm sorry, Tucker, she wouldn't take no for an answer."

"It's fine, Mrs. P." He checked the clock. "After five. Why don't you head on home? You can finish up those depositions in the morning."

"You sure?" Mrs. Prescott, who was sixty-five if she was a day, shot her gaze to Malika.

"Positive. And thanks for all your hard work today."

"I'll see you in the morning. Come in late. You aren't scheduled for court tomorrow, and you need some sleep," she ordered.

That was the truth. "Yes ma'am."

Once she was gone, Malika shut the door. "I heard about you and Corinne."

Tucker leaned back in his chair. "Are you here to deliver retribution of some kind? Because if she actually told you what it was I did wrong, you're more in the know than I am."

"No. Not retribution. But I think I may know what went wrong. Some of it anyway."

He hadn't actually expected that. Rising, he circled around his desk and gestured to one of the chairs. "Please, have a seat. I'd actually been hoping to talk with you, but I didn't know your last name and hadn't quite had time to track you down." Not the full truth, but admitting he'd been drunk off his ass or hungover for much of the last three days didn't seem the right move.

She sat, tucking her purse neatly in her lap. "How well did you know Corinne in high school?"

Not the tack he'd expected. "Better than she probably realizes. I've known her since elementary school."

"Was she really the mean girl she says she was?"

"Sometimes. Her parents put her under a lot of pressure and that led to some...less than noble behavior. But everybody grows up. She's not like that anymore, and she's worked really hard to prove it."

"Seems like memories here are pretty long."

"You're not wrong. What happened when she went off with you Friday night?"

"We were out in the lobby talking, catching up. Talking about you. She was happy." Those big dark eyes drilled into his, bringing home the point. "You make her happy."

He'd certainly thought so. "Go on."

"She saw somebody she knew, got this real concerned look on her face, so we ended up following this couple down the hall toward the bathrooms. The guy was being rough with her and Corinne intervened."

"Intervened how?"

"Asked the woman if she was okay. The guy hid it fast, but I could see he was really angry she'd said something."

Tucker leaned forward. "Did he do something to Corinne? Say something?"

"No, but after he left—without his wife, I might add—*she* said something. She was in total denial there was a problem and Corinne kept pushing her to let her help, to trust her. I guess they must've had bad history because the other woman—Whitney, I think, was her name—she got all snappy and ugly with Corinne."

Of course, it would be Whitney Harrington. Because, for whatever reason, Corinne would never fight back against her. "What did Whitney say?"

"That she'd trusted Corinne once and Corinne had turned on her, acted just like her mama."

If there was a bigger insult to Corinne, Tucker didn't know what it was. His hands clenched to helpless fists. "What else?"

"That nobody believed Corinne had changed and she was still the same hateful person she was back in high school. And..."

"And?"

Malika winced. "And that one of these days you'd figure it out and drop her because she wasn't worth your time."

Tucker swore. "What did Corinne say?"

"Nothing. She just told Whitney to get some help, if not from her then from somebody else. And then Whitney left. I knew Corinne was upset. She wanted to find you. I didn't know she'd do something drastic. I thought when I left her with you that she'd wanted you because you make her feel better."

He did make her feel better. And that was entirely the problem.

Tucker dropped his head, shoving both hands through his hair and sighing. This was the same old shit. Guilt about her past was eating her up inside and convincing her she didn't deserve to be happy. They'd been through this. What more did he have to do to convince her? And why the hell should Whitney's opinion matter so much that it overrode everything he'd said, everything he'd done?

"Tucker?"

"Yeah?"

"Look, I know Corinne's maybe not the easiest person to deal with. She's got some issues. I don't know how much she may have told you about them."

He straightened to look at her then. "Not nearly enough."

Malika shrugged. "She hasn't told me much, but I've inferred plenty. She's had a rough road. I just...I came because I wanted to tell you I don't think any of this is your fault and to ask you not to give up on her."

Tucker didn't want to give up on Corinne. He liked what they were together, and he liked the possibility of what they could be. But the things at the root of this whole mess were bigger than him, bigger than both of them, and he didn't know if he had it in him to keep fighting.

CORINNE SAT in her car in front of the sprawling, two-story brick house, one of several McMansions peppering one of the nicest neighborhoods at the edge of Wishful. Her stomach twisted into a sick knot in her gut. It was so like the house she'd shared with Lance. The garage door was down, so she couldn't tell if anyone was home. She hoped she hadn't come all this way for nothing. It had taken most of the drive back from Tupelo to get up the nerve to come over here, and she wasn't sure if she could do it again.

Bright seasonal flowers lined the long walk, bobbing in the hot breeze. The vast expanse of lawn was a healthy green, and huge, curving flowerbeds accented the house and the few young trees. In her experience, people who lived in places like this didn't actually do yard work. The whole point was to have a showpiece of a yard and a service to maintain it, which served double duty in showing off the wealth behind it.

With a bracing breath, Corinne got out of the car. Even from thirty feet away, she could hear the sounds of shouting. She broke into a run, headed for the double doors.

"What were you thinking?" The angry roar carried through the wood and brick and had Corinne trying the knob. Locked.

She circled around the house, fumbling with the gate of the low, wrought iron fence and hurrying past the pool to the back door. It opened into the living room. Inside, off to the right, she could see Garrett looming over Whitney in the kitchen. Tears streaked her face as she cowered back against the counter, saying something too low for Corinne to hear. It wasn't the right answer. Garrett drew back his arm, backhanding Whitney across the face, knocking her into a cabinet.

Corinne was through the door, into the living room, before she could think better of it. "Get away from her!"

Garrett turned, startled, and she used the instant of surprise to grab up the nearest thing that could be used as a weapon. He didn't move, though she doubted it was because of the fireplace poker in her hands. A man like him didn't see women as a threat.

"What the fuck are you doing here?"

"The police are already on their way." Belatedly, it occurred to Corinne that she absolutely should have called 911 before she decided to play hero. Too late now. She tightened her hands on the poker and advanced into the kitchen. "Back away from her. Slowly."

"She's my wife. I'll do with her as I choose. That's no one's business but mine."

"You need to leave." Corinne edged around the big center island, coming up behind where Whitney lay sprawled and dazed on the floor. Blood streamed down from her temple. Jesus. "Whitney, can you hear me?"

She groaned. "Corinne?"

Still conscious.

"You're getting arrested, Garrett," Corinne said.

He smirked. "I'm doing no such thing. She fell."

"Not gonna work since you've got a witness to the contrary."

"Who do you think the cops are gonna believe? A piece of trash waitress or a candidate for state senate?"

Corinne advanced on him, choking up on the fireplace poker like a baseball bat as she put herself between him and Whitney. "They'll believe the evidence. Falling doesn't give you a black eye on one side and a concussion on the other. You weren't careful this time."

He looked down at Whitney, where the side of her face was already purpling with bruises from where he'd struck her, and the first hints of doubt flickered in his eyes.

"Get the fuck out of here," she demanded. "Or don't. You could always stay. I'm sure plenty of your neighbors would love to see the senatorial hopeful get carted away in handcuffs. In these days of smartphones, I'm sure it'll wind up on YouTube. That'd be great for your campaign."

"You bitch," he snarled.

"That's Queen Bitch to you. Leave, Garrett. Before I remind you up close and personal that I played varsity softball."

"This isn't over."

No, it was just beginning, and it would be ugly.

But he left. Corinne held her position until the garage door slammed and a car cranked up. Then she dropped into a crouch, already assessing Whitney.

"What are you...doing here?"

"Trying to save your ass." She grabbed a dish towel and blotted at the gash on Whitney's temple. "Here, can you hold this?"

She lifted her hand and Corinne was relieved to see she could hold the pressure. Corinne rose, tugging open drawers until she found the Ziploc bags to make an ice pack. "We need to get out of here."

"But the police..."

"I was bluffing. And I don't know how long Garrett will stay gone."

"He'll be furious if I'm not here when he gets back. It'll be worse."

"There will always be some reason, some excuse, for it to be worse. Has he hit you before today?"

Whitney started to shake her head and winced. "Jerked me around some. Yelled a lot. But I never thought he'd hit me."

Corinne had to tamp down the simmering rage, to do what needed to be done. "They always make you think that. And when they finally snap and do hit you, they make you feel like it's all your fault. That you deserved it."

"I did deserve it. I—"

"I don't care what you did. No man should ever hit a woman. No one should hit, period. You have to leave him." She carefully pressed the ice pack to Whitney's cheek.

"I can't leave. Everything's in his name. If I leave, I'll have nothing."

"You'll have your life."

Whitney's eyes widened. "He wouldn't..."

"He would. Sooner or later, he would. He's an abusive son of a bitch. I knew this was coming when I saw you together the other night."

"How?"

"Because I lived it." How much time had passed? Was Garrett coming back yet? "There's not time to get into this now. We need to leave. You need to be checked for a concussion, and you absolutely need a couple of stitches."

"But I—"

"Look, I know you have no reason to trust me. I know I can't ever make up for the things I said and did to you in high school, and I'm sorrier and more ashamed than I can say that I had any role in starting you down the path that landed you here in this situation. But, Whitney, Garrett isn't going to stop. You can plead and you can promise and try to predict him, but, sooner or later, he's going to snap again, and next time it might not be just a black eye or a concussion."

Whitney exhaled long and slow, resting her head back against the cabinet. "I don't know how to start over. I don't know the first thing to do."

"I do. You just have to take the first step and come with me."

Her eyes began to droop, and Corinne knew she had to get Whitney on her feet.

"Why would you help me?"

"Because I can. After tonight, if you never want to see or talk to me again, fine. I don't blame you. But let me help you now. Let me see you safe."

Her eyes slid closed.

Corinne's hand shot out, taking her by the shoulder. "Whitney!"

"I'm not passing out," she said, though her voice sounded leaden. She heaved another heavy sigh before curling her fingers around Corinne's arm. "Help me up."

Relieved, Corinne levered Whitney to her feet. "We're going to get you taken care of. Just hang in with me for a little while longer."

CHAPTER 17

*T*UCKER WOKE FROM A fitful doze. The digital clock read 11:37. Barely an hour since he'd fallen into bed. On the nightstand, his phone vibrated again. He answered without checking the display, his heart leaping into the thundering tattoo of *Emergency! Emergency!*

"Tucker, it's Lily Mae."

Not his parents. Not his friends. He exhaled some of the anxiety.

"I'm sorry to call so late, but we've got a sensitive case here and we'll need a restraining order filed first thing in the morning."

He scrubbed a hand over his face, palm rasping over stubble. "On my way."

Pulling on jeans and a polo, he gave fleeting thought to coffee, but Lily Mae had an eternal pot going out at the shelter. He'd get a cup there while he took the victim's statement. His lone concession to professionalism before heading out the door was to grab his briefcase.

A Wishful PD cruiser was parked in the driveway when he arrived. They'd left the porch lights on. Tucker climbed the steps and, as usual, the door swung open before he could knock, Lily

Mae filling the doorway. Her eyes glittered with temper and a muscle jumped in her jaw. Tucker knew that look, knew that whoever had come in tonight was in bad shape.

"Thanks for coming."

"Of course." He followed her inside.

"Can I get you a cup of coffee?"

"I'd happily give up my first born for one."

"I'll see to it. They're in the study."

He saw the cop first. Judd Hamilton stood in the doorway of the study, thumbs hooked in his duty belt. "There's been no sign of him back at the house, but we've got officers posted. Can you think of anywhere he might go to ground?"

"I don't—wait. There's a hunting cabin. Somewhere up near Sardis. I don't know where exactly. I wasn't ever allowed to go there." The woman's voice quavered.

"It's okay. We'll track it down." Judd turned as Tucker stepped up. His expression was set in reassuring lines, but Tucker could see the snap of fury in his eyes.

He understood why as he stepped into the room and caught sight of the woman's face. Vicious bruising colored one side from temple to halfway down her cheek. Her blonde hair was pulled back to reveal more bruising on the other side, along with a row of neat stitches holding together a gash near her hairline. The swelling so altered her appearance, it took him a moment to recognize her.

"Whitney."

"Tucker. Thank you for coming. I hate that I've put so many people out."

"Think nothing of it. We're all here to help." He took a seat across from her, at the tiny desk and pulled out a legal pad to take notes.

"Found it."

It was the last voice Tucker expected to hear. His chest squeezed as Corinne walked in, a tube of something in her hand.

She stopped dead at the sight of him, stark pain flickering over her face before she got it under control. "Tucker."

"Corinne." It cost him to stay put, but now wasn't the time to address whatever was between them.

She moved to Whitney. "This is arnica gel. It will help with the bruising."

Corinne unscrewed the cap and gently dabbed some of the gel onto Whitney's face.

The other woman winced, but held still for her ministrations. "They teach you this in nursing school?"

Corinne met her gaze. "I learned this a long time before nursing school." A wealth of history underscored the simple statement. History she'd never trusted him enough to share.

"I'm going to follow up on that hunting cabin," Judd said. "We'll keep you posted. Once the order of protection is filed tomorrow, one of us will escort you to the house to pick up some things. Meanwhile, you'll be safest here."

"Thank you," Whitney murmured.

"You can swing by the station to get a copy of the police report," Judd told Tucker.

"I'll do that."

As soon as Judd left, Corinne rose, too. "I'll give you some privacy."

"No!" Whitney's hand shot out, grabbed hers. "Please stay."

Corinne sank back down, holding tight to Whitney's hand. "As long as you want."

How absolutely unexpected.

"It's going to be okay. You'll tell Tucker what happened, and he'll file for a temporary order of protection."

"Temporary?" Panic made Whitney's voice squeak.

"In Mississippi, we can file a temporary order that lasts for ten days," he explained. "After that, a hearing is required in chancery court to acquire something more permanent."

"A hearing? I'll have to see him?"

"Not alone," Corinne assured her. "We won't let him get to you."

"What about you? He's still out there and he's so angry. What if he comes after you?"

"I don't think he's that stupid, but if he is, I can handle myself," Corinne said.

"I'm sorry, why would he come after you? And I assume the 'he' in question is Garrett?"

Corinne nodded. "Because I'm the one who got her away from him."

"With a fireplace poker," Whitney added.

Garrett Harrington was a bull of a man, powerfully built like the linebacker he'd been in high school. At the mental image of Corinne facing him down with nothing but a fireplace poker, the blood drained out of Tucker's head. Everything in him wanted to gather her up in his arms, check her for injuries, though evidence to the contrary was sitting right in front of him. He struggled for composure. "Do we need to worry about assault charges being filed against you?"

"I didn't hit him. If I had, we'd know exactly where he was because he wouldn't have gotten back up." Her voice held grim promise.

Tucker exhaled. "Why don't y'all start at the beginning and explain what happened?"

So they did. He listened, taking notes, asking the occasional question to clarify. He didn't know whether to be impressed by Corinne's bravery or appalled at her stupidity for not immediately calling the police. Some of both. But he didn't remark on either.

"Are you willing to testify to what you witnessed?" he asked Corinne.

"Absolutely. I'll do whatever is necessary to help her sever ties with the bastard."

"All right. We'll cross that bridge when we get there. You know how that process works." He didn't make it a question.

Corinne angled her head in acknowledgment.

"I'll file for the temporary order of protection as soon as the courthouse opens in the morning, and we can go from there. You can discuss your other legal options with me, or I can make recommendations for some other good attorneys in the area."

"I'll stick with you. Corinne trusts you."

She didn't. Not where it mattered with them.

"Then I'll see you tomorrow, and we'll decide what comes next. In the meantime, try to get some rest." He shoved his legal pad into his briefcase and rose.

Corinne didn't move.

"Aren't you going to walk him out?" Whitney asked.

"I—We're not...together," she stammered.

Those bruised brown eyes slitted in a glare aimed squarely at him. "You *idiot.*"

Tucker opened his mouth—to say what, he had no idea—but Corinne beat him to it.

"He's not the idiot in this scenario."

Did that mean she regretted walking away? Tucker quashed the surge of hope. He wasn't about to pin anything on an off-hand remark.

Whitney stared at her. "Please don't tell me you chose Friday night to actually listen to anything coming out of my mouth."

Corinne ducked her head. "You weren't wrong."

"Oh for pity's sake. I *was* wrong. I was hurt and angry, and I said it to get a rise out of you. And apparently it did. Why should you ruin a perfectly good fifteen-year streak *now?*"

Tucker watched this play-by-play and decided he'd never understand women.

Whitney pointed at him with an imperious hand. "Go fix it."

"But you're not settled yet—" Corinne began.

"I'll see to that," Lily Mae said, coming into the room. "Whitney's right. Go fix it."

Corinne looked his way, a mixture of panic and resignation on her face. "It seems we need to have a conversation."

So he was finally going to get that explanation? Tucker spread his hands. "I'm all ears."

EXHAUSTION DID nothing to keep the nerves at bay as she followed Tucker back to his apartment. She wasn't ready for this. Truth be told, she might never be ready for this, so maybe being railroaded into it was for the best. She owed Tucker an explanation. She didn't dare hope for more than him maybe not hating her when she finished, because Whitney was right. She *was* an idiot.

"Want wine?" he asked, ever the congenial host.

"It'd put me to sleep."

"Okay then." He kicked back against the kitchen counter and crossed his arms.

For the first time since she'd known him, he didn't turn on the stereo, so there was no music to set the tone. His usually open expression was shuttered, and Corinne had the sudden thought that she'd hate facing him from the witness stand. This wasn't her kind, funny Tucker. She'd given him up and hurt him in the process. Now he stood, closed off and remote. A stranger.

"I don't know where to start."

"How about starting with why the fuck you thought it was a good idea to go up against a guy twice your size, who could've done to you exactly what he did to Whitney?"

Corinne refused to flinch, though she recognized the foolishness of her actions. Instead, she squared her shoulders. "Because I've survived worse. She hasn't."

He swore, low and vicious.

She *hated* talking about this. But she'd opened this subject, so she might as well get it all out there. She waggled the middle fingers of her right hand. "These fingers were jammed when I tried to block a blow. He was upset I didn't have dinner ready on time." At the time she'd managed to convince herself it'd been an accident. That Lance had just been gesticulating wildly, and she got caught in the crossfire.

Holding up her left hand she said, "This wrist was broken when he shoved me back, yanking the phone away to prove I was talking to another guy. It was the cell phone company calling to offer us an upgrade." The stunned shock of that moment still reverberated through her, but Corinne didn't focus on it, moving instead to the next thing. "He dislocated my left shoulder when I talked back to him because he didn't like how I'd cut my hair. And of course there were countless bruises for doing nothing more than breathing too loud or interrupting his TV time. The coup de grace was when he broke my collarbone because he said I looked at another man on the street. I left him that night with nothing but Kurt, his diaper bag, and the clothes on our backs."

Tucker's hands clenched into fists but she saw no gut level shock. Neither did she see the pity she'd expected. This wasn't news to him. He'd suspected, but he'd never pried, never asked, and he could have.

"Is this supposed to be some kind of badge of honor?"

She shook her head. "No. It's evidence I knew exactly what I was getting into when I ran into that kitchen, and I knew exactly what would happen if I didn't. I had to get her out, Tucker. Because it's my fault she was with him in the first place."

His head kicked back in surprise. "How the hell do you figure that?"

"Abuse is a self-perpetuating cycle. My parents were never violent, but they spent a helluva lot of time and effort tearing me down. They verbally abused me from the time I was Kurt's age. Made me feel like I was never good enough, never pretty enough, never doing enough. And since I couldn't lash out at them, I lashed out at someone weaker."

"Whitney? What does that have to do with us?"

She'd have to spell it out. And then he'd know, without a doubt, who she really was. This conversation would be over in a hurry after that, and then they'd be through for good. The knowledge of that made the bad hospital coffee and vending machine crackers that had been dinner want to come back up in revolt.

"I'm the one who started the cycle for her. I'm the one who tore her down, made her feel like less. I knew her better than anyone, so I knew exactly how to do it for the most damage. When we hit high school, I used that knowledge to get in with the popular crowd. I hurt and embarrassed her, and then over the next four years I *kept* doing it. I broke her, Tucker. I'm the one who primed her for that asshole to come along and prey on her poor self-esteem. I'm the one who set her up for that. And when I realized it, I just couldn't—be with you. Because I didn't deserve something so good, so wonderful when I'd done that. I didn't deserve you." She wasn't sure she deserved him now, but it wasn't because of Whitney.

"So this is all about some misguided sense of guilt?"

Why wasn't he looking appalled? "Haven't you been *listening* to me?"

"Yeah. I'm hearing you had a shitty family and an even shittier marriage. And you did some shitty things to someone who used to be a friend, and somehow you think that places the blame for her asshole's fists on you. I call bullshit." He shoved away from the counter. "Corinne, life isn't a balance sheet. What we had didn't have anything to do with Whitney."

What we had. Past tense.

She didn't flinch at that blow either, though it hurt worse than all the rest combined. *You brought this on yourself. You walked away. You screwed this up. This was the only possible outcome here because you didn't listen to the voice that mattered.*

"You're right," she said.

"Come again?"

"You're right. You've been right since you slipped all those notes in my locker in high school. I didn't deserve what was done to me. I didn't deserve what was said. You always tried to build me up, to remind me of that. Then and now. But your voice has been drowned out by so, so many others over the years. I thought if I could get Whitney out, get her away from Garrett, I'd somehow redeem myself. That it would make up for the past and make me feel like the kind of person who could be worthy of the way you looked at me."

"And now?"

Now she just felt soul weary and sad. But she'd finish this and say what she'd come here to say. "Now I realize that in your eyes I was always worthy. It's not your good opinion I needed to earn. It was mine. Because nothing you could say or do would ever make up for what I believe of myself."

"What do you believe, Corinne?"

"I'd rather tell you what I know."

"Okay."

Because her knees weren't quite steady, now she was the one leaning back against the counter. "I know I made mistakes in the past. I know I've bent over backward trying to make up for them, to be a better example for Kurt. I know I did the right thing going after Whitney today. Maybe we won't ever be friends again, but it went a long way toward healing the hurt between us. Either way, I'll sleep easier knowing she's away from him. I know I'm strong. Strong enough to break the cycle of abuse for my son, so he'll never grow up feeling the way I did. And—" She swallowed, thinking that if this was the last chance she got to speak to him like this, she'd at least leave him with the truth. "—I know I'm in love with you and walking away from you was the dumbest thing in a long line of dumb things I've done in my life."

Tucker stared at her, face inscrutable. She'd put herself out there, admitted she loved him, and he just stood there. Abruptly angry, Corinne thought of the one useful thing she'd ever learned from her mother. *No one's going to hand you anything. If you want something, you have to go after it yourself.*

She wanted Tucker McGee.

Shoving away from the counter, Corinne crossed to him, wishing he'd say or do something—*anything* to indicate how he was feeling.

"I hurt you. I'm so sorry for that. But I'm asking you for a second chance because I deserve it. *We* deserve it." She hadn't thought so when she came over here. But she believed it now, and she wanted with every fiber of her being for him to believe it too. Reaching out, she framed his face in her hands. His stubble rasped her palms. "Please give me another chance."

Eyes never leaving hers, Tucker's hands curled around hers, pulling them away from his face and her heart all but stopped.

It was truly over.

CHAPTER 18

NO ONE HAD EVER accused Tucker of being a man of few words. But despite all his theater training, all his hours in front of judge and jury sometimes pulling arguments out of his ass, right this moment he couldn't think of the right words to express how proud he was of her. She'd finally figured out what he'd known from day one—that she was worth it.

He reached up to take her hands, pulling them away from his face. Her eyes shattered with grief, and he realized he'd taken too long to answer. She started to pull away.

He tightened his grip on her hands and pressed his lips to each of her palms. "I'm in love with you, too."

"But?"

Tucker pulled her in, hating that he'd given her another moment's doubt. "No buts. It's a complete, unqualified statement and the answer to all the important questions. I love you. And if I took a little longer to get it out, it's only because you cut the knees out from under my whole list of arguments, and I had to fast forward through the script in my head."

On a half laugh, half sob, she wrapped around him. "There was a script?"

"Oh yeah. I wasn't letting you walk out of here without throwing every reason in the book at you to give us another try." He stroked the hair back from her face, hand lingering on the cheek now wet with tears. "What changed your mind?"

"Brody. I called him out on his mistake. He called me out on mine. Quid pro quo and all that. He followed me all the way to Tupelo and waited outside the testing center to tell me."

"Your test was today? How the hell did I forget that? How did it go?"

Corinne shook her head. "I don't want to talk about the test, Tucker. I don't want to talk at all." Rising to her toes, she brushed her mouth over his. "I need you."

Tucker skimmed his hands down her back. "Is your mom expecting you back at any particular time?"

"I didn't know how long things would take with Whitney, so I told her not to expect me until the morning."

"Then stay with me. Spend the night in my bed and wake up with me in the morning."

She glanced past him, toward the clock on the stove. "Not a whole lot left of the night."

"Then let's make it count."

He took her mouth, gorging himself on the flavor of her as he backed her toward the bedroom. How had it only been days since he'd tasted her? Greedy for more, he licked into her mouth. She met him with equal hunger, her hands shoving his shirt up and off with a hurried gasp before her lips came back to his.

Some dim part of his mind urged him to slow down, find some of the finesse he'd planned that night at The Babylon. But it was drowned out by a primal need to take and claim, to eradicate the distance between them. They tugged and circled until, at last, they found skin. Her breasts spilled into his palms, full and heavy and perfect. He took one taut peak into his mouth and her head fell back on a moan, the hands at his belt abruptly stopping. A quick glance at her face, suffused with pleasure, assured him he'd just temporarily scrambled her dexterity.

Not wanting the other breast to feel neglected, he shifted over, giving it the same treatment. At this, Corinne groaned his name and gave up on the belt entirely, reaching into the waistband of his pants and curling those strong fingers around him. Now it was his turn to gasp, to press into her touch.

"Too many clothes," she said.

"God, yes."

By tacit agreement, they released each other, stripping out of the rest of their clothes in moments, before falling in a tangle of fevered limbs on the bed. They rolled, touching and tasting whatever they could reach. When she rose up over him, her dark hair brushing the dusky tips of her breasts, he'd never seen anyone so beautiful.

Corinne leaned forward to kiss him, tongue thrusting against his as she shifted to take him inside her.

"Wait."

She froze.

"Condom," he managed.

"Birth control."

"Are you s—"

She put an end to the discussion by sinking down onto him. Her scorching heat closed around him like a fist, and Tucker cursed with reverence. Corinne brought his hands back to her breasts, using them to knead their fullness as she began to move. And, oh yeah, he could handle that demand. Her eyes stayed on his as she rode him. There was no patience here, only pure unadulterated need. Her hips began to piston faster, sinking down hard to take him deeper with every stroke. The glorious, erotic friction drove him out of his mind.

Her skin flushed, and she whipped forward. "So close. So close, Tucker."

The sound of his name on her lips tasted like heaven as he

clamped his arms around her and thrust deeper, burying himself to the root in all her wet heat and swiveling to rub the base of his cock against her most sensitive flesh. Corinne whimpered, a wordless plea, so he did it again and again. Tension coiled in his shoulders, shooting down his spine and into his balls. She cried out, her body clamping around him and pulling him over the edge. He came hard and fast, shouting her name as he spilled into her.

Corinne collapsed across his chest, her hair sticking to his sweat slicked skin. Tucker held her to him, until their hearts began to slow. She pressed a kiss to the underside of his jaw, where her head was nestled. He could probably stay like this for the rest of his life, cozied up, still inside her. Smug and happy, he felt so goddamned lucky not to be that guy again.

He didn't realize he'd spoken aloud until she asked, "What guy?"

Well shit. He hadn't meant to get into this.

She stirred, shifting just enough to look into his face, concern lighting up those sky blue eyes as she waited for an explanation.

Tucker exhaled and stroked a hand down her back. She'd bared her scars to him. "The guy who gets left."

Realization dawned. "Laura?"

He nodded.

"We don't have to talk about this. I don't know why I was so angry, except that everybody knew and I was sensitive right then. We don't have to—"

"No, listen. I want to tell you this. I haven't even thought about my marriage in a long time, but being with you has made me look at things in a new light." Because it pleased him, he rubbed circles at her nape. She stretched against him, arching into his touch like a big cat.

"We were supposed to be the perfect couple. And less than a year after we took our vows, she left me for her high school sweetheart. You, at least, had the decency to say something when you walked away. She just had me served with divorce papers. Never said a word about being unhappy. We never fought."

"That's horrible."

"Blindsided me, for sure."

"The others don't know, do they? Piper's too bloodthirsty and protective of you to speak so casually of her otherwise."

"They didn't know, no. It came out this weekend when I lost my shit."

"That's so hard to imagine. You're always so calm and together."

"There was a lot of alcohol and self-pity involved. And generally wondering what it was about me that made me so easy to walk away from."

Her kiss tasted of apology. "Walking away from you wasn't easy. It tore me in two. I never wanted to leave you, Tucker. I just thought I had to."

"I know. And I get that now. You needed to do it for yourself or we'd have ended up circling back around to this same issue at some other point."

"If you always felt like the guy who gets left, I always felt like the girl who wasn't good enough. Not for my parents. Not for my ex. But for you, I'm not just good enough. I'm just *good.* You make me a better person. I can't promise I won't still have rough patches. But I'm finally making peace with my past and moving on from it. And I want to move on with you. I *like* who I am with you. I like who we are together."

"Me too." He levered up to kiss her, rolling her beneath him because he already wanted her again. "It's worth noting, I didn't lose my shit when Laura left me. I was upset. Embarrassed. But not devastated. In the end, she did me a favor."

Corinne dragged her hands down his back and arched into him. "Yeah?"

"I wasn't in love with her. Not the way I should've been. But I am in love with you and with Kurt. And I look forward to every messy and challenging second with you both."

She framed his face. "You're a good man, Tucker McGee, and I'm so proud to call you mine."

He sank into her and spent the rest of the night proving he was up for the job.

CORINNE STEPPED out the automatic doors of Wilton Memorial Hospital with a spring in her step. Credit for that went largely to Tucker. Amazing what stupendous makeup sex would do for a girl's confidence, despite the almost total lack of sleep. Regardless of what happened in the end, she'd done her absolute best in the panel interview with the hospital board. If the various members who had direct or indirect history with her couldn't look past that history to see she was the best candidate for the job, well, that was on them. She'd find something else.

Her phone rang as she crossed the parking lot. Fishing it out of her purse, she checked the display, but didn't recognize the number. "Hello?"

"Corinne? It's Whitney." Her voice sounded hesitant and put Corinne on immediate alert.

"Are you okay? Is Garrett giving you trouble? Did he find you?"

"I'm fine. Well, as fine as I can be. I'm still out at the shelter."

Corinne let out a sigh as she unlocked her car. "Have the police tracked him down yet?"

"No, but Tucker called. He said the restraining order is filed. And there's been an officer posted at the house all night. That's why I'm calling, actually. I was wondering if you'd go over there with me. Help me pack up some stuff?"

The request took her by surprise. Surely there was someone else she'd rather have with her. Then again, if Garrett held true to the typical pattern, he'd cut Whitney off from all her friends and family, isolating her in order to keep her in line. Because of the interview, Corinne had taken off work, but she had about seventeen other things she should be doing. "Of course. I'll come get you."

Whitney rose from the porch steps as Corinne pulled up. Her bruises stood out in all their multi-colored glory behind the oversized sunglasses, but her movements weren't stiff as she climbed into the front seat.

She took one long look at Corinne. "You fixed things with Tucker."

"Am I wearing a sign?"

"Might as well be. Everything about you says 'well-loved woman'." Whitney paused. "I'm glad."

Corinne glanced her way. "Are you?"

"Well, it's nice to have a different reason to call you a bitch."

Corinne just lifted a brow.

Whitney blew out a breath. "Sorry. Old habits. I didn't call you so I could abuse you to your face."

"Why *did* you call me?"

"Because as olive branches go, saving me from my abusive husband with a fireplace poker is a pretty damned big one. High school Corinne wouldn't have done that. And I thought maybe if you could turn over a new leaf, so could I."

A knot she'd been carrying around for years finally loosened. "I'd like that."

"As for Tucker, I *am* glad. A tad jealous, maybe. He's the genuine article—a truly good guy. And he adores you. It's what we all want. It's a little easier knowing you have that now, when you went through the same hell I did. Gives me faith that there's life on the other side of all this."

Reaching out, Corinne squeezed Whitney's hand. "There is. It's not easy, and it's not fast. But I promise life will be better on the other side."

"I sure as hell hope so."

As they turned onto Whitney's street, Corinne asked, "How are you feeling?"

One blonde brow arched above the glasses.

"I didn't just mean physically," Corinne clarified. "You did a huge thing yesterday. You're doing another big one today. It's natural if you're scared."

"Were you?" Whitney asked.

"Every single time. It took a while before Lance was willing to waive custody. I vomited on almost every trip to drop Kurt off or pick him up for visitation."

"Did he ever hurt Kurt?"

"No. Thank God. If I'd stayed, I think he might have eventually. Especially once Kurt hit that point of wanting independence and defying all rules to try and get it. It was a blessing when he gave up all parental rights."

"I can't even imagine how much more terrifying this would have been if we'd had a child."

That, at least, wasn't something Corinne had to worry about anymore.

As she pulled into the drive, the driver's side door of the police cruiser parked across the street opened and a tall black man slid out.

"Oh good. Looks like Darius is on duty."

"I don't think I know Darius."

"Darius Greeley. Not a local. Moved in a few years ago with Wishful PD. His people are from Baltimore. He married Mama Pearl's almost youngest this summer. Tucker's law partner, Vivian."

"One of the twins, right?"

"Yep."

They climbed out of the car.

"Corinne! I hear tell I'm gonna be losing my favorite waitress," Darius called.

"From your mouth to God's ear. My interview at the hospital was this morning."

"Yeah? How'd it go?"

Corinne shrugged. "As well as it was gonna. Panel interviews are a thing of the devil. How's Viv?"

"Good. She said she's taking over some of Tucker's cases this week to give y'all some extra rehearsal time."

"Blame it all on your mama-in-law. She's got a competitive streak ten miles wide." And she knew they were behind on practicing their freestyle routine. "Has it been all quiet?"

"Nary a peep other than nosy neighbors. Can't complain too much. Mrs. Carsen brought out fresh cookies."

"She bakes amazing cookies," Whitney put in.

"That she does," Darius agreed. "Y'all go on in, do what you need to do. I'll be right here if you need anything."

Whitney's hand trembled as she tried to insert the key into the lock, so Corinne took it from her, doing the honors herself and pushing open the door into the kitchen. They stepped inside. The bloody kitchen towel she'd used to stanch the bleeding the night before still lay crumpled on the counter.

"I don't know why I expected it to look different," Whitney said.

"Because today you're different." Corinne wrapped an arm around her, pleased when her friend did the same.

"I don't know where to start."

"Let's start with a couple of weeks' worth of clothes and anything that's really important to you. Pictures, heirlooms. Anything Garrett might destroy out of spite. We'll load up your car with whatever will fit, then go from there."

"Okay."

They climbed the stairs together.

"I didn't know you were interviewing out at Wilton Memorial."

"It won't be the only place I'll apply, but it's the most obvious. I did my clinical hours there, and I really like the staff, the work. I feel like it'd be a good fit."

"They'd be lucky to have you."

Because Whitney's voice sounded a little choked, Corinne tried to lighten the mood. "Hey now, I know we're doing this whole turning over a new leaf thing, but let's not go crazy with the compliments."

Whitney gave a watery laugh. "I know. Someone should check to see if hell froze over. But I mean it. They'd be lucky to have you. *I* feel lucky to have you. And I didn't say it last night because there was just so much going on and I was so overwhelmed, but... thank you. For helping me. For deciding to be my friend again."

Feeling a little watery herself, Corinne wrapped the smaller woman in a hug. "Thank you for letting me."

CHAPTER 19

"—AND AS WE STAND here at the start of the final performance of Dancing With Wishful, I want to thank everyone involved in the project."

From his position on the sidelines, Tucker watched Norah on the big screen they'd set up at the opposite end of the ballroom.

"The fundraiser has been a total success and our local women's shelter will be able to break ground on a new addition later this fall!"

Applause and cheers broke out. Beside him, Cam gave a two-fingered whistle.

"Looks like your girl pulled it off again," Tucker observed.

Cam slapped him on the back. "Brother, we all pulled this one off."

"You ready to have your ass kicked?"

"Dream on, Tuck. Cam and I have this in the bag," Tyler said.

Tucker just slid his arm around Corinne and smiled. "May the best pair win." She leaned into him, and he decided all was right in his world.

Out front, Norah handed off the mic to the emcee, who rolled immediately into clips from the interviews they'd done throughout competition. With only two performances, they had to fill the extra time with something. Beside him, Corinne fairly vibrated.

"Are you nervous or excited?" he asked.

"Both. Hyped up about the competition. Excited by the possibility of winning. And also relieved it's nearly over. I've been burning the candle at both ends for so long at this point, and I need a serious break."

He'd been thinking on that subject for a few weeks now. But before he could respond, he caught sight of Corinne's mom and Kurt making their way through the crowd. "I had some ideas about that. Remind me to tell you about them later. Meanwhile, I think our cheering section has arrived."

Corinne turned, smiling and waving when she saw her son. The grin dimmed a fraction as she realized her mother was with him. "I didn't know she was coming."

That put Tucker on red alert. She'd told him about their fight the previous weekend. The two hadn't exactly been on speaking terms.

As soon as Kurt spotted them, he tugged free from Marianne and made a beeline in their direction. Tucker broke away and met him halfway, initiating the complicated fist bump/handshake routine they'd established, before scooping the giggling boy up for a hug. "How you doin' kiddo?"

"Good! I earned three R2-D2 stickers on my chore chart this week!"

"That's awesome."

"Kurt Dawson, you know you're not supposed to run from me." Marianne sounded faintly winded.

Tucker set him down and pointed out Corinne in the long dark cloak hiding her costume. "Why don't you go wish your mom luck?"

"Okay!"

Marianne started toward Corinne. "There's something I need to tell her."

As Kurt scampered off to his mother, Tucker offered his arm to Marianne with a courtly bow.

With some surprise, she took it. "Such pretty manners."

"Only to a point. If you say anything at all to upset Corinne, you'll have me to deal with. I won't have tonight ruined for her. Are we clear?"

Rather than offense or irritation, it was approval he saw in her eyes. "You'll do, Tucker McGee."

Kurt was chattering a mile a minute by the time they reached Corinne.

"And it was awesome! Can we bring Tucker to the water park before it closes for the summer?"

"It so happens, I love water parks," Tucker informed him. "And the beach. Ever been to the beach, Kurt?"

"Just the beach at the lake. I've never seen a real beach before, except on TV."

"We'll have to see what we can do about that."

Corinne and her mother were in a staring contest.

"Thank you for coming, Mama. You didn't have to."

"I wanted to support you." There was something more under her statement, an earnestness he hadn't heard from Marianne before.

The emcee's voice boomed. "And now, let's put our hands together in a warm Wishful welcome for the first of your final competitors! Team Wishful Nursery and Garden Center—Tyler Edison and Cam Crawford performing their freestyle."

"You should find your seats," Corinne said.

"Good luck, Mommy!"

Her dimple flashed. "Thanks baby."

"Good luck. Both of you." With one last look, Marianne herded her grandson away.

Tucker laced his fingers through Corinne's as they moved to watch Cam and Tyler's performance. "Okay?"

"Yeah, I'm fine. Just ready to do this."

The music poured out and their friends leapt into motion. The routine was fast and flashy—at least on Tyler's part. Tucker and Corinne hadn't had time to put together anything so complex, so Tucker made the choice to play their audience. The crowd had followed their love story from the beginning, so he'd designed a routine to showcase it and tug on the heartstrings of anyone watching. If they won tonight, it was more likely to be from an influx of popular votes rather than the judges' decision. Either way, he figured he owed Norah one for giving him the opportunity to woo Corinne in the first place.

The number ended to cheers and wolf whistles. Tyler and Cam moved toward the dais, awaiting the judges' decisions. After some discussion among themselves, they lifted their paddles. Ten. Nine. Ten.

"Tough scores to beat," Corinne observed.

"It ain't over 'til the fat lady sings. Besides, it doesn't matter if we win."

Her brows arched up in surprise.

"The fundraiser was a success, and we got each other out of the deal. Those are both wins in my book."

Corinne rose to her toes and brushed a kiss over his mouth. "That's sweet and noble, but the difference is, I'm in the mood to kick a little ass."

He was still laughing as they got the signal to take their positions. She shrugged out of the cloak to reveal her costume, a long, glittering gold confection that was Babette's modernized take on Belle to his Beast. They walked out on the floor with the lights lowered. Before they snapped up, he pressed a kiss to her hand. "In case I haven't mentioned it, you're gorgeous."

Her face glowed with a smile as the lights came up and the music started. Tucker pulled her in, sliding into the dance and into their own little world. No crowd, no competition, only the woman he loved. The dance was part waltz, part foxtrot, all love story. When the final bars played, he eased her into a dip and pressed his lips to hers.

The applause apparently went on for a bit before he registered the sound.

Corinne was laughing as he pulled her vertical. "Nice improv."

"I enjoyed it." Grinning, they made their way to the judges' dais.

Almost before they'd stopped, the paddles came up. Nine. Ten. Ten.

"A tie, ladies and gentlemen! That means the final results are up to you voters here and at home. Audience members will find a ballot card at your seat. Our ushers will be collecting them shortly. At home, you can go online and vote for the next half hour." He gave the web address for voting. "While we await the exciting conclusion of Dancing With Wishful, let's review some of the highlights from the competition."

Everybody converged as soon as they left the floor.

"The Disney vote? Come on!" Tyler complained.

"Hey, no rule against it," Tucker argued. "And we've been pulling the nostalgia thread from day one."

"And rocking it," Piper observed. "Nicely done." Her gaze slid up and down Corinne. "Not gonna lie. I'm having some dress envy right now."

Corinne laughed. "I admit, I'll be sad to give it back. What girl *didn't* want to be Belle?"

"You make a pretty princess, Mommy!"

Tucker snagged Kurt and scooped him up before he could leap into Corinne's arms and muss her costume. "She does, doesn't she?"

"Thanks. I think both my men are looking pretty handsome." She gave them both noisy kisses on their cheeks.

A flustered Marianne was half a dozen paces away. "Sorry. He keeps getting away from me."

"Are you sad it's nearly over?" Brody asked Corinne.

"No. It's been fun. But it's been so long since life was anything resembling normal, I'd kinda like to figure out what that looks like."

"How did your test go?" Piper asked.

"Don't know yet. I'll probably have to take it again. I wasn't in the greatest headspace when I went in."

"That's what I wanted to tell you earlier. The results came in." Marianne pulled an envelope from her purse.

Corinne eyed it like it might bite her.

"You don't have to look at it yet," Tucker told her. "Enjoy tonight, wait until tomorrow."

"But it's *there*. I can't *not* look at it." Blowing out a breath, she took the envelope from her mother and tore open the flap.

With Kurt perched on one hip, Tucker reached out to press a hand to her back as she pulled out the sheet of printed paper inside. She skimmed the contents twice before lifting her gaze to his.

"Well?"

"I passed," she whispered. Thrusting both hands into the air, she spun in a circle. "Thank you, sweet baby Jesus, I *passed*."

More cheers and congratulations broke out. Kurt was juggled, kisses were given, shoulders were squeezed. Corinne glowed with relief and joy. Until she came face-to-face with her mother.

Marianne caught her by the hands. "I'm so proud of you, Corinne. Of everything you've done."

Corinne swallowed. "But?"

Her mother winced. "No buts. No qualifiers. No suggestions for how you could've done it better. I'm just proud of you. Period. I should've told you that a long time ago."

Corinne's mouth dropped open. "Thank you, Mama."

When Marianne moved in for a hug, Corinne didn't stop her.

The whole thing was stiff and awkward, obviously not something the two women were used to. But it was real. And Tucker hoped it was the start of a new chapter there, as Corinne had started so many others.

The emcee's voice boomed over the crowd. "If our dancers will return to the floor, we have the final tallies to deliver."

A few minutes later, the four of them stood before the judges as the emcee reminded the crowd of the individual performances and scores the two teams had earned over the course of the competition. "Through the entire process, these two teams have been neck-and-neck. So we turned over the decision for the final winners of Dancing With Wishful to you, our audience. Results have been tabulated from our in-house audience and online. And the winner of the first annual Dancing With Wishful competition is—" He paused for effect, looking out over the crowd. "Team Dinner Belles, Tucker McGee and Corinne Dawson!"

Tucker scooped Corinne up in a bear hug.

"We did it!" she shouted.

"We absolutely did."

They turned to accept congratulations from Tyler and Cam. As the four of them traded handshakes and hugs amid the deafening applause, Tyler spoke up, "Hey, did anybody else catch that whole 'first annual' part of the spiel?"

"I did notice that," Tucker said.

They all looked at Cam, who lifted his hands in peace. "What can I say? It's Norah."

CORINNE SLID A TOWERING slice of coconut cream pie in front of Malika before settling across from her with her own slice of peach pie. A la mode, of course.

Malika forked a bite into her mouth. "Oh my God."

"Good, isn't it?"

"I think I just had a foodgasm. I take it back. This is so much better than champagne for celebration."

"We'll revisit the champagne once we are gainfully employed in our chosen profession."

"You didn't have any after winning Dancing With Wishful?"

Corinne grinned. "Tucker had other ideas for how to celebrate our win." Her cheeks heated just thinking about it. Who knew he liked a little role play *off* the stage?

Malika shot her a knowing grin.

Corinne scooped up a bite of pie and studied her friend. "He told me you came to see him."

One dark brow arched up. "Mad I interfered?"

"Do I look mad?"

"You look happy. He makes you happy. I'm so glad you gave him another chance."

"Me too. He *does* make me happy." And at last, finally, she didn't feel guilty about it.

"How was y'all's weekend down in Lost Beach?"

Tucker's answer to some downtime was to sweep her and Kurt off to the Mississippi coast for a long weekend beach vacation. Corinne had worried about taking more time off work, but Mama Pearl was so excited about the win, she'd practically shoved them out the door.

"It was fun. Kurt *loved* the ocean. He and Tucker swam and made sand castles, and I got to lay on a towel and do nothing for whole hours at a time. I actually *napped*. It was glorious." And for those three days, they'd felt like a family. Everything in Corinne wanted that future, that life, with him. Tucker wanted them—both of them—but that kind of dream was a ways off. Despite how long they'd known each other, they'd only been together for a little while. She couldn't let her heart run away with the rest of her. But it was hard to hang on to practicality when faced with such a man.

"You absolutely deserved the break," Malika declared.

Checking the clock, Corinne said, "Speaking of break, mine's nearly over. I should finish my pie." She dug into it in earnest.

They chatted a few more minutes as they demolished the pie, discussing other job opportunities and plans for upcoming months. Malika was considering a traveling nurse position to see some more of the country. Corinne had the sense she'd prefer that to being locked in at the hospital here. It was good money and a good opportunity since her friend wasn't tied down by anything. But, man, she'd miss her.

At the end of her break, Corinne rose, plate in hand to head back to the kitchen. The bell over the door jangled as another customer came in.

"I'll be right with you. I just need to…" She trailed off as she recognized Patton Holifield, Managing Director and CEO of Wilton Memorial. Hastily, she set the plate back on the table, surreptitiously wiping her hands on her apron. "Mr. Holifield. What can I get for you, sir?"

"I actually came to speak with you, if you can spare a moment."

"Of course." Corinne's heart beat thick in her throat. Why was he *here?* Surely, they didn't give rejections in person. Maybe it had nothing to do with the hospital job at all.

God, she needed something to do with her hands. "Can I get you a cup of coffee?"

"No, that's all right. This won't take long." He gestured toward the door. Away from prying ears.

Swallowing back the nerves, Corinne caught Omar's eye through the window into the kitchen and jerked her head to indicate she'd be right back. Then she followed Mr. Holifield outside.

"I'm sure you're wondering why I'm here, so I'll get straight to the point."

"Thank you, sir."

"We had two dozen applicants for the two nursing positions open at the hospital. As you know, we conducted panel interviews with all the candidates. Though yours went well, certain members of the board had some concerns about your suitability as a candidate."

Corinne's heart fell. So this was a rejection. She'd known there was a strong chance she wouldn't get the job, but this? The head of the board had come all the way down here to tell her in person. What? The form letter rejection wasn't good enough? She'd earned personal humiliation?

"I see," she said, though she didn't.

"I'm not finished."

What more was there to say?

"When pressed to provide reasons for those objections, it became clear they were allowing personal feelings to get in the way of their decision making. Your three recommendations were excellent, as were all your performance reviews during your internship at the hospital."

Corinne blinked. "I'm sorry. My *three* recommendations? I only submitted two."

"Only two were required. But a third one came in last week that I simply couldn't ignore."

"From who?"

"Whitney Harrington. My goddaughter."

This was Whitney's godfather? Corinne's mouth opened, but nothing came out. Mr. Holifield didn't seem to need her acknowledgment to continue the conversation.

"You fought for her. Literally. You succeeded in getting her out of a horrific situation where many of the rest of us failed. I want that kind of strength and passion in my hospital, Miss Dawson. So I'm here to offer you the job."

Corinne stared at him. She'd gotten the job?

He continued on, reeling off starting salary, benefits and the like, but she heard almost none of it until he asked, "What do you say?"

"Yes." She had to force the word past lips frozen with shock. "Yes, I'd love to take the job. When do I start?"

"First of the month. You'll need to come by human resources and fill out some paperwork, of course. But we look forward to having you as part of the Wilton Memorial team." He offered his hand.

Corinne took it. "Thank you. Thank you, sir. I can't tell you what this means to me." It was everything she'd been working for. The thing that would mean her independence from her mother. What would allow them to move out into their own place and *finally* have more than the bare minimum in their life. She'd done it.

She had to tell Tucker.

They said their goodbyes and Corinne watched as he got into his car. Before his tail lights disappeared around the corner, she'd hit a dead run. People stared as she raced across the town green, but she paid no attention. She didn't stop until she stumbled, gasping for air, through the front door of Tucker's office.

Mrs. Prescott looked up from her desk, "Well, my Lord. Are you okay, honey?"

Unable to speak for sucking in air, Corinne just nodded and gestured vaguely toward Tucker's office, hoping the woman would understand the question of whether he was in and if he was alone.

The man himself emerged, a folder in hand. "Mrs. P, do you know if— Corinne?" He dropped the folder, crossing to her in two strides. "What's wrong? Did something happen to Kurt?"

Corinne shook her head. "Nothing wrong." Gracious, she hadn't run full tilt like this since high school. She sucked in another lungful of air. "Got the job."

"You got the hospital job? Here at Wilton Memorial?"

She nodded.

He gave a great whoop and spun her around in a bear hug. "That's fantastic!"

Getting her breath back, she grinned. "Ran all the way here to tell you."

"So I see. Aren't you on shift?"

"I am. And I—" She hissed a breath. "Oh, good Lord, I left Malika sitting at the diner."

Tucker laughed. "You could've called."

"Never even crossed my mind. I wanted to tell you first."

Vivian stuck her head out from her office down the hall. "Hey Corinne, Mama's on the phone. She's looking for you."

"Tell her I'm bringing her back now," Tucker said, "and to ready the celebratory pie."

"I just finished a piece in honor of passing the NCLEX."

He held open the door for her. "And your point is?"

She laughed. "You're as bad as Kurt wanting second dessert."

"My dear girl, life is far too short not to celebrate all the great moments with pie. This is another of those moments."

Corinne slid her hand in his, not caring about the pie but just that she got to celebrate this with him. "Point taken."

EPILOGUE

2 Months Later

"Speakeasy is jumping tonight, so they said the pizza will be ready in about an hour," Corinne said.

They weren't actually *that* busy, but Tucker had enlisted Natalie Mercer, the manager, to give him the necessary lead time to execute his plan.

"Well that's fine. I've got something in mind to kill some time before we go pick it up. You up for a little adventure, Kurt?"

"Always!" He leapt up and Tucker watched him like a hawk.

Maybe it wasn't a hundred percent smart to loop the five-year-old in on things. Tucker didn't have complete confidence the kid wouldn't blow the surprise in his excitement. But so far, he'd managed to sit on the piece he knew without saying a word.

"What did you have in mind?" Corinne asked.

"I know you're still looking for a place. A guy I know has one for rent that I think might be perfect. I thought we could take a field trip to go see it."

"Getting kind of dark out for peeking in the windows," she observed.

"I borrowed the keys. He said we could take all the time we wanted to look around."

She gave him a little bit of side eye but didn't argue. So they loaded up in the car and drove the couple of miles from his office to the two-story brick house on Barnard Street. The sun had already sunk behind the big trees shading the yard.

"Are you insane? There's no way this is in my price range. And there's not even a for rent sign."

"He just put it on the market. And before you say no, let's at least look. Gotta kill some time before we get the pizza."

Again with the side eye, but she got out of the car. Kurt scrambled up the walk ahead of them. It was a little weedy and the flowerbeds needed some TLC, but some fresh plantings and mulch would go a long way. The front door and shutters had a fresh coat of dark brown paint that set off the cream painted brick.

"It's a bit of a fixer upper, he told me." Tucker unlocked the door and stepped inside, flipping on lights as he went. "Three bedroom, two-and-a-half bath, with a sort of office space. It's a couple of decades old, but solidly built. Original hardwoods throughout. Kinda scuffed, but they'd refinish easy. And the walls are all pale neutral, so you'd have the option to paint whatever colors you wanted without needing to prime."

"Since when do landlords allow tenants to do that kind of home improvement?"

"Well, he ran out of get up and go to do more himself, so I think he'd love it if somebody'd fix up the place some more. Pending his approval, of course."

Tucker led her into the kitchen. "It's dated, but paint and new hardware would go a long way toward helping that. And the appliances are new in the last five years."

Kurt wandered over to peer out the big picture window overlooking the backyard. *"There's a fort!"*

He was already racing for the back door when Corinne called, "Slow down, don't run, and stay in the yard!"

"Okay!" In a flash, he was out the door.

"The people who lived here before had kids. Left the playset behind when they moved."

"This is the kiss of death, Tucker. He's going to be crushed when I tell him we aren't moving here." Her expression of exasperation and longing almost made him smile, but he managed to keep a straight face.

"Don't make a decision yet. You haven't seen the rest of the house yet."

"I don't need to see the rest of the house. I don't need to fall in love with it any more myself. There's no way this is in the budget."

"So you admit you like the house?" he pressed.

"Of course, I like the house. It's a great house. Good bones, lots of potential. There's even a fenced yard for the dog Kurt's been begging for. You're right, it is perfect. But I'm just not there yet. Maybe after I finish my BSN and get the commensurate pay increase, but that'll be a good long while."

Tucker reeled her in, lacing his hands at the small of her back. "The landlord's flexible on rent."

"Unless he's a candidate for Cirque de Soleil, I doubt it'll be enough. It was a sweet thought, Tucker, but I don't think this is going to work out." She pulled away and went to the door to call Kurt back inside.

Tucker snagged her hand again. "We've got some more time before we need to get the pizza. Let him play a bit."

She relented and followed when he pulled her toward the family room. "He's really motivated to get a family in here. It's a great neighborhood for kids. And it's a cul de sac, so no worries about a lot of traffic."

"I'm sure it's a great place for kids but this guy is not going to agree to what I could afford to pay."

"Oh, I think he might. He was really clear family is a lot more important to him than the money. Look, he's left a picture of them on the mantle."

She wandered over to peer up at the lone frame set on the rough wood mantle. As her steps slowed, Tucker's heart began to thud. He slid his hand—sweaty now—into his pocket. Corinne reached to pick up the frame that held a picture of the three of them from their weekend on the coast, grinning in all their sunburned glory at the camera.

Eyes wide, she stared at him. "I don't understand."

"It's our house. I bought it for us."

"You bought a house?"

Okay, stupefied wasn't necessarily bad, was it?

Tucker crossed over. "I did. For our family. Because that's what I want us to be, Corinne. A family."

"You bought a house?" she repeated.

"Not just a house." He pulled out his hand and her stunned gaze fell to the ring in his palm.

"Ohmygod."

"This wasn't necessarily how I planned this part, but I seem to recall a conversation about how you didn't need to hang out in the slow lane. I'm not much interested in the slow lane either. I love you. I love Kurt. And I don't see any reason to put off what I already want." She still wasn't saying anything and Tucker started to feel the first flickers of panic. Had he screwed this up? "Unless you don't want this or aren't ready. I can put it away for later, when you are—"

Corinne pressed the fingers of her free hand to his lips to stop the flow of words. Tucker shut his mouth.

She set the picture carefully back on the mantle and turned to him. "Is there an actual question in all that?"

He took a breath and sank to one knee. "Will you and Kurt marry me, be my family, and come live here in this house?"

Her eyes were glassy, but her lips curved, dimple flashing. "Seems like that's a lot of questions."

"They're all rolled up together. Package deal."

She pressed a hand to her mouth for a moment. "It's a pretty awesome package."

"Well?"

"Say yes, Mama! Say yes! Tucker said if you say yes, I can get a puppy!"

Corinne slid Tucker a Look.

Tucker gave Kurt the side eye. "You weren't supposed to mention that part yet."

"So," she said. "Marriage, family, house, and dog? In that order?"

"In whatever order you want," Tucker told her.

"Well then," she dropped to her knees before him, "I think the answer is a resounding yes."

∼

Choose Your Next Romance!

Next up in Wishful is the Christmas novella most often described as a Hallmark Christmas movie on the page! *Dance Me A Dream* is a delightful, heartwarming, holiday tale about an older sister who's working her tush off to provide for her younger half-sibs, and the guy who comes along to make their Christmas dreams come true.

Or maybe you're looking for some tighter family ties? If you haven't checked out my Misfit Inn series, now's your chance! *When You Got A Good Thing* is a second chance, homecoming romance—the first in a quartet about the Reynolds sisters in tiny Eden's Ridge, Tennessee. It's all the Southern charm and sass you've come to expect, in a whole new series!

Can't decide which to grab? Keep reading for a sneak peek of both!

DANCE ME A DREAM

WISHFUL ROMANCE, BOOK #7

Jace Applewhite is home for the holidays, helping out on his family's Christmas tree farm and enjoying some much needed downtime between semesters of grad school. He's intrigued by the sexy and serious barista from The Daily Grind, but she's got a Hand's Off vibe that can be seen from miles away.

Tara Honeycutt missed most of her college years being single parent to her two younger half siblings. Working multiple jobs, she's forgotten what it's like to be a normal twenty-something. All her focus is on giving the kids some new holiday memories.

When a major gas line breaks, leaving them with no heat, no hot water, and no way to cook for Christmas, Jace invites Tara and her sibs out to Applewhite Farms. Will a good old fashioned farmhouse Christmas be enough to get Tara to give him a second glance?

Chapter One

ROST GLISTENED ON THE carved stone of the fountain that was the jewel of the Wishful town green, looking candied and fanciful, like something out of a fairy tale. Tara Honeycutt hunched her shoulders against the cold, watching her breath puff out in clouds. She really needed to get going. The window between when she dropped her siblings off at school and when she had to be at The Daily Grind for her shift was already narrow, and today she needed to swing by to pick up a check for her sales at the artisan market where she sold her hand-crafted jewelry. But the fountain had drawn her. Maybe because of the dream.

Last night she'd been back in her old life. On the stage. Preparing for the season's opening performance of *The Nutcracker*. She'd woken out of sorts, with a gut-deep yearning for what used to be. And so, here she was, a coin in her fist, about to make a wish in the fountain that gave the town its name.

I wish...

What did she wish? Did she really want to go back to professional dance? To the brutal schedule? The grueling competition? The loneliness? No. Whatever she may have missed about performing, it wasn't that. She'd traded her career for family and she wouldn't—couldn't—go back on that.

But God, to be a normal twenty-one year old girl, free of all these responsibilities...

I wish I could be normal girl, just for a little while.

Tara tossed the coin into the water and immediately felt guilty for making such a selfish wish. She found herself digging into her purse for another coin.

I'll just make another wish. Surely that's not breaking the rules.

Clutching this one tight in her hand, Tara stared hard at the fountain, as if that would somehow impress upon whatever powers that be that she was really serious about this one.

I wish I could give Austin and Ginny a good Christmas. The kind of Christmas they truly deserve.

The nickel hit the water with a thunk, joining the legion of others from wishers who'd come before.

Okay, that was enough of that foolishness. She needed to get going. With long-legged strides, she headed across the green toward Wishful Discount Drugs.

The historic downtown pharmacy was decked out for the holidays in true Currier and Ives style, with swags of greenery, twinkly lights, and festoons of ribbon. The windows had been flocked with fake snow, and somebody had even found a vintage Christmas village to set up in the front window. Tara made a mental note to bring the kids by to see it. Ginny would absolutely love it, and even Austin would be charmed by the train circling on a track. Bing Crosby crooned "White Christmas" over the loudspeakers as Tara stepped inside.

"Be with you in a sec!" Pharmacist Riley Gower's voice floated from somewhere below counter level.

Tara crossed over, trying to think if she needed to pick up anything else while she was here. Ginny's insulin supply was good, and they'd just restocked syringes last week.

Riley popped up, a pair of felt reindeer antlers perched in her glossy dark brown hair. "Tara! Merry Christmas!"

Tara grinned. "Nice antlers."

"I drew the line at the nose."

"I think the rosy cheeks and sparkle in your eyes make up for it. They've been a permanent addition since you and Liam got engaged."

Riley beamed and blushed. "I keep thinking I'll get used to it. But I don't."

"Don't ever get used to it. I think that's the key to staying in love. And it looks good on you," Tara added. If she felt just a wee pinch of envy, it wasn't big enough to note. Riley and Liam were two of her favorite people—kind and generous to a fault. Tara was delighted they'd found each other.

But a tiny part of her—the small, self-absorbed part wishing for a normal life—wondered if she'd ever get the chance to find someone of her own. At least before her siblings were grown and out on their own. What did the dating scene look like for thirty-two year olds? It didn't bear thinking about.

"I'll get your check. You've had absolutely outstanding sales. If you've got any other stock to load in, now's the time. The last minute shoppers are picking up and everybody's loving the new artisan market."

"I've got a few more things I can bring by in a day or two."

Riley disappeared into the office.

If she stayed up a couple extra hours tonight, she could probably stretch that to more. Tara's mind was already spinning new jewelry designs based on the supplies she had left when Riley came back out.

"Here we go." She handed over the check.

Tara took it. "Thanks. I've gotta jet. I'm gonna be late to my shift at The Grind and we've been hopping with all the holiday shoppers."

"I'll see you in a few days when you bring in the new stock."

Tara turned toward the door, glancing down at the check. She took in the number of zeroes. Blinked. Looked again. "You forgot to take out the booth rental fee."

"Nope. The amount is right. You've sold out all but two pieces."

Tara stared at her. "You're kidding."

"Make that all but one," Jessie Applewhite said. Riley's pharmacy tech wandered in from the market side of the store. "I'm nabbing that turquoise pendant necklace right now. And if Eli comes in looking for ideas, I want the earrings, too. Just sayin'."

"Well, sweet little baby Jesus," Tara muttered.

"Told you. Enjoy it!" Riley urged.

Two wishes, one of them answered in fifteen minutes. That

had to be some kind of record. Batting 500—and the more important 500 at that—was pretty darn good odds. She didn't have a
prayer of a shot at being a normal girl, but this year—this year
she'd be able to give her brother and sister a *real* Christmas. One
with new traditions and festivities that would make up, at least a
little, for the absence of their parents.

Tucking the check carefully into her purse, Tara hurried to
work.

THERE'S *no place like home.*

Jace Applewhite took his time crossing the town green,
enjoying the sight of the enormous town Christmas tree. The
Bradford pears lining Main Street were wrapped in twinkle lights,
and the light poles had regimented lines of lit wreaths marching
all the way around the green. Beautiful. And with the unseason-
ably cold weather, it actually felt like winter. Of course, give it a
day or two and it'd be 75 degrees. Such was the nature of
December in Mississippi. His sister Livia and their cousin Jessie
had a long-running bet on whether they'd be able to wear t-shirts
for Christmas Day.

Jace stepped into The Daily Grind, scanning the faces for his
friends. Grad school exams had wrapped a bit earlier than
expected, so he'd come on home to Wishful to help with the
family business for the remainder of the holiday. He'd head out to
the farm and surprise his parents after catching up with the guys.

Across the room, Eli lifted his hand in a wave.

"Well, you're a sight for sore eyes," Jace said, pulling him into a
back thumping hug.

"That's what you get for doing the grad school thing, man.
Lots of tiny print. While you're up to your eyeballs in textbooks,
I'm out in the good clean air."

"And how's the Forestry Service treating you?"

"Can't complain," Eli said.

"How's my cousin treating you? Or maybe I should ask how you're treating Jessie."

"He's whipped," Zach Warren announced, rising from his chair to repeat the man hug routine.

"As he should be. She's too good for him. Where are Leo and Reed?"

"Leo's running the lighting and sound for the community theater's production of *White Christmas*, and Reed is in Connecticut with his lady love and her parents."

"That sounds serious," Jace observed. "Is there a ring involved?"

"If there is, he hasn't told us," Eli said.

"Given the way such news spreads in this town, that's probably wise. Let me grab some coffee." Jace joined the short queue at the counter, tapping a finger against his leg in time with the rhythm of the music playing over the sound system. What was that? *Charlie Brown Christmas?*

"Welcome to The Daily Grind. What can I get you?"

Jace focused on the girl behind the counter. *Your number.*

Tall and willowy, her sandy blonde hair was piled on top of her head in some updo that left her long, graceful neck bare. His fingers itched to trace it, to see if her skin was as soft as it looked. Her hazel eyes were expectant, and Jace realized he hadn't said anything. He cleared his throat. "Um, what do you recommend?"

"For light roast today, we've got a Nkurubuye from Rawanda. Our dark roast is an Idido from Ethiopia. This late in the day, I'd be inclined to go for the dark. Less caffeine."

"Really? I thought darker roasts had more caffeine."

"Other way around," she said. The name tag on her holly red apron read *Tara*. "The roasting process destroys some of the caffeine, so the lighter the roast, the more potent."

Her voice was deeper than he expected. A throaty, rich alto. Talk about potent.

"I'll have the dark then. Just black."

Tara punched at the iPad mounted at the register. "Any nibbles to go with it?"

Jace could think of several of her inches he'd like to nibble. Jesus, he really had been stuck in a book too damned long. "No, nothing to eat, thanks."

Her slender fingers punched in the rest of the transaction and tipped the iPad toward him to pay. "I'll just get this started for you."

Jace pulled out his wallet and swiped his card before he forgot how to use it. Tara seemed to float across the floor, graceful and unhurried, almost like a dance. How did she do that?

"Here you go."

He took the steaming mug she offered. "You aren't from around here."

She tipped her head in question.

"I'd remember if I'd seen you before," Jace clarified.

"You haven't been in for coffee in a year and a half? I know all the regulars."

"Grad school at Mississippi State," he explained. "I've been having my caffeine directly by IV drip."

Her lips curved a little, and Jace found himself wanting to see her full smile. He'd bet it was stunning.

"Home for the holidays, then," she concluded, friendly but not exactly a green light to his flirtation.

"I am indeed. A full month until I have to go back. I'll be one of those regulars before you know it." Jace grinned, hoping she'd respond in kind.

But Tara wasn't quite paying attention. Her head angled slightly, her eyes unfocused and heartbreakingly sad.

The sight of it struck a deep, painful chord in him, reminding him of another pair of somber eyes. He wanted to reach out and stroke her cheek. *Don't be sad*. The music on the sound system had shifted to *The Nutcracker*. Not exactly a melancholy tune.

Before he could work that out, she shook herself, plastering on a smile that was stiff around the edges. "You have a merry Christmas."

It was a polite brush off with an underlying message of *hands off.*

"You, too," Jace murmured, lifting the coffee in a toast and heading back to his friends.

"Need a fire extinguisher?" Eli asked.

"Huh?"

"Because you just crashed and burned, brother."

Jace glanced back at Tara, who was helping another customer. "What's her story? Is she seeing somebody?" Which was only half what he wanted to know. He wanted—needed—to know what had put that look in her eyes.

"Oh no, the Snow Queen shoots down all comers," Eli said. "Many have tried. No one has succeeded."

"Snow Queen? Isn't that kinda harsh?" Jace felt offended on Tara's behalf.

"She's never rude, just kind of holds herself apart. More important things to worry about than dating."

"You're taken," Jace reminded him. "By my cousin."

"I'm off the market. I'm not blind," Eli protested.

Zach picked up the thread. "She's been here a bit over a year, I think. Not sure where she came from, but she's got guardianship of her two half-siblings."

"She's young for that isn't she?" Jace didn't think she was more than twenty-two.

"Got them at nineteen."

"Holy crap. Why?"

Zach sipped at his coffee. "Mom left for parts unknown a few years back. And their dad is in jail on burglary charges. Tara's the only other family they've got."

That was certainly adequate reason to be sad. "Wow. How old are the kids?"

"Third grade and fifth from what I remember when I did school pics earlier this fall," Zach reported.

So, for the time being, anyway, she was a single sort-of mom. The hands off vibe made total sense in that context. Jace should probably respect that. But as he sat catching up with his friends, he knew he'd spend the next month feeding his coffee habit.

Get your copy of *Dance Me A Dream* today!

WHEN YOU GOT A GOOD THING

THE MISFIT INN, BOOK #1

*I*n the mood for more Eden's Ridge? Check out Sheriff Xander Kincaid's story!

Charming, poignant, and sexy, *When You Got a Good Thing* **pulled me in with its sweet charm and deft storytelling, and didn't let go until the very last page. It has everything I love in a small-town romance!** **~USA Today Best-Selling Author Tawna Fenske**

She thought she could never go home again. Kennedy Reynolds has spent the past decade traveling the world as a free spirit. She never looks back at the past, the place, or the love she left behind —until her adopted mother's unexpected death forces her home to Eden's Ridge, Tennessee.

Deputy Xander Kincaid has never forgotten his first love. He's spent ten long years waiting for the chance to make up for one bone-headed mistake that sent her running. Now that she's finally home, he wants to give her so much more than just an apology.

Kennedy finds an unexpected ally in Xander, as she struggles to mend fences with her sisters and to care for the foster child her mother left behind. Falling back into his arms is beyond tempting, but accepting his support is dangerous. He can never know the truth about why she really left. Will Kennedy be able to bury the past and carve out her place in the Ridge, or will her secret destroy her second chance?

~

Chapter One

"WELCOME TO O'LEARY'S PUB. What can I get you?" The greeting rolled off Kennedy Reynolds' tongue as she continued to work the taps with deft hands.

The man on the other side of the long, polished bar gaped at her. "You're American."

Kennedy topped off the pint of Harp and slid it expertly into a patron's waiting hand. "So are you." She injected the lilt of Ireland into her voice instead of the faint twang of East Tennessee. "You'd be expectin' somethin' more along these lines, I'd wager. So what'll it be for a strapping Yank like yourself?"

The guy only blinked at her.

So she wasn't exactly typical of County Kerry, Ireland. Her sisters would be the first to say she wasn't exactly typical of anyone, anywhere. It didn't bother her. But there was a line stacking up behind this slack-jawed idiot, and she had work to do.

"Can I suggest a pint of Guinness? Or perhaps you'd prefer whiskey to warm you through? The night's still got a bit of a chill."

He seemed to shake himself. "Uh, Jameson."

She poured his drink, already looking past him to take the next order, when he spoke again.

"How's a girl from—is that Texas I hear in there?—wind up working in a pub in Ireland?"

This again? Really? Kennedy repressed the eye roll, determined to be polite and professional

A big, long-fingered hand slapped the guy on the shoulder hard enough to almost slosh the whiskey. "Well now, I suppose herself walked right in and answered the help wanted sign." The speaker shifted twinkling blue eyes to Kennedy's. "That was how it happened in Dublin, now wasn't it, darlin'?"

"And Galway," she added, shooting a grin in Flynn's direction. "I'd heard rumor you were playing tonight. Usual?"

"If you'd be so kind. It's good to see you, *deifiúr beag.*" His voice was low and rich with affection, the kind of tone for greeting an old lover—which was laughable. Flynn Bohannon was about as far from her lover as he could get. But it did the trick.

With some relief, Kennedy saw the American wander away. "Thanks for that."

"All in a day's work," Flynn replied.

"I've missed your pretty face." She glanced at the nearly black beard now covering his cheeks as she began to pull his pint of Murphy's Irish Stout. "Even if you are hiding it these days."

He grinned, laying a hand over his heart. "Self preservation, love."

"You keep telling yourself that." Kennedy glanced at the line snaking back through the pub. "I'm slammed here, and you're starting your set shortly. Catch up later?"

Flynn lifted the beer and toasted her before making his way toward the tiny stage shoehorned beside the fireplace, where the other two members of his trio were waiting.

Mhairi, one of the waitstaff, wandered over, setting her tray on the bar as she all but drooled in his direction. "Well now, I'd not be kickin' that one out of bed for eating crisps."

"Wait 'til you hear him play."

Mhairi glanced back at Kennedy, lifting a brow in question. "Are you and he...?"

"No. Just friends. The way there is clear, so far as I know."

The waitress smiled. "Brilliant." She reeled off orders and it was back to the job at hand.

As Kennedy continued to pour drinks, Flynn and his band tuned instruments. They weren't the same pair who'd been with him in Dublin, whom she'd traveled with for several weeks as an extra voice. That wasn't much of a surprise. It'd been—what?—a year or so since they'd parted in Scotland. Flynn would, she knew, go where the music took him. And that sometimes meant changing up his companions. He was as much an unfettered gypsy as she was, which was why they'd become such fast friends. But whereas he didn't mind a different city or village every night, she preferred to take a more leisurely pace, picking up seasonal work and staying put for two or three months at a stretch. Really immersing herself in the culture of a place. The ability to pause and soak in each new environment gave her both the thrill of the new and kept her from feeling that incessant, terrified rush of not being able to fit in everything she wanted to see or do. It was important to her to avoid that, to take the time to be still in a place and find out what it really had to teach her.

The itinerant lifestyle worked for her. She'd seen huge chunks of the world over the past decade, made friends of every stripe, picked up bits and pieces of more than a dozen languages. Many people saw her life as unstable. She preferred to think of it as an endless adventure. What did their stability give them? Consistent money in the bank, yes. But also boredom and stress and a suffocating sameness. No, thank you. Kennedy would take her unique experiences any day. Never mind that the desk jobs and business suits had never even been a possibility for her. She'd been ill-suited for the education that led to those anyway.

Across the pub, Flynn drew his bow across his fiddle and launched into a lively jig. The crowd immediately shifted its focus. Those who knew the tune began to clap or stomp in time, and a handful of patrons leapt up and into the dance. Kennedy loved the spontaneity of it, the unreserved joy and fun. As jig rolled into reel and reel into hornpipe, she found herself in her own kind of dance as she moved behind the bar. Flynn switched instruments with the ease of shaking hands, playing or lifting his voice as the tune dictated. He even dragged Kennedy in for a couple of duets that made her nostalgic for their touring days. His music made the night pass quickly, so she didn't feel the ache in her feet until she'd shut the door behind the last patron.

Flynn kicked back against the bar. "A good night, I'd say."

"A very good night," Kennedy agreed.

"Help you clean up?"

"I wouldn't say no."

They went through the motions with the other staff, clearing tables, wiping down, sweeping up. Mhairi went on home—disappointed. And Kennedy promised Seamus, the pub's owner, that she'd lock up on her way out. Then, at long last, she settled in beside the remains of the fire with her own pint.

Flynn lifted his. "To unexpected encounters with old friends."

"Why unexpected?"

"You said yourself you rarely stay more than three months in a place. You've already been from one coast of Ireland to the other. I didn't expect you back."

"I always seem pulled back here," she admitted. "The people. The culture. As a whole, I suppose Ireland has been as close as I've had to a home base over the past ten years. I've spent more collective time in this country than anywhere else combined since I started traveling."

"How long have you been in Kerry?"

"Coming up on three months."

"Thinking of settling?" he asked.

Was she? No. She still felt that vague itch between her shoulder blades that she got every time she'd been long enough in a place. She knew she'd be moving on soon, searching for the next place to quiet the yearning she refused to acknowledge. "Not exactly. I haven't decided where I want to go next. Which isn't the same thing." She took a breath and spilled out the news she'd told no one. "I've been contacted by a book editor in New York. She wants me to turn my blog into a book."

"Really?" Flynn's grin spread wide and sparkling as the River Liffey. "That's grand!"

It was the most exciting thing to ever happen to her, and she was glad to finally get a chance to share it. "I haven't said yes."

"Why not? Are the terms not to your liking?"

"We haven't gotten that far. I'm still thinking about it." Still looking for reasons to talk herself out of it.

"What's there to think about?" Flynn prodded.

"A book means deadlines and criticism and working on other people's schedules. None of those are exactly my strong suit."

"Bollocks. Every job you've had has been on someone else's schedule. As to deadlines, how hard can it be to take what you've already written and turn it into a book? *Not All Who Wander* is well-written, engaging, and personal. You're a talented writer."

On her better days, Kennedy could admit that. But it was one thing having her little travel blog, with its admittedly solid online following, be read and commented on via the anonymity of the internet. It was a whole other animal turning that into a book that lots of people could read. Or not read, as the case might be. That was opening herself up to a level of failure she didn't even want to contemplate.

"She's offered to fly me to New York to meet with her, and I'm thinking about taking her up on the offer. I might feel better about the idea of the project if we talk about it in person."

"And if you go back across the pond, will you finally take a detour home?"

At the mention of Eden's Ridge, Kennedy felt some of her pleasure in the evening dim. "It hasn't really been on my radar as an option."

"Maybe it should be."

She lifted a brow. "This from the man who's been on the go nearly as long as I have?"

"I travel and often, yes, but I've been home. I've seen my family. You've been running."

"I'm not running," she insisted.

"All right, not running. Searching, then. For something. In all your travels, have you found it?"

"How can I even answer that? I don't know what I'm looking for." But that was a lie. She knew what she was looking for and knew she wouldn't find it in any new country, on any new adventure.

"I'd say that's an answer in and of itself."

Kennedy scowled into her beer. "I've had my reasons for staying away from home."

"They aren't family. You've seen them since you left. So who?"

Her gaze shot to his.

Flynn jerked his shoulders and gave an easy smile. "Deduction, *deifiúr beag.* Who was he?"

Someone better off without me.

She was saved from answering by the ringing of her mobile phone. "Late for a call." Fishing it out of her pocket, she saw her mother's number flash across the screen. "Not so late back in Tennessee." She hit answer. "Hey, Mom."

"Kennedy."

At the sound of her name, she felt her stomach clench into knots. Because it wasn't her mother, and the strain in her eldest sister's voice was palpable. "Pru?"

"Are you sitting down?"

Absolutely nothing good could follow those words. "What?"

Beside her, Flynn straightened, setting his pint to the side.

"You're not on the street where you can accidentally walk into traffic or something are you?"

"I'm sitting. What the hell is going on? Where's Mom?"

Her sister took a shaky breath. "Kennedy, Mom was in an accident. Her car was in the shop, and she was in a loaner. We've had a cold snap."

"What?" Kennedy whispered.

"She…" Pru gave a hiccuping sort of sob. "She didn't make it."

The earth fell out from beneath Kennedy's chair, and she curled her hand tighter around the phone, as if that pitiful anchor would help. She didn't even recognize her own voice as she asked, "Mom's dead?"

She wasn't aware of Flynn moving, but suddenly he was there, his strong hand curling around hers.

"The doctors said it was all but instant. She didn't suffer. I…we need to make arrangements."

"Arrangements." She needed to get the hell off the phone. She needed to move, to throw something, to rail at the Universe because this…this shouldn't be happening. "I have to go."

"Kennedy, I know this is hard but—"

"I'm coming home. I'll be there absolutely as soon as I can. Call you back as soon as I know when." She hung up before Pru could answer.

"Do you want me to come with you?" Flynn asked.

He would. He'd cancel whatever bookings he had and fly across an ocean with her to face the grief and demons that waited in Eden's Ridge. But this was for her to do.

"No. I… No." Lifting her eyes to his, she felt the weight of grief land on her chest like a boulder. She'd never again hear her mother's laugh. Never smell her mother's favorite perfume. Never get a chance to tell her the truth about why she'd walked away. "Flynn."

Without word, without question, he tugged her into his arms, holding tight as the first wave crashed over her, and she fell apart, the phantom scent of violets on the air.

～

CHIEF DEPUTY XANDER KINCAID parked his cruiser in front of the rambling Victorian that had been Joan Reynolds' home. He retrieved the covered dish of chicken enchiladas sent by his mama —the first wave of death casseroles that would soon fill the old kitchen to bursting—and headed for the front door. Despite its size, with its muted gray paint, the house tended to blend into the woods and mountains around it. Joan had loved this house. She'd always said it was a peaceful spot, a good place to heal and a good place to love. And she'd done exactly that for nearly twenty-five of her sixty-two years, filling the over-sized house with foster children who'd needed a home and someone to love them.

No telling whose home it would become now. Pru had moved back in. As the only one of Joan's adopted girls who hadn't moved away, she'd immediately stepped in to take over guardianship of Ari Rosas, Joan's most recent—well, her last foster child. But he didn't imagine Pru could afford the upkeep of the place on her income as a massage therapist—especially after the death taxes and probate lawyer had their way with the place. And what, he wondered, would happen with Ari, whose adoption hadn't yet been finalized?

Juggling the casserole dish, he rang the bell and waited. And waited.

Backing up on the porch, he craned his head to peer around toward the barn. Pru's car was there. He tried the knob and found it unlocked. Making a mental note to have a word with her about security, even here on the Ridge, he stuck his head inside. "Pru?"

She appeared at the head of the stairs, her big brown eyes red-rimmed from crying. "Sorry. I was just…" She tailed off, waving a vague hand down the hall.

"It's fine." He lifted the enchiladas. "Mama wanted me to bring these by. She thought with your sisters coming in, the last thing you or any of them would want to do is cook."

Xander watched as manners kicked in. Her posture straightened, her expression smoothing out as she locked down the grief.

"That's so kind of her." She came down the stairs and reached for the dish. "I'll just go put this in the kitchen."

He followed her back.

"No one's here just yet," she said, a false bright note in her voice, as if everything was fine and her world wasn't falling apart.

Xander waited until she slid the casserole into the fridge before he simply wrapped his arms around her. "Pru. I'm so sorry."

For a long moment, she stood there like a wooden post. Then a shudder rippled through her as her control fractured. Her arms lifted and she burrowed in.

"This shouldn't have happened," she whispered. "If she'd been in her own car instead of that tin can loaner, it wouldn't have."

Xander wasn't sure Joan's SUV would've handled the patch of black ice any better, but he remained silent. The fact was, nobody expected black ice in east Tennessee in March. Not when daytime temperatures were almost to the sixties. Joan's hadn't been the only accident this week. But she'd been the only fatality.

He ran a hand down Pru's silky, dark brown hair, hoping to soothe, at least a little. But this wasn't like middle school, when he'd been able to pound Derek Pedretti into the ground for making Pru cry by calling her fat. There was no one he could take to task, no one to be punished. Grief simply had to be endured.

"There are all these arrangements to be made," she hiccuped.

And no one here to help her do them, with Maggie off in Los Angeles and Athena running her restaurant in Chicago. Xander deliberately avoided thinking about the final Reynolds sister, though he was sure that this would bring even her home. The idea of that caused his gut to tighten with a mix of old fury and guilt.

"What can I do to help?"

"Let me make you some coffee."

"Pru—"

"No really," she sniffed, pulling away. "I'm better when I'm doing something."

Xander didn't want coffee, but if she needed to keep her hands busy, he'd drink some. "Coffee'd be great."

She began puttering around the kitchen, pulling beans out of the freezer and scooping them into the grinder. Joan had loved her gourmet beans. It'd been one of the few luxuries she'd always allowed herself. As she went through the motions, Pru seemed to regain her control.

"Maggie's taking the red eye from LA, and Athena's flying out as soon as she closes down the restaurant tonight."

"Do either of them need to be picked up from the airport?"

"They're meeting in Nashville and driving up together in the morning, so they'll be here to help me finish planning the service. It's supposed to be on Thursday."

Xander didn't ask about Kennedy. Both because he didn't want to care whether she showed up, and if she wasn't coming, he didn't want to rub it in.

Pru set a steaming mug in front of him, adding the dollop of half and half he liked and giving it a stir. "Kennedy gets in day after tomorrow. There was some kind of issue getting a direct flight, so she's having to criss-cross Europe before she even makes it Stateside again. She's coming home, Xander."

He wasn't sure if that was supposed to be an announcement or a warning, but it cracked open the scab over a very old wound that had never quite healed.

She laid a hand over his. "Are you okay?"

This woman had just lost her mother, and she was worried about whether he'd be okay with the fact that his high school girlfriend, whom he hadn't seen in a decade, was coming home.

"Why wouldn't I be?"

Pru leveled those deep, dark eyes on his. "I know there are unresolved issues between you."

God, if only she knew the truth—that he was the reason Kennedy had left—she wouldn't be so quick to offer sympathy.

"It was a long time ago, Pru. There's nothing to resolve."

Kennedy had made her position clear without saying a word to him. At the memory, temper stirred, belying his words. There were things he needed to say to her, questions he wanted answered. But whatever her faults, Kennedy had just lost her mother, too, and Xander wasn't the kind of asshole who'd attack her and demand them while she was reeling from that. Chances were, she'd be gone before he had an opportunity to say a thing. He'd gotten used to living with disappointment on that front.

He laid a hand over Pru's. "Don't worry about me. How's Ari?"

She straightened. "Devastated. Terrified. And…" Pru sighed. "Not speaking."

"Not speaking?"

"Not since I told her. She'd come so far living here with Mom, and this is an enormous setback. No surprise. Especially having just lost her grandmother last year." Pru continued to bustle around the kitchen, pouring herself a cup of coffee and coming to sit with him at the table. Her long, capable fingers wrapped around the mug.

"She upstairs?"

"Yeah. I was trying to get her to eat something when you got here."

"Poor kid. Have you talked to the social worker yet?"

"Briefly. Mae wants to let us get through the funeral and all the stuff after before we all figure out what to do."

"Who would've been named her emergency guardian if the adoption had gone through?" Xander asked.

"The four of us, probably. I know it's what Mom would've wanted. But there are legal ramifications to the situation, and the fact is, I'm the only one still here." She sighed. "We'll have to talk about it after. The one thing I know we'll all be in agreement on is that we want what's best for Ari."

"All four of you have been in her shoes, and you turned into amazing women. I know you'll do the right thing." Whatever that turned out to be.

Xander polished off the coffee. "I'm on shift, so I need to be getting back. But, please, if you need *anything*, Pru, don't hesitate to call. I'm just down the road."

She rose as he did and laid a hand on his cheek. "You're a good stand-in brother, Xander. Mom always loved that about you."

He felt another prick of guilt, knowing his own involvement with this family had been heavily motivated by trying to make up for Kennedy's absence. "Yeah well, I ran as tame here as the rest of you when we were kids. Especially when Porter was around." Giving her another squeeze, he asked, "Can I do that for you? Notify the rest of her fosters? I know you've covered your sisters, but there were a lot of kids who went through here over the years. I'm sure they'd like to pay their respects."

Her face relaxed a fraction. "That would be amazing. I'm sure we'll have a houseful after the funeral, but I need a chance to gird my loins for the influx. Mom kept a list. I'll get it for you."

As she disappeared upstairs, he wandered into the living room. Little had changed over the years. The big, cushy sofas had rotated a time or two. And there'd been at least three rugs that I could remember. But photos of Joan and her charges were scattered everywhere. Xander eased along the wall, scanning faces. A lot of them he knew. A lot of them, he didn't.

A shot at the end caught his attention. The girl's face was turned away from the camera, looking out over the misty mountains. She was on the cusp of womanhood, her long, tanned legs crossed on the swing that still hung from the porch outside, a book forgotten in her lap. Her golden hair was caught in a loose tail at her nape. Xander's fingers itched with the memory of the silky strands flowing through his fingers. She'd been sixteen, gorgeous, and the center of his world. The sight of her still gave him a punch in the gut.

"Here it is."

At the sound of Pru's voice, Xander turned away from Kennedy's picture. *Over and done.*

He strode over and took the pages she'd printed. "I'll take care of it," he promised.

"Thank you, Xander. This means a lot."

"Anytime." With one last, affectionate tug on her hair, he stepped outside, away from memories and the looming specter of what might have been.

Get your copy of *When You Got A Good Thing* **today!**

OTHER BOOKS BY KAIT NOLAN

A complete and up-to-date list of all my books can be found at https://kaitnolan.com.

THE MISFIT INN SERIES
SMALL TOWN FAMILY ROMANCE

- *When You Got A Good Thing* (Kennedy and Xander)
- *Til There Was You* (Misty and Denver)
- *Those Sweet Words* (Pru and Flynn)
- *Stay A Little Longer* (Athena and Logan)
- *Bring It On Home* (Maggie and Porter)

RESCUE MY HEART SERIES
SMALL TOWN MILITARY ROMANCE

- *Baby It's Cold Outside* (Ivy and Harrison)
- *What I Like About You* (Laurel and Sebastian)
- *Bad Case of Loving You* (Paisley and Ty prequel)

- *Made For Loving You* (Paisley and Ty)

MEN OF THE MISFIT INN
SMALL TOWN SOUTHERN ROMANCE

- *Let It Be Me* (Emerson and Caleb)
- *Our Kind of Love* (Abbey and Kyle)

WISHFUL SERIES
SMALL TOWN SOUTHERN ROMANCE

- *Once Upon A Coffee* (Avery and Dillon)
- *To Get Me To You* (Cam and Norah)
- *Know Me Well* (Liam and Riley)
- *Be Careful, It's My Heart* (Brody and Tyler)
- *Just For This Moment* (Myles and Piper)
- *Wish I Might* (Reed and Cecily)
- *Turn My World Around* (Tucker and Corinne)
- *Dance Me A Dream* (Jace and Tara)
- *See You Again* (Trey and Sandy)
- *The Christmas Fountain* (Chad and Mary Alice)
- *You Were Meant For Me* (Mitch and Tess)
- *A Lot Like Christmas* (Ryan and Hannah)
- *Dancing Away With My Heart* (Zach and Lexi)

WISHING FOR A HERO SERIES (A WISHFUL SPINOFF SERIES)
SMALL TOWN ROMANTIC SUSPENSE

- *Make You Feel My Love* (Judd and Autumn)
- *Watch Over Me* (Nash and Rowan)
- *Can't Take My Eyes Off You* (Ethan and Miranda)
- *Burn For You* (Sean and Delaney)

MEET CUTE ROMANCE

SMALL TOWN SHORT ROMANCE

- *Once Upon A Snow Day*
- *Once Upon A New Year's Eve*
- *Once Upon An Heirloom*
- *Once Upon A Coffee*
- *Once Upon A Campfire*
- *Once Upon A Rescue*

SUMMER CAMP
CONTEMPORARY ROMANCE

- *Once Upon A Campfire*
- *Second Chance Summer*

ACKNOWLEDGMENTS

First and foremost, I have to thank my twitter pal @JAScribbles for putting this bug in my ear after you read *Be Careful, It's My Heart*. I would never have thought of pairing these two. Without you, this story wouldn't exist. As always my undying gratitude to my awesome editor, Susan Bischoff of The Forge Book Finishers. You pushed me to challenge myself as an author, asking me to redeem a character I'd have been content to leave a mean girl. I'm a better writer because of you.

To Kady Weatherford for answering all my thousand questions about *Dancing With The Stars* and for all those hours we lost to YouTube research.

And to the members of the Squee Squad, who are the great champions of my work. I couldn't do this without you!

Deniz Bevan, Gabryyl Pierce, Erica Turnipseed, Maria McConnaughy, Rose Kelley, Nancy Nicholson, Angela Zommers, Dawn Foss, Evelyn Nathalia, Naomi Nelson, Susan Bischoff, Barb Redner, Elizabeth Laurie, Cindy Thoennes, Caitlin Mannarino,

Faith Wanjala, Annie Allen, Jay Perantoni, Barbara OBrien, Shelby Forbes, Karen Demeyere, Yasmeen Elfar, Alexis Roark, Lisa Orthmann, Vera B. Bolcevic, Carol McCarthy, Jacki N, Janice Richard, Vera Mallard, Leah Hughes, Sandra Mason, Margarita Gayle, Sheryl McNaught, Michael Lang, Irene Shea, Marjorie Mindel, Beth Colon, Pearl Moreno, Michelle Myre, Deborah Hawley, Melissa Riddle, Eunice Aleon, Mark Kyhl, Cathy Glenn, Christine Jordan, Lisa Benison, Connie Nowakowski, Andy Smith, Nicki Conroy, Mignone Chaves, Jessye Chevere, Beverly Pugh, Rebecca Donkin, Paige Ng, Deborah Bennett, Debra Punjabi, Kay Sterling, Theresa Morris, Amara Marcoccia, Elaine Boone, Suzy Perez, Lauren Dabney, Wendy Wright, Bernice Vigne, Meeta Mohabeer, Bert Blume, Andrea Partee, Tracey Landa, Trish C., Lesa Green, Ashley Nunn, Sharon Hughson, Angie McCaslan, Jackie Camire, Lorie Davis, Jo-ann Stenton, Heather Deal, Lynne DiTizio, Kathleen Kirkwood, Corlia Boshoff, Priya Prithviraj, Jami Plambeck, Bonnie Laurenzi, Wendy Jermier, Linda Dillbeck, Jennifer McMaster, Amy Drummond, Amanda Proch, Sinthia Hernandez, Heather Bahm, Fi Axford, Brandy Caywood, Carla Ellison, Reita Frazier, Sanet Steenkamp, Amy Webb, Alisa Price, Kassi Wanamaker, Carey Colton, Carol Fraley, Cori Plastina, Tammy Jordan, Jen Apfel, Annett Krumske, Shayna Tyann, Carol Downer, Donna Rumfelt, Timothy Hendricks, Jessica Ramsay-Taylor, Susan Reis, Marietjie De Waal, Michele Perry, Pamela Mingus, Preot Oaks, Grace Adeleke, Josey Wales, Lacey Frink, Diane Klingman, T Clark, Jeri Denniston, Claire Spencer, Shayna Tyann, Susan Clement, FD Noz, Marci Higgins, Liz Smith, Wendy Edwards, Lisa Roth, Andrea Romero, Courtney Ludwig, Melissa Feriancek, Yolandi Henry, Georgina Akins, Mary Sundra, Myla Fujimoto, Lola Gillies, Loes Lotze, Brandy Nelson, Chelsea McNeil, Ava Grant, Patricia Parker, Jo Ladkin, Debbie Knieper, Wunmi Ayodele, Kady Weatherford, Melody Metz, Brianna Harvey-Khowley, Louisa Stewart, Lynn Henning, Georgine Kasprazak, Kathy Broggy, Roger Gisseman, Mary Miltier, Deena Knight,

Nancy Kenney, Cynthia Duffee, Patricia Merritt, April Johnson, Gail Frankowiak, Sheila Waldner, Tammy Turnbow, Jean Pierson, Phyllis Souder, Paula Hurdle, Jen Roemershauser, Dawn Sablan, Carol Dominick, Becky Weldon, Theresa Denton, Holly Geer, Cindy Snider, Karissa C, Beth Blackmore, Sharon Shakinovsky, Deb Wagner, Tammie Neuenfeldt, Karen Beliveau, Jodi Lattanzio, Doris Chase, D C, Karan Jordan, Melanie Groff, Lynn Welborn, Eunice Elkins, Michelle Davyduke, Bev Harcourt, Sue Schultz, Loretta Cergol, Karen Call, John Alliapoulos, Lynn Cooke, Beverley Ettinger, Ronalee Coppock, Dawn Kuhn, Diane Harness, Glynneth Mathis, Priscilla Smith, Tracy Welsh, Ann Richardson, Judy Chamberlin, Karen Thompson, Ellen Ondo, Grace Ryan, Jodi Dawson, Dana Mullican, Susy Wolf, Shirley Pea, Joy Hack, Colleen Taylor, Margaret Ball, Yvonne Holste, Theresa Grant, Karen Nelson, Trudie Denton, Barbara Dombrowski, Cheryl Meyer, Charmaine Franklyn, Sharen Sherman, Kathryn Greiner, Rebecca Remley, Beverley MacMillan, Marilyn Burrows, Sue Everhart, Betty Caruthurs, Diane Gacki, Heiddi Zalamar, Richard Fetrow, Charlotte Holt, Kjristi Burningham, Noreen Chase, Karen Wilson, Deb Hazelton, Joyce Beard, Karen Baxter, Karen Cherry, Debra Turcotte, Alicia Muller, Barbara Rincon, Brbara Ultan, Alana Erstad, Jan Kingery, Janet Grindon, C Fannin, Larry Barlow, Rachel Burke, Marj Hodgins, Susan Byrd, Lori Tillman, Kim Bauer, Shaleen Varner, Beth Zone, Tondi Sorenson, Karen Kelder, Arielle Wood, Carol Sobeski, Kirstie Ibrahim, Joyce Insley, Michele Brooks, Jack Brumbarger, Martha Tippett, Kim Garman, Patty Garrett, Carol Kaczmarek, Anna P, Priscilla Patel, Betty Hopkins, Irene Griffin, Aimee Vanduyne, Gail Bell, April Angle, Annette Papageorgiou, Jeannine Muhn, Sue Mehr, Kristine Hoover, Debby Ong, Aren Ar, Anne Dallara, Lynette Elson, Katy Staley, Pam Walker, Sara Zuckerman, Cathy Wittie, Kim Jennings, Paula Pardue, Marian Andersen, Renae Bohnet, Kat Murray, Anne O'Brien, Suan Felts, Rita Aquino, Glenna Durst, Dorinda Perez, Sylvia Cole, Cathy Percae, Jackie Peters, Gisele Nicholas,

RoxAnne Simon, Pam Skaggs, Joniara Orr, Martha Vega, Kimberley Goetz, Wenonah Schwedler, Samantha Roseberry, Karen Scheffler, Linda Trappe, Susan Gannon, Marlene Weber, Roberta Webb, Bernice Tresemer, Betty Martin, Narda Snell, Marilyn Ruediseuli, Elsie Thompson, Prathima Shetty, Penny Berry, Taylor Holden, Debbie Tolbert, Dorothy Scorr, Amanda Humphrey, Kimberley Capel, Kelli Prue, Kelly Jesso, Desiree Boettcher, Samie Hill, Dana Redding, Stephanie Smith, Eva Petelin, Jeslie John, Kerry Hackenberg, Cathy Long, Susan Kluchin, Susan Shrode, Cheryl Underwood-Eginton, Debbie Shepler, Marie Rogers, Jeannette Bruun, Anita James, Vicki Hammond, Marie Dehaas, Maria Drakopoulos, Stephanie Alexander, Debbie Keith, Donna Russell, Marilyn Hartz, Carol Pearson, Linda Denouden, Irene Heijser, Mabelisse Gonzalez, Alison Ritchhart, Gloria Kietzke, Anita van Vuuren, Cheryl Kendall, Edith Abraham

ABOUT KAIT

Kait is a Mississippi native, who often swears like a sailor, calls everyone sugar, honey, or darlin', and can wield a bless your heart like a saber or a Snuggie, depending on requirements.

You can find more information on this RITA ® Award-winning author and her books on her website http://kaitnolan.com. While you're there, sign up for her newsletter so you don't miss out on news about new releases!